KICKED

Celia Aaron

Let Trent through your uprights.

xoxo,
Celia Aaron

Kicked

Celia Aaron

Copyright © 2016 Celia Aaron

Cover art by Mr. Aaron
Content Editing by J. Brooks
Copy editing by Spell Bound

ISBN: 1535453443
ISBN-13: 978-1535453448

OTHER BOOKS BY CELIA AARON

The Acquisition Series
Dark Romance Trilogy
***

The Forced Series
***

A Stepbrother for Christmas
The Hard and Dirty Holidays, Book 1

Bad Boy Valentine
The Hard and Dirty Holidays, Book 2

Bad Boy Valentine *Wedding*
The Hard and Dirty Holidays

F*ck of the Irish
The Hard and Dirty Holidays, Book 3
***

The Cleat Catcher Duet
Romantic Comedy written with Sloane Howell

Sign up for my newsletter at AaronErotica.com and be the first to learn about new releases (no spam, just free stuff and book news.)

Twitter: @aaronerotica

CONTENTS

"I'll put you through hell, but at the end of it all, we'll be champions." *Bear Bryant*

CELIA AARON

CHAPTER ONE
CORDY

I HAD THAT FEELING. You know the one. When your heart is beating against your ribs. Your ears are hot, your fingers are numb, and you could vomit any second. I tried to take a deep breath, but the announcer crowing and the crowd roaring weren't helping me any. Being in the claustrophobic tunnel with fifty of the largest men in a hundred-mile radius wasn't helping much, either.

They jostled against each other, their white jerseys with blue numbers taking up every square bit of space I could see. The stadium was full, the fans anxious to see if their team had what it took to be a contender. After all, football season would forever be a big deal in any state south of the Mason-Dixon line.

"You ready, princess?" Ethan Granger, a good defensive lineman but a *great* dickbag, squeezed my ass. He leaned over and spoke in my helmet's ear hole. "I think one of these days I'll dress out with you in the girls' locker room. Sound good?"

I shoved him, but he barely moved. He was six-five, two hundred and seventy-five to my five-seven, one-forty. I had a better chance of being a star quarterback than moving his chunky ass out of my way.

"You'd faint if you ever saw a girl naked." I kept my eyes straight ahead and raised my voice so he'd hear me through the helmet. "Now get the hell away from me. I'm trying to concentrate, and your wildebeest stench is making it impossible." A couple guys turned to look at me and my apparent case of Tourette's.

"See you, princess." Ethan stepped away, and another meathead took his spot beside me in the crush of bodies.

I tried to keep it together, to think about what I'd do after the game, or my homework, or the last poem I read that really spoke to me. My conjured distractions failed, and the mass surged as the players burst forward. The lights were bright beyond the dark tunnel, and I was carried out into the stadium by a wave of blue and white. The cheerleaders yelled, smoke billowed, and the band played the Billingsley fight song.

I broke into a trot along with the hulking men, sticking close to them so no one noticed me. Fat chance. After Bill the Bobcat, I was more or less the team's second mascot. I liked to refer to myself as "Mav." Sadly, it wasn't because I was capable of shooting down fighter jets or winning homo-erotic games of volleyball like Tom Cruise in *Top Gun*. Instead, my nickname stood for Mascot with a Vagina (the "w" didn't count.)

My university—Billingsley—had recently lost a particularly vicious Title Nine lawsuit where several women alleged discrimination in sports spending. To mend the school's reputation, the president decided to add a female kicker to the football roster. Ornamental only, of course. But it provided a partial scholarship, so I was all over it.

I needed the money; the school needed a female who could kick. That was how I wound up on a football field with the crowd cheering, the Gatorade flowing, and the testosterone reigning.

After a pat on my helmet from the weathered coach, I

took my seat on the farthest bench. My long brown hair was braided down my back, and I didn't bother with any eye black. I wouldn't have bothered with pads, either, but the dean wanted it to appear as if I were ready to go at any second. I could have laughed at the idea. The only place I got—or wanted—playing time was on the soccer field. Football was a means to an end, nothing more.

I pulled off my helmet and stowed it next to me, the thick plastic thunking onto the metal bench.

The stadium lights, hum of the crowd, and smell of popcorn and beer mixed to create a familiar cocktail of college football. I used to love going to games with Dad when I was little. But now, dressed out as number three of the Billingsley Bobcats, I'd rather have been reading, or kicking the soccer ball around, or getting my nether regions waxed.

I glanced down the row of players standing and chatting before the game. They were nice guys for the most part, each of them doing his best on the field while getting a top notch education on the hallowed grounds of Billingsley. Despite their politeness, the team hadn't been welcoming. But that assessment wasn't exactly fair. I hadn't warmed to them, either. Getting close to them would have meant getting close to Trent Carrington. No, thank you. I was more than happy to remain the outcast, the hood ornament, and the Mav if it kept me away from him.

Sitting alone, I had a decent view of the field, and no one to bother me. I preferred it that way. It was the second game of the season, and I was third-string. I didn't need any last minute coaching or warming up. Riding the bench, keeping to myself, and earning a chunk of tuition money was the plan for the rest of the year. Easy.

I'd grown up watching football, going to games with my father, and following the state teams. Soccer was my sport, but football was in my blood. All the same, I wasn't here to play. Not really. I was just a Mav with a front-row seat for every game of the season.

The bench shifted as someone sat beside me, and the band began playing at my back. "Hey."

I knew that voice. Trent. Goose bumps rose along my arms, but I didn't look at him. I hadn't been able to look him in the eye since freshman year, and I didn't expect that to change anytime soon.

"Cordy?" He used my nickname.

"Yep." I gripped the edge of the bench, the metal warm in the muggy air. "Shouldn't you be, I don't know, flipping coins or something?"

The deep bass of the band thumped through my heart, forcing it to keep a quicker beat than usual. It was the band that sped it up. Not Trent.

"The coin toss doesn't happen until after the national anthem."

"Right." I reached beneath my jersey and yanked out a composition notebook. My pen was trapped in the binding. If I had to be at the games, I figured I might as well get some writing in.

"Still write poetry?"

"Yes. Don't you have a pep talk you should be doing? You know, like *'let's go pluck those Eagles*?'" I wasn't going to talk about myself with him. His easy charm fooled me once. I wouldn't let it happen again.

"I already gave that." I could hear the smile in his voice.

"Well, then"—I sighed, trying to fight my irritation and losing—"maybe you should talk to Coach about how you throw off your back foot too much."

He laughed, the sound deep and rolling like the thundering bass behind me. "Is that so?"

"You throw across your body and into traffic too much, too. Might want to have that chat. You have a million other things to do other than being here right now."

"Maybe. But I only want to do this—sit here and talk

to you." The bench shifted, and the heat from his arm radiated against mine. "Besides, this has been enlightening. Any more pointers, coach?"

Before I could inform him that his choice of taking a sack instead of throwing the ball away in the last game almost cost us the win, the band started the national anthem. We both stood and put our hands over our hearts. The singer began off pitch and continued her flat spiral with each note.

He leaned closer, his arm brushing against mine. "I haven't had a chance to really welcome you to the team yet. But I'm glad you're here. Do you still play soc—"

"Shh." I would have rather heard the dying cat sounds of the national anthem singer than listen to his rich, sexy baritone a moment longer.

He sighed and quieted. The song continued, and I glanced at him. My eyes only came up to his chest pads, so it was easy enough to avoid his gaze. Instead, I noted his tan forearm, muscled with veins popping. He was even bigger than I remembered, filled out and ridiculously masculine.

I dropped my gaze as the song finally finished. The crowd gave a roar as hype music began pumping through the stadium once again.

He rocked up onto the balls of his feet and then back down. "That's my cue."

"Okay." I sank back onto the bench. "Break a leg."

He leaned down, his mouth close to my ear. "I think that's only for the theater, Cordy."

A tingle of pleasure ran down my spine as his warm breath tickled my ear. And just like that, I broke my rule.

Leaning away, I met his green eyes with my light brown ones. "What are you doing?"

He smiled, his perfect dimples complementing his square jaw and bright eyes. "Flipping a coin." He rose to his full height and jogged out onto the field, joining two other team captains and heading toward the referee in the center.

I took a deep breath, my heart hammering, my poise broken. Once I'd looked, I couldn't stop staring. His muscled ass filled out his football pants just right. The pads exaggerated the width of his shoulders, but not by that much. He was the perfect 'V'—broad shoulders, narrow hips, and made of corded muscle. He'd been beautiful when we'd first met, his boyish good looks the first step in my downfall. But now, he was beyond attractive. He was sexy, powerful—a perfect mix of masculinity and grace that had my body warming.

He swiped his hair from his eyes and called heads. The referee flipped the coin. It landed and bounced on the grass before lying flat. It was heads. Of course it was. Not even the whims of chance could deny Trent Carrington.

I dropped my eyes to my notebook and tried to ignore him again. Why was he even talking to me? We weren't friends. We were barely acquaintances anymore. Taking my pen out, I hovered it over the page as the teams took the field. The stadium vibrated with the fury of the crowd. So far, we were undefeated. The pressure would build with each game to keep it that way. Not that I cared.

I forced my pen to make words on the page. The words turned into doodles of the number nine. I glanced up to the field, my eyes invariably straying to Trent. It was as if that simple "hi" opened the floodgates. I watched him through the first quarter and into the second, pausing to doodle when the defense or special teams were on the field.

Halftime came and went, and the game finally wound down to one minute left in the fourth quarter. Our offense was on the field. Trent was in control. He'd been steadily driving down the field, all the way to the two, but a missed assignment caused a fumble behind the line of scrimmage. We recovered, but lost a yard. Second down was a busted pass play.

On third down, he called an audible and changed the

play. The runners scurried to switch positions as the defensive line tried to adjust. The center hiked the ball. Trent caught it and dropped back, his helmet on a swivel as he scanned downfield for a receiver. There were none. Each eligible player who could catch the ball was well covered.

The box of linemen around Trent gave way, and a defensive back broke through and drove him to the ground. I bit the inside of my cheek. After a small scuffle between the defender and a couple of linemen, Trent jumped up and headed to the sideline, knocking the grass out of his helmet grill.

The prolonged play had eaten clock. There were only nineteen seconds left, and we were tied. That left only two ways to win the game on this set of downs—the offensive line could go for it on fourth down and hope for a touchdown, or special teams could try for a field goal.

The refs moved the chains to the seven-yard line. It would be a twenty-four yard field goal. I shot a look over to Jared Link, the first-string kicker. He had leg for days and served as the field goal kicker and punter. He pulled on his helmet and pushed through the crowd of players. After a swift chat with the coach, he ran out onto the field with the kicking team at his back. The crowd hushed.

Trent was the ball holder, so number nine was still on the field, still catching my eye. Jared walked up to Trent, who gave him a light tap on the helmet. The special teams settled into place at the line of scrimmage, and I couldn't tear my eyes away. This was for the game. Half the stadium held its breath, and the other half gave raucous shouts and jeers to try and distract our kicker. Jared backed away from Trent and took two steps to the right. He lined the shot up with his arm, then squared his shoulders and gave the signal.

The center hiked the ball. Trent caught it and held it perfectly in place as Jared ran forward. Jared kicked hard, plenty of leg for a makeable field goal. But the kick pulled to the left. Worse, an Eagles defensive player broke through the line and ran right into Jared's outstretched leg after the kick. He went down and clutched his knee as the crowd booed and the ball sailed to the left, no good.

Yellow flags flew to the spot where Jared lay on the turf, holding onto his knee. A ref picked up a flag and signaled a roughing the kicker foul against the defense.

"Half the distance to the goal, replay the down." The ref's voice boomed around the stadium via his mic.

That meant we had another shot, but with only a twelve seconds left and the first-string kicker still on the grass.

"Get up Jared. Up, up!" I clenched the bench as our trainers ran out to check on him. He wasn't rising, just clutching his leg and rolling back and forth. A sick feeling gurgled in my stomach at the pain telegraphed by Jared's movements.

Pate, our second-string kicker, stood and began practicing. He wobbled for a moment, then squared off and kicked into the small net behind the benches.

Jared was still down, and a hush fell over the crowd. Three trainers knelt around him, trying to get a look at the injury as he groaned and shook his head each time they touched his right leg. Coach Sterling ran out to check on him and wound up supporting him under one shoulder as the trainers helped him off the field. It didn't look good. A leg injury was the worst news for a kicker.

I turned to look at Pate. Right at that moment, he retched all over Coach Carver. Even though Pate was at least ten yards away from me, I cringed. The poor guy bent over at the waist and vomited again, this time all over the ball he'd set up to kick into the practice net.

The hairs on the back of my neck stood on end and a litany of "oh fuck" began playing in my head on repeat when the realization hit me. If Pate couldn't pull himself together, there was only one other kicker on the team. Me.

Coach Sterling called our second time-out and hustled

over to me as I watched Pate hurl yet again, vomiting every last bit of his stomach's contents into the too-green grass of the well-kept field.

My hands went numb as Coach clapped me on the shoulder. He'd always been kind to me, welcoming even, though somewhat aloof. After all, he had real players to take care of. I was just the Mav.

He gave me a thin smile. "You ready?"

I stared up into his weathered cheeks and watery eyes. "I-I'm—"

"Good! Now get your helmet on and get out there!"

I looked from him to the field, and then to Trent, his green eyes focusing on nothing else. It was time. Time to kick.

CHAPTER TWO
CORDY

COACH STERLING SIGNALED FOR our third and final time-out as Coach Carver—still covered in Pate's lunch—tried to give me some last-minute pointers. "Get your foot under it. You need lift. I've seen you do it in practice."

"Right." I nodded, feigning a confidence I didn't feel.

"Do it just like we practiced."

When I saw a chunk of hotdog dangling from his shirt, I dry heaved and backed away. "I can't. That smell."

He glanced down and rolled his eyes. "Fucking Pate."

"I got this." Trent's voice washed over me, and the number nine obscured my view of the vomit-covered Coach Carver.

I was too shell-shocked to try and avoid his gaze, so I stared up at him. His eye black was smeared, and his hair was a sweaty mess, but he had a smile for me. Encouragement lived in the small upturn of his lips, and I needed all the help I could get.

"Look. We're tied. Twelve seconds left. After the penalty, it's going to be a twenty to twenty-one yard kick. If you miss it, we go to overtime, and then it's on me. No pressure. We can still win it. You can do this. The team needs you, but it's not life or death." He put a hand on my shoulder pads and pinned me with his green gaze.

I wanted to shrug him off, but I needed the comfort. My knees turned to jelly as the kicking team crowded around Trent and me. The other players watched us, most of them with an "oh shit" look on their faces. I didn't blame them. Counting on the third-string Mav to win the game wasn't a very comforting proposition for anyone, especially me.

"Cordy." Trent moved his hand closer to my neck and his thumb grazed my bare skin. "We can do this. Together. Okay?"

He rubbed his thumb back and forth against my collar bone. The stadium noise, the glares of my teammates, and even the fear that bubbled in my heart all faded as I focused on that one single point of contact. I hated Trent, but I was also starved for him. How could I still crave him after all this time?

Don't fall for it.

I stepped back, and he dropped his hand as his smile faltered.

"Time-out is almost over. Get out there!" Coach yelled, and the mass of players around me pushed onto the field.

The Eagles defense was lined up and waiting.

I snugged my helmet over my hair and ran out onto the field. A couple of the red-jerseyed defenders whistled and cat-called as I approached the left hash. My heart had never beat so quickly, and I thought I might go the way of Pate and lose my lunch all over the field.

The crowd roared as the announcer called out my number and name. "She's a Lady" played over the speakers, and the chances of vomiting rose exponentially. My knees wobbled, and my hands went numb, but I kept trotting to the line of scrimmage. There was nothing else I could do.

"Remember, we can still win even if you miss it." Trent trotted at my elbow. "I'll take it to overtime and shove it up their tailpipes with a touchdown. Just do your best. And get the kick off as quickly as possible." Trent pointed to the play clock. "They will be diving to block this ball."

I needed to get my bearings, but my brain didn't respond to my request, only sort of fizzed and tingled. *So screwed.*

He moved me back a foot or so and pointed to the ground. "I'll have the ball ready for you on this spot. So, line up from here."

I froze. I'd practiced and made these kicks a few times with Coach Carver, but I'd never actually had to try it with the team on the field.

When Jared went down, I was worried. When Pate upchucked, I was scared. But now that I stood on the field, I realized I was screwed.

"Cordy." Trent leaned down and bumped his helmet into mine so we were face to face. All I could see were his light green eyes. "Calm down. Breathe. This is just like soccer, okay? The only difference is that you can't line drive it. Get your foot under the ball and you'll be fine."

"I-I don't know if I can do it." I hated the tremble in my voice. Even worse, I hated that I was desperate enough to rely on the most unreliable man I'd ever met.

"You have to. The team needs you, and I know you can do it. Pretend like it's just another practice." He patted my helmet. "It's a chip shot. You got this." He walked to the line and gave our players some last-second instructions as the other team's taunts continued filtering through my helmet.

"This is definitely not soccer." I craned my head back to stare at the goal posts as the ref blew the whistle.

"Cordy, get set." Trent knelt, ready to catch the ball and hold it for me to kick.

The play clock ticked as I took a few steps backwards and then shimmied a few steps to the left. Trent stared back at me, his eyes shadowed by his helmet.

Maybe he was right. Maybe I could do this. *Just like*

kicking a soccer ball. I'd kicked thousands upon thousands of times. This time wasn't any different, really. A different sort of ball, but the same principle. I just had to get under it more. Totally doable. *You got this.*

I relaxed my shoulders and lined up the shot, gauging the distance I'd need to get the ball through the uprights. I started my forward momentum, leaning forward the way Coach Carver had shown me. The defensive players surged forward as the center hiked the ball.

Trent caught it and set it on the ground, holding it upright for me to kick. I took my long steps, planted my left foot, and let my right leg fly. My foot made contact with a thud.

The ball sailed upward, but the angle was all wrong. I watched in horror as it bounced off one of my own players' helmets, flew straight up, then came down into the arms of a hulking defender. The line of red surged toward me, the big linebacker plowing ahead with the ball tucked close to his body.

Trent scrambled from the ground and dove for him, but another linebacker moved forward to take the hit. They fell in a tangle as my teammates ran after Big Red. The other defenders blocked my players until I was the only one left between Big Red and a touchdown. He lumbered past me, his feet thundering on the turf. I turned and sprinted after him.

With a leap, I jumped onto his back and wrapped my arms around his neck, trying to bring him down. He kept running as if I weren't even there. The crowd roared as he carried me across the fifty, never breaking his pace as I tried to strip the ball from his grip. He threw an elbow back and nailed me in the ribs. I grunted from the sharp pain, but didn't let go.

"Fuck. Off." Big Red panted and kept hulking toward the end zone.

By the time we were at the twenty-five, another defender tried to shove me off. I held on and pawed at the brute's arm, but he'd tucked the ball perfectly.

He carried me across the goal line. My heart deflated like a Patriots football as the announcer's voice boomed, the game clock ticked to zero, and we lost.

The linebacker spiked the ball as I still clung to him. Then he bent over and flipped me to the ground. I landed hard on my back, and all the air left my lungs. I lay there as a sea of players in red rushed the field. It was like *The Shining*, all that red crashing down while all I could do was watch in horror and try to breathe.

Fuck my life.

Big Red's teammates congratulated him on his run for glory and completely ignored me as I tried to catch my breath. I wanted to sink into the grass and disappear. No such luck. A white jersey appeared above me, the number nine written in the signature Billingsley blue.

Trent knelt next to me and yanked his helmet off. "You okay?"

"I'm fine." *I just want to die is all.*

The celebrating players formed a cocoon of noise and bodies around us. The Eagles fight song mingled with the yells and the din of the crowd.

Trent took my hand and pulled me into a sitting position. Then he undid my chin strap and lifted my helmet off.

"You don't hurt anywhere, right?" He placed his hands on my cheeks and stared into my right eye, then my left.

"No. I'm not hurt. Just embarrassed. I lost the game." I tilted my head back. I refused to cry. I hadn't cried on the field since the peewee soccer days.

"We're a team, Cordy. *We* lost the game. Not you." He stood and pulled me to my feet. "It's okay."

"Way to go, short stuff." Big Red clapped me on the back. "Carrying your sorry ass to the end zone will get me on the highlight reel for sure."

Think of a comeback. Think of a comeback. I blanked and stared, only adding to my humiliation.

"Don't touch her." Trent threw an arm around my shoulder and walked me through the mass of players. Our sideline was glum, many of the guys already heading to the locker room or staring at me and whispering to each other.

"Good work, princess." Ethan smirked as I walked to my bench and retrieved my notebook.

"Lay off." Trent tossed his helmet to the equipment handler.

"She loses the game, and you want me to lay off?" Ethan stepped toward Trent.

I snagged my notebook and darted past them. I had to get off the field, away from Trent and Ethan, and somewhere private. Crying on the field wasn't going to happen, but I didn't have a rule against crying in the women's locker room.

"Cordy, wait," Trent called.

I sped faster, weaving between players until I made it to the tunnel and veered away from the crowd. I pushed into the empty women's locker room and let the dam burst, tears flowing down my cheeks as I sank onto the nearest bench. I hadn't failed this badly since I missed the winning goal in a junior varsity soccer practice.

My side hurt as I stripped off my pads and tossed them onto the floor. With my head in my hands, I cried until I was a snotty, teary mess. I hated crying, but sometimes it was necessary. Losing the game and tanking the season? Definitely time for a cry. I lay down and stared up at the fluorescent lights above me as my tears tapered off.

After a few quiet moments, a crazed snort escaped me. Because, at that moment, I empathized with the football. I finally knew what it felt like to be kicked.

CHAPTER THREE
CORDY

"BETTER LUCK NEXT TIME?" Landon, my best friend, forked a piece of my pancake into his mouth.

I wasn't hungry, my stomach still in knots from the previous night. The familiar hum of chatter and the intermittent kitchen noises soothed my jangled nerves, but I still kept picturing that kick. That total clusterfuck of a kick, the ensuing tears, ugly looks from players and students, and the self-loathing inherent in all of it. Shifting in my seat, I smoothed my hand along my ribs, still tender from the linebacker's elbow.

"There won't be a next time." I sipped my coffee and stared out across the quad.

"What do you mean?" He leaned back and ran a hand through his sandy blond hair. He had it cut close on the sides and long on top, giving him a hipster look that I enjoyed ridiculing him for. "Why not?"

"They're going to have walk-on tryouts."

He frowned, the morning light glinting from the spider bite piercings in his lower lip. "When?"

"This week. They'll need a new kicker before the game Saturday. They can't risk using me again, and Jared is out for the season."

"What about the second-stringer, what's-his-face?"

"I don't think they can count on Pate. Poor guy." I winced at the memory of him hurling on the football. "So, a new kicker is in order. Now that they have one loss—"

"A loss that was in no way your fault." He pointed at me.

I sighed. "Come on, Landon. It was completely my fault. If I'd made the field goal, or hell, if I'd manage to get it above the line of defenders even, we would have had a chance. But that touchdown killed us, and it was all my fault."

"No kicker is one hundred percent."

"I'm running at zero percent. Maybe even a negative percentage. I saw ESPN. They're calling it the Kick Six of the century." *Mortifying.* I set my coffee cup down and pulled my blue cable knit cardigan closer around me. "I wasn't supposed to kick. That's not my thing. I'm just there for appearances. The Mav."

He took a swig of his orange juice and stared at me. I knew that look—eyebrows up, mouth curled at one corner. He'd given it to me only a few times since we became best friends freshmen year, and it basically said, "you're full of shit, Cordy."

I sighed. "Do you remember when we met?"

"What is this, *The Notebook*? Of course I remember. You stole my soccer ball." He draped his arm over the back of the chair next to him, his long, lean frame taking up his side of the table.

"I didn't *steal* it. You kicked it into the bleachers. I was trying to do homework."

"Sure you were." He winked. "I'm pretty sure you were just checking me out."

I snorted. "In your dreams, pretty boy. And then, after I retrieved your ball for you, I kicked your ass in our little shootout."

He made a pffftt sound. "You've lost your mind. That

one goal you scored didn't even count. Just dumb luck, really."

"I got it past you. The net was all that mattered."

"Okay, whatever." He darted his gaze around the cafeteria, lingering on a cluster of girls at a table in the center. "What's your point?"

"Can you focus for two seconds, manwhore?"

"Firstly, I learned in my women's studies class that the term 'manwhore' is sexist because it assumes all whores are women. Secondly"—he finally tore his eyes away from the girls—"I'm focused. So shoot."

I cocked my head at him. "And just how many women from that class did you study?"

He shrugged and stared up at the ceiling, clearly trying to remember. "I think I studied maybe three, possibly four, in depth."

"Figures." I tried not to give any hint of a smile, though I was still amused at the fact he'd voluntarily signed up for a women's studies class.

He snapped his head back down. "What can I say? I'm a feminist. I love women."

I snorted. "You are so full of shit. Now can we get back down to discussing me for once?"

"I'm all ears. You were telling me about how you scored a lucky goal on me when we first met."

I let the "lucky" bit slide to keep the conversation on track. "Soccer. That's what I want to do. When the season starts, I want to be on the soccer pitch. Not on the football field. Soccer is where I need to focus."

He shook his head. "Tell me something, Cordy. Do you have a soccer scholarship?"

I crossed my arms and leaned my right side against the cool wall beside the window. Landon knew I had no funds from home or rich parents to see me through undergrad. My first two years of school, I'd relied on a full scholarship for students from my small coal mine of a county in West Virginia. But the money ran out when the sponsor, Reliant

Coal, closed its doors. So, for the third and fourth years of school, I would have to depend on the slight scholarship money from my kicker spot and the dreaded student loans that would eventually come calling.

My dad spent most of his time at the bottom of a bottle, and I sent him what money I could. Mom was long gone, having left when I was a baby. For the past few years, I relied only on myself. It had been working so far, but the loss of the coal scholarship had been an unwelcome surprise.

"Well, do you?" Landon drummed his fingers on the table. "Have you been granted some full-tuition bomb from the soccer gods that you haven't mentioned?"

"You know I haven't."

"But you *do* have a football scholarship."

"Yes."

"Then use your brain for something other than headers." He tapped his index finger on his temple. "*Think*. Be smart about this. Could you have made that kick?"

I chewed on my lip and looked out at the falling leaves. I'd screwed it up so badly that I wasn't sure anymore. I'd made field goals in the few practices I'd attended, but the pressure during an actual game was different. "I think I could have."

"I *know* you could have. You've got a lot of leg. So, why did you miss it?" He leaned forward, his light brown eyes searching my face.

"I didn't get enough lift, so it bounced off of—"

"Nope. That's what happened, but that's not the why."

I shifted in my seat. I knew the answer; I just didn't want to give it to him.

"Come on, Cordy, fess up." He gave me a dazzling smile—the same one that dropped panties all over campus.

I huffed out a breath. "Fine. I missed the field goal because—"

"Because you need to practice." Trent's voice washed

over me like a Gatorade ice bath. But instead of freezing, heat grew in the pit of my stomach.

Trent pulled out the empty chair beside me and sat down. He was smaller without pads, but still a large man. His thigh touched the side of mine, and I shrank away despite the pleasant warmth.

Landon glanced at me and then back to Trent. "Who's this guy?" His mouth turned down in a glower. "Wait, is this—"

"Trent Carrington." He held his hand out across the table.

Landon's eyes narrowed and he avoided Trent's proffered hand. "What do you want?"

Landon knew all about what happened freshman year. He'd pulled every detail from me one night after I'd had a few too many shots at a campus party.

"I overheard your conversation and thought I might be able to add some information." Trent withdrew his hand. He wore a gray long-sleeved t-shirt and jeans. He must have just showered because a clean, woodsy scent drifted around me.

Landon pushed his chair onto its back two legs, balancing while he studied Trent with a critical eye. "What do you think you have to offer?"

Trent turned to me, a sparkle in his light green eyes. My heart hammered against my ribs, and I forced myself not to fidget. Jesus, he was still just as beautiful as he was back then, maybe more so. The sun had graced him with a warm tan, and his dark hair tickled his ears. I remembered it was soft and shone a gorgeous chocolate in the sun. Without the bright stadium lights and the eye black, he was only the most handsome man I'd ever seen. No big deal.

He smiled, and my eyes were drawn to his lips. Memories of a stolen kiss danced around in my mind, but I closed the door on them. Trent wasn't the man he pretended to be. He was much, much worse.

CHAPTER FOUR
TRENT

I UNDERSTOOD THE DISTRUST in her amber eyes. But the way she pulled away from my touch left me scalded.

"Talk, man." Her friend, Landon, smirked at me.

I cleared my throat. "I was just saying that first-string kickers get full scholarships."

She chewed her bottom lip. "I know."

"What do you mean 'I know'?" Landon dropped his chair onto all fours with a clack and leaned across the table toward her. "Full scholarship? You didn't tell me that. You need this, Cordy. Go for it."

"But soccer—"

"Fuck soccer. Try for first-string." Landon opened his palm.

She reached out and lay her small hand in his. Something rumbled deep in my heart, and I had the urge to knock his hand away. I knew all about him, his many conquests, and his constant need to be close to Cordy. He may have had her fooled, but I wasn't buying the "just friends" routine.

Instead of starting something that would end with Landon in a heap on the floor, I slung my arm over the

23

back of her chair.

He gave me an acid look and turned back to Cordy. "You need to try for it at least. You could get your tuition paid for the rest of the year and next year, too, if you stayed on."

"They aren't going to let a girl be first-string." She shook her head, her long brown hair tickling the back of my hand. "Especially not after what happened yesterday."

I took in her scent, sweet and warm. Keeping my hand out of her hair was taking an effort. I leaned closer. "You don't know that. I saw what you did yesterday. You have enough leg to get the ball between the uprights from thirty yards out. You just set up wrong and didn't get enough lift."

She glanced at me and pulled her hand away from Landon. I had to stow my goofy smile and the juvenile feeling of triumph that bloomed inside me.

Tucking her hair behind her ear, she frowned down at the table. "You saw what happened. It bounced off *my own player*. The defenders didn't have to do anything other than stand there. I sank the whole thing myself. Besides, I can't kick a fifty-yard field goal, or even a forty-yarder, most likely. They won't let me be first-string if I can't make distance kicks."

She finally looked at me, a full-on view of her radiant face. My heart stuttered and kicked as my chest warmed. Her amber eyes were like pools of gold, and her lips… Damn, her full lips were made for kissing. I'd only ever gotten a taste of them in that one stolen moment two years ago, but I wanted more. If I told her how far I'd gone to ensure I'd get the chance to be near her again, she might knee me and run.

"You don't need to be able to kick a fifty-yarder or even a forty-yarder to be first-string. Plenty of teams have a first-stringer that kicks within a set number of yardage. Your range could be forty yards and under, or whatever you're comfortable with." I found myself leaning closer to her, drawn in by her wide eyes and the pensive look crinkling her small nose. "You need accuracy. You have the leg. I could see it when you kicked yesterday. But it'll take practice, and we have to keep an eye on the walk-ons to find a guy who kicks it long like a champ, but doesn't have your accuracy up close."

Her eyes flickered as if she wanted to look away, but she couldn't. Her pink lips parted the slightest bit, and I forced myself to keep a reasonable distance, despite my burning need to kiss the breath out of her. Being near her was proving more of a challenge than I'd expected.

Landon stood, his chair scraping across the floor. "Hey, asshole, do you have a point or are you just going to keep eye fucking her in front of me?"

"Landon!" Heat seeped into her luminous cheeks. God, she was beautiful.

I cleared my throat and continued, trying to make my plan sound as nonchalant and off-the-cuff as possible. "They're going to have walk-on tryouts on Wednesday. You need to practice for the next three days. You have to be accurate—not miss a single kick—during tryouts. That's the only way."

"Let me guess." Landon glared down at me. "You want to help her practice?"

"I'm the holder. It only makes sense for me to be the one—"

"No, not a chance." He balled his fists at his sides. "You need to move along."

"I'm not going anywhere." I measured my words. Landon was Cordy's friend, and I hoped he'd eventually be mine, but backing down now wasn't an option. I was too close.

"I don't give a damn that you're the holder or star quarterback. I'm going to kick your ass." Landon flexed his fists until his knuckles gleamed white.

This was not going how I'd hoped. No surprise there. Landon was just as territorial as I'd guessed.

"Landon?" A blonde sauntered up, her athletic shorts barely bigger than a pair of panties. She smiled up at him and ran a hand down his tattooed forearm.

"I'm busy." He didn't break eye contact with me.

"You weren't too busy for me last weekend." The blonde pouted, her duck lips larger than life. She stood on her tiptoes and whispered something into his ear before dropping back down.

Landon's jaw went slack and his eyes seized on her ample chest that was covered with only a sports bra. He swallowed hard. "Cordy, I ah—"

"Just go. I'm fine." She turned so her back was against the wall, then pulled her sweater tighter around her like it was some sort of armor.

She felt like she needed to defend herself. Against me. For the millionth time, I cursed myself for ruining things with her two years ago. But I could fix it. I would do anything in my power to make her see me again the way she had then—with bright eyes and a trusting heart.

The blonde molded herself to Landon's side, but he turned back to Cordy. "No, I can stay. I don't want to leave you alone with—"

"We aren't alone." Cordy waved her arm at the busy cafeteria. "It's not like he's in the back of a windowless van offering me candy."

I arched an eyebrow at her comparison between me and a kidnapper. I should have been offended. Instead, I laughed. She wasn't that far from the truth. If I could have tossed her over my shoulder and run with her, I would have. But that move didn't exactly strengthen trust, and I wanted her trust more than anything. All I needed was for her to give me a chance.

"I don't like leaving you with him." Landon shifted his gaze from her to me.

"I don't like you going to jail for indecent exposure." She gave a pointed look at the blonde whose hands roved along Landon's torso and began inching lower. "So you should probably go somewhere private."

The blonde tiptoed again and whispered something that made Landon's eyes close. Once finished with whatever scandalous words she'd chosen, she eased her body down his side with a breathy sigh.

He opened his eyes. "Okay, I'm going, but I'll see you this afternoon. And you." He stabbed a finger at me. "If you so much as look at her wrong, I'll kick your ass."

"I'll keep that in mind." I smirked up at him as the blonde took his elbow and pulled him away.

Finally, it was just Cordy and me. The way it was supposed to be. I was going to get the chance I'd been dreaming about for two years. I had so much to tell her, so many things to explain.

The chair next to me pushed back from the table.

I turned to see her gathering her bag and grabbing her tray.

"Wait, where are you going?" I stood, worry icing the steady pace of my heart.

She gave me a piercing look, her head cocked slightly to the side as if my question was the dumbest thing she'd ever heard. "Isn't it obvious? Away from you."

CHAPTER FIVE
CORDY

I MARCHED THROUGH THE cafeteria and dumped my tray. Landon was long gone, probably locked in a maintenance closet with his blonde-of-the-week. It didn't matter. I'd planned to finish my homework and do some writing for the rest of the day.

"Cordy, please." Trent followed me out of the cafeteria and into the fall air. Leaves swirled from the oaks that towered over the edges of the quad, and a few students played Frisbee in the fading grass.

I pulled my cardigan closer and followed the concrete sidewalk away from the heart of campus and toward my dorm. Trent dogged my steps, but I didn't want to talk to him. He almost fooled me in the cafeteria. His earnest eyes, sweet smile, and the rich sound of his voice—I'd fallen for all of it before. His feigned interest seemed real just like it had the last time.

He had been so cute, so endearing when we'd first met. But it was all an act. We'd been in the same speech class together when I was a freshman and he was a sophomore. The teacher had randomly paired us together. Having been president of the drama club in high school, I loved the thrill of speaking in front of a crowd.

Trent, on the other hand, visibly paled when we received our final assignment—tell the class a simple story about what you did on your summer break. He'd been terrified, but we'd worked through it together. After he'd successfully given his speech to the class, he'd picked me up and twirled me in the air. My gaze slid toward the arts hall, to the spot where that twirl had happened.

I almost smiled at the memory of his hands on me and the giddy sensation of spinning. I shook my head against the memories. I couldn't just remember the good. There was plenty of bad to go with it. The problem was that when he looked at me or came too close, I was spinning again.

"Cordy—"

I whirled on him, anger overcoming my need to escape. "What do you want from me?"

He stepped closer, and I fought to remain still. I wouldn't back down from him. His eyes softened, and he held up his hands, as if I were wielding a gun.

"I just want to help, okay? That's all I want." A breeze blew by, tousling his hair and bringing the homey smell of wood smoke to my nose.

"Why?"

He lowered his hands and stuffed them into his pockets, his wide shoulders rising in a shrug. "You helped me one time, remember?"

"I remember plenty." I hiked my bag farther up my shoulder and turned my head to watch the boys throwing the Frisbee. Light filtered through the trees overhead, the sun playing along the fallen leaves on the path.

"Cordy." His voice was almost a whisper. He pulled his right hand from his pocket and slowly reached for me.

I held my breath. His fingertips, calloused from years of throwing perfect spirals, brushed my hair from my cheek with gentle pressure. Warmth sparked from his touch and spread everywhere in my body. I was caught up, dragging my attention from the players and back to him. His bright eyes held me in their gaze. I refused to lean into his touch, but how I wanted to do just that.

"Let me help, please?" He dropped his hand and gave me a sober stare.

Pounding feet and crunching leaves distracted me, and before I could move, Trent yanked me into his arms. One of the Frisbee players ran into Trent's back and bounced off while Trent scarcely moved.

"Watch it!" Trent yelled, his voice rumbling in my ear.

I was pressed to him, his strong arms wrapped around me. He was so much larger than me. I couldn't even peek over his shoulder or see past the wide expanse of his chest.

"Sorry, man. Didn't see you there." The student darted past and picked up the Frisbee, then returned to his friends. "My bad."

Trent pushed me back and held me at arm's length. "Sorry about that. You okay?"

He was so close now, and I was surrounded by his scent, by *him*. My eyelashes fluttered, and I couldn't catch a full breath.

"I-I'm fine." I shrugged him off and backed away a step. He'd felt so good. Too good. I wouldn't let anything like that happen again. I couldn't go down the path that I already knew would end in disappointment.

But he had a point about the scholarship and the kicking. If I could get a full scholarship, then I would be able to do what I wanted after graduation without student loans hanging around my neck. Instead of switching majors to something more "practical" as my student advisor would call it, I could stay in the arts, graduate, and teach. That was my dream, and it could actually come true if I practiced. And even if I didn't make first-string, at least I would have tried.

"I owe you one, okay?" He shrugged. "The only reason I'm able to do press conferences after games is because of you. Just let me help you and try to repay the favor that you did me. That's all I'm asking." His words seemed reasonable, but I couldn't miss the eagerness in his tone.

I chewed my lip and considered him. "If we do this, then we're even, right? You won't bother me anymore?"

His face fell, but he nodded. "Right. Even."

"Fine." *What am I doing?* "We can...we can start this afternoon at the practice field."

He looked at me through his lashes, and one corner of his mouth quirked up. Warmth bloomed up my neck and blossomed in my cheeks. God, he was gorgeous.

I took another step backward. "Two o'clock."

He focused on me, not letting me go. "Two, sure."

"Okay."

His smile spread across his lips and reached his eyes. "Okay."

I realized I was still backing away when a normal person would have turned and walked by then. "Okay, so bye."

"Right."

Do not think about kissing him. Do not think about kissing him.

I turned and hurried away.

But the wind still carried his low, sexy voice to me. "Bye for now."

CHAPTER SIX
TRENT

I TOSSED THE BALL above my head and caught it easily, the leather slapping against my palms. The sun shone high and bright, warming the exposed skin of my arms and neck. I tried not to stare toward Cordy's dorm, but I couldn't stop my gaze from returning there again and again.

Five minutes before two, and I'd already been at the field for half an hour, waiting. All I could think about was her in my arms, where she belonged. She fit perfectly against me. I'd enjoyed holding her so much that I could have kissed the wayward Frisbee player for making it happen. I wanted it again, her trembling against me—but not out of fear, and preferably naked. The thought sent a jolt to my cock, though I'd given it quite the workout earlier today while I imagined Cordy beneath me.

Focus. Even though the whole "practice kicking" idea was, at its heart, a scheme for me to get close to Cordy again, I did intend to help her become first-string. She needed the scholarship, and I would do everything I could to help her win it. She belonged on the team, with me. I just needed her to believe it as much as I did.

Finally, I saw two figures approaching the field. My heart leapt at the sight of her luscious frame—high tits, smaller waist, flaring hips, and strong, shapely legs from years of soccer. She wore athletic shorts and a white logo t-shirt, the kind you get for free at college fairs. My joy was only slightly dampened by the sight of Landon at her side.

They walked onto the neatly-kept grass, Landon looking out of place in his black death metal t-shirt and jeans with a long chain hanging down his leg and attached to his wallet. He leaned down and whispered something in her ear. I squeezed the ball between my hands until my fingers ached. When she laughed, I forced myself to breathe. They were friends, nothing more.

He gave her a half-hearted salute and peeled off to sit on the bleachers. She kept walking toward me and pulled an elastic from her pocket. Whipping her hair into a ponytail, her t-shirt rode up, and I got a glimpse of the paler skin of her stomach. My cock tried to join in the fun, but I looked away—and specifically, at Landon, and the mutiny down below quieted. A boner in my athletic shorts wouldn't inspire Cordy's trust.

"So, what are we doing?" She didn't raise her eyes to me.

I grinned and placed the ball on the ground. "First, we run some laps to get warmed up."

She wrinkled her nose. "Fine." Then she took off running toward the edge of the field.

I caught up with her easily, keeping my stride slow so we ran at the same pace.

"Run Forrest, run!" Landon leaned back and slid a pair of shades over his eyes before popping in some earbuds.

"Why is he even here?" I tried to keep my tone even as we cut across behind the yellow goal post, circling the field at a steady pace.

"He doesn't trust you." She kept her eyes forward. Her ponytail bounced back and forth with each of her steps.

"What does he think I'm going to do? Maul you on the

practice field?" I didn't think it would be wise to mention that I would love to pin her to the ground and make her come so many times she passed out from exhaustion.

She glanced at me. "Maybe."

"I thought we already cleared up that I don't have a kidnapper van."

We jogged past Landon, who was laid out on the bleachers, hands behind his head, one knee bent with his foot tapping to a rhythm only he could hear.

"Just because you don't have the van doesn't mean you don't have a thing for snatching girls and putting them down the well with the lotion basket." She smirked.

I wanted to kiss that little quirk of a smile right off her lips.

"I don't have lotion in a basket, but I do like to dance around and talk about how fuckable I am."

She snorted. "Do you make videos, too?"

We rounded the other goal post and headed up the visitor's side.

"Sure do. There's an entire YouTube channel dedicated to them. Very popular."

"Good to know. I'll have to check that out later."

"You do that." I smiled. Did we just have a fun conversation about serial killers like normal people do? *Yes, we did.* "One more lap."

"You're slow, QB." She increased her speed.

I lengthened my stride, getting out ahead of her as we came around to the first goalpost again.

She sped to my elbow and then cut ahead of me to the inside as we ran around the end zone.

"Whoa." I darted to her left so I didn't trip all over her.

She reached out and ran her fingertips along the black padding at the base of the goalpost as we passed. "Try and keep up," she said over her shoulder, her amber eyes taunting me.

My heart sped up a beat at even the hint of competition. Athletes, from the lowliest third-stringer to the top quarterback, have always thrived on competition. To beat another person at something that person thought they were good at? Nothing better. To see that competitive glint in Cordy's eye? I knew I'd need a cold shower after the training was over.

I stayed at her elbow and fought the desire to smoke her to the opposite goalpost. We reached it at the same time and spent a few moments catching our breath.

I pointed to the turf. "Stretch."

She widened her stance and bent over at the waist.

Don't stare at her ass. Don't stare at her ass. I did the same, stretching along with her to keep me from doing exactly what I was telling myself not to. We went through the regular positions—yanking our heels to our asses, loosening our shoulders, and finally ending up on the ground, legs spread in front of us while we pulled on our toes.

Making a very diligent effort not to follow the line of her legs to her pussy, I got to my feet. "Ready?" I offered her my hand.

After a moment of hesitation, she took it, and my heart swelled from that one tiny bit of trust.

"Yes." She stood and trotted over to the ball holder, a three-legged contraption that held the ball upright for her to kick it.

I picked it up and set it on the ten-yard line, right hash. Once the ball was in place, I backed away to watch her form.

"This would be about the distance you'd have for the point after touchdown. Show me your usual set up, but don't kick. Stop right before your foot impacts the ball." I tried to turn off my appraisal of her body—the way the t-shirt clung to her breasts and how her shorts gave me an excellent view of her thighs. Instead, I focused on her posture and balance as she lined up behind the ball, took three steps back, then two steps to the left.

She took a deep breath and started with long striding

steps toward the ball, stopping right before kicking just as I'd instructed. Like any right-footed kicker, she stopped her forward motion by landing on her left foot to brace, then swinging with her right.

I walked the few paces to her and dropped down to my haunches. The smooth curve of her left leg called for my fingers, but I kept my hands to myself. This time.

"You're planting your left foot wrong, for starters." I pointed. "Your heel should be in line with the ball, about a foot away. You've got the distance right. There's a foot there, but you've lined up with your laces next to the ball. That little bit of difference can cost you a lot of lift once the ball comes off your shoe." I peered at her kicking foot. "This is good, turned to the side perfectly. But"—I gripped her heel and pulled her foot down an inch—"if you could make contact with the ball lower, then you have a better chance of getting it over the defenders."

She put her kicking foot down and placed her fists on her hips. "Coach Carver always told me to line the ball up with my shoelaces. And he always put a two-inch tee under the ball for practice."

"You've been using a kicking tee?" *How in the hell did she ever manage to get it off the ground on Saturday?*

"Yeah."

I stood. "You don't need a kicking tee. It's a crutch. You have to learn to kick from the ground, not on a tee. Got me?"

She nibbled her bottom lip. "Yeah. I guess Coach just never thought I'd actually have to kick, so—"

"So he went easy on you. I won't. Your posture needs work, your balance is atrocious, and first we need to get your feet set correctly. Now do your setup, and stop again before kicking. I want to see that heel planted even with the ball or you'll have to do a lap."

"What?" Her mouth opened, her pink lips glistening in the sunlight. I wondered if she'd taste the way she did two years ago—like fruity gum.

"You heard me." I adopted the same stern expression I used during the high school quarterback camp I guest-taught during the summer.

She glowered right back, but marked off her backward steps, then took two more to the left. Taking her long strides, she stopped right before making contact with the ball.

I knelt down and inspected her left foot with a smirk. "Even with the laces. Take a lap."

CHAPTER SEVEN
CORDY

FOUR HOURS AND TWICE as many laps later, I finally planted my heel even with the ball each time I set up to kick. Though, during the entire afternoon, Trent had yet to let me actually make contact with the pigskin.

Landon had eventually grown bored and come over to lie in the grass next to us. His light snores became the background music to Trent's criticism.

After I set up perfectly ten times in a row, Trent ran a hand through his dark hair. "I think your approach is as good as it can be."

I wiped the sweat from my forehead with the back of my hand. The sun sat low on the horizon, casting an orange glow on everything and lengthening each shadow to monstrous proportions.

Trent leaned over and grabbed the ball and the holder. "I have team practice in the morning and classes right after, but I can meet you out here at three. Sound good?"

"Yeah. I can do that." Despite my athleticism, my legs were sore and my back ached from the posture corrections Trent had instituted. I needed a shower and some rest.

"Why don't you ever come to team practice?" He

followed me over to Landon.

"I don't have to go, and I'd rather do other things."
And you're always there.

"Wake up. Time to go." I toed Landon's side.

"Good. I'm hungry." Landon sat up, then rose to his feet before brushing all the grass off his jeans. "I may have dozed off for a second. Did he touch you?" He lowered his mirrored sunglasses and glared at Trent.

"A second? Try two hours. And no, he didn't touch me."

"Then I won't kick his ass." Landon slung his arm around me, even though I was sweaty and pretty certain I had that 'just worked out' smell. "Can we do tacos?"

I laughed. "Not again." Landon would be content if he ate nothing but tacos for the rest of his life. Me, not so much.

He pulled me along with him toward my dorm. "Come on. It's buy-one-get-one-free night at MegaTaco. I'll pay and everything."

Trent walked on my other side. "I'll take her for a real dinner. She needs protein and plenty of fluids."

Landon tensed, but kept walking. "And I bet you're just the guy to give her fluids, right?"

"Ew." I disentangled myself from Landon and walked out ahead. "I'll just shower, hit the caf, and take the food back to my room. I've got reading to do for class."

"You sure? Did you hear the part about MegaTaco?" Landon pouted.

"I did, but I'm just not down for taco night. Can you pencil me in for Tuesday? Taco Tuesday?" One taco night a week was my limit.

He shrugged. "I guess I can make that happen. Let me walk you to your room."

A white car parked along Campus Circle chirped and lit up. It was some sort of Mercedes, but identifying hood ornaments was the extent of my car knowledge.

Trent headed for it and placed the ball and the holder

in his trunk. "I'll catch you guys later."

A pang of something sparked in my chest. Disappointment? It grew as Trent dropped into the driver's seat and started the engine, a smooth purr cutting through the cooling air.

"Rich guys." Landon shook his head and led me toward Hope Hall, my dorm.

I didn't let myself watch Trent drive away. Even so, the familiar feeling of abandonment rattled around inside me. Of course Trent left. That was his thing. Like a catch phrase or a signature style. If Trent Carrington had a calling card, it was that he always walked away first.

The knock on my door shocked me from sleep. It was dark outside, and I was still wearing a towel. *What time is it?* Then I remembered. I'd taken a shower and laid on my bed to cool, but fell asleep. The kicking practice had taken more out of me than I'd thought.

The knock came again.

"Hang on!" My roommate was out. Maybe she'd forgotten her key again.

I rose and stretched, my damp hair hanging down my back. Pulling my towel tighter around myself, I opened the door.

"Shit!" I slammed it closed.

"Ow." Trent's voice filtered through the wood.

"Oh my God. I'm sorry. Hang on. Just a minute, okay?" I turned and dashed to our small closet. Tossing my towel on the floor, I donned some underwear, a tank, and athletic shorts, then returned to the door. I opened it and saw Trent again, his hands full of take-out and drinks. "Come in."

I backed up, and he walked in, glancing around the

room before going to my desk and laying the food out.

He gingerly wiggled his nose back and forth.

"Oh no." I walked to him and stared up at his perfect nose. "I didn't break it, did I?"

"No." He smiled, his eyes warming as he looked down at me. "You gave it your all, though, and I can respect that."

I backed up until my legs hit my bed, and I sat in a whoosh. My knees felt like jelly, though I blamed my lack of food. It wasn't Trent's presence *in my room* or anything.

I cocked my head at him. "Wait, how did you get in here? This is a girls-only dorm."

"I know Brandy at the front desk."

I couldn't stop the frown that tugged at the edges of my mouth. "I'm sure you do."

"No, not like that." He shook his head, then bobbled what looked like a container of hummus. He set it on the desk and turned around. "I'm going about this all wrong." He dropped down, sitting on his haunches like he had on the field earlier. It put him almost at eye level with me. "I know her from a class. I came in, hoping to bribe whoever was at the desk so that I could come up and see you, but Brandy was there, so it all worked out."

Why did my heart lighten at his explanation? I shouldn't have cared who he was with. It was none of my business. Any chance we had together was long since passed. My stomach grumbled, and I winced with embarrassment.

He glanced to my middle. "Exactly. I figured you might have been too tired to make it to the caf, so I brought you some stuff." He rose and began separating out the food. "Here." He tossed me a blue energy drink.

I caught it, practically ripped the lid off, and chugged it. My gaze traveled from Trent's dark hair, down the thin material of his t-shirt to the waistband of his jeans, and stopped on the perfect expanse of ass beneath his belt. *Holy shit.*

When the last of the drink was gone, I wiped my mouth on the hem of my purple tank top and tossed the empty bottle into the small wastebasket.

"Another." He held the bottle out behind him.

I took it and drank more slowly this time. "How did you know this was my dorm?"

He froze for a split second, then turned around and handed me a paper plate laden with food. "I just guessed from the way you and Landon were heading after practice." He looked away as I took the overloaded plate.

"Okay." I wanted to investigate further, but the smell of freshly grilled chicken with Mediterranean seasoning almost turned me into a ravenous wolf. I set the plate on my lap and dug in with the plastic ware. Chicken, salad, rice, and hummus beckoned.

"Where did you get this?" I asked around a mouthful of food.

He pulled out the chair from my desk and turned it around to face me. He ate with me, though not half as rudely. "There's a little deli on the south side of town. Pita Stop. Best hummus in the city."

"You aren't kidding." My manners were sorely lacking, but Trent didn't seem to mind.

We ate for a while, both of us chewing instead of making conversation. When I got to the point where I couldn't eat another bite, I cleaned up for both of us before plopping back down onto my bed.

I met his eyes and realized he'd been watching my every move. Warmth seeped into my cheeks. "Thanks for the food."

"You're welcome."

Silence fell, and it truly dawned on me that I was alone, in my room, with Trent Carrington. The "oh shit" bells began ringing, but it was too late. I couldn't just kick him out after he fed me.

"So, are you ready for the Tigers on Saturday?"

He smirked, that one little move that had every girl in

school at his feet. I pushed my shoulders back. Every girl in school *but me*.

"I think we can handle them as long as we have a great kicker." He rubbed a hand along his square jaw, the stubble there making a *whisk* sound against his palm. What would it feel like against me? I let my gaze slide down the length of him and then back up to his face.

He'd matured in the two years since we'd spent time together. He'd been big then, but now he was NFL-sized. And he'd filled out, his face more angular somehow, and his voice a notch deeper. There were other differences too—a certain reserved nature about him that he didn't have before. At least he seemed reserved on the surface. Underneath, I could sense him simmering, thinking, watching. My nipples tingled and hardened at the thought of him simmering for me. I crossed my arms over my chest to hide it.

He licked his lips, the silence doubling between us like dough in a warm bowl. I needed to remember the Trent who'd abandoned me, the one who'd never called, never even acknowledged my existence. I wanted to ask him, demand he tell me why he'd acted so horribly. But I wouldn't lower myself to bring it up. My pride wouldn't allow it. I deserved an explanation without having to ask for it.

I shook myself inwardly. This man before me seemed different, but deep down, he was the same. We both knew the score. Our history wasn't erased by a few kicking lessons and some food.

He rubbed his palms down his jeans. "I should go."

"Yes, you should." I said, more sharply than I'd intended. I rose from the bed to follow him.

He took a step toward the door, then stopped and turned.

We were standing close, too close. I held my breath and stared up at him. *He is the same. Don't fall for it.* His eyebrows rose slightly, but then his eyes darkened, and I could sense he wanted more from me. Things were sliding out of control in the space of a moment, and that look of his made me want more, too.

He leaned toward me. "Fuck it." In a smooth movement, he put his palm to my cheek and claimed me in a kiss that took my breath away.

He wrapped one arm around my back and crushed me to his hard chest. My eyes fluttered closed as his firm lips took my mouth. A giddy sensation, like the first tinge of alcohol in your system, rushed through me. He moved his hand into my hair and tugged gently, craning my neck back. He licked along my lips, sending a chain reaction of heat skating down my body all the way to my pussy.

I put my hands on his chest to push him away, but my fingers clutched at him. He felt so right, but I knew everything about this was wrong. He was going to use me and throw me away. Again.

I opened my mouth to protest. Bad idea. He ran his tongue along mine and let out a masculine groan that curled my toes. My body melted for him, and my mind was soon to follow. Had I ever been kissed before Trent Carrington? His tongue caressed mine, and I answered, tasting him and venturing into his mouth as he clutched me to him. I gave in and wrapped my arms around his neck, savoring the feel of him against me, the past be damned.

We kissed until my breath belonged to him. I'd never been so hot, my panties sticking to me, and my skin oversensitive to every point of pressure from his touch. I ran my fingers through his soft hair, the strands like silk. His five-o'clock shadow scraped against the tender skin around my mouth, but I didn't care. I wanted him, just like I'd wanted him two years ago. But this time my want had matured into something greater. I didn't just want him. I *needed* him. My body craved his touch, and the thought of him on top of me had me moaning into his mouth.

He broke the kiss and traced a scorching path to my

neck. His lips moved over me like lava, burning me and thrilling me all at once. I opened my eyes and took a full breath as he nipped at my collar bone and moved one hand to my ass.

I can't see you anymore. I'm just not interested. His voice, two years younger, came out of nowhere like a blindside punch. I thought that specific memory was long gone, but it was there, haunting me.

I froze and pulled away. "I can't."

His eyes were wild, and I'd managed to give his hair the "freshly fucked" look that male models would kill for.

"What? Why?" He didn't release me, his eyes flickering to my lips.

I ignored the deep ache he set off inside me, the skittering sensation of pleasure rushing through every nerve in my body, and the hungry way he looked at me. "Please."

His grip on me softened, and he gave me some space. "I'm sorry. I got caught up—"

"You can't touch me like this. You can't kiss me... I-I—you should go." My breathy voice shook, because I wanted his hands on me again.

"Right. Sorry." He turned and walked toward the door, tension written in the stark lines of his shoulders. "I'll see you tomorrow. The practice field."

"Three o'clock." I didn't walk him out, just stood as he swung the door open and stepped into the hall.

He turned to me. Under his stare, I felt naked, as if his kiss had exposed the me I kept hidden from men like him.

"Three o'clock. See you then. Sorry again." His tone spoke of regret, but his eyes still had that predatory glimmer that turned my insides to mush.

It's an act. He'll just get what he wants, and then he'll walk away. I steeled my spine and walked over to him. "Good night." With a firm touch, I shut the door.

His footsteps retreated down the hall.

The boy who'd stolen my heart and then trampled on it

two years ago was gone. In his place, there was a man who kissed like the devil and made me stupid with just a look. I bounced my forehead on the door, trying to knock some sense into my brain since my heart sure wasn't listening.

He's an asshole. A complete and utter asshole.

I backed away and sank onto my bed. I couldn't trust a man like Trent with my heart. Not again. Opening up would only give him the chance to hurt me. I took a deep, shaking breath and let it out.

I would keep our practices professional, win the scholarship, and never let my guard down again.

CHAPTER EIGHT
TRENT

MY HANDS ALREADY ITCHED to hold her again. I would. It was only a matter of time. Leaning against the wall of my shower, I let the cool water cascade down my body. She was all I could see when I closed my eyes, her touch the only thing I could feel.

'Obsession' would have been putting it lightly. Cordy had ensnared me from the start. And even when I tried to free myself from the trap, there was no way out. She had me from the moment I first saw her in that speech class when she was a freshman.

She had only grown more beautiful each day since I left her. Watching her had become my favorite pastime. I knew her schedule, her friends, even her habits. I knew she only saw comedies at the movies, no horrors or tearjerkers. Her favorite ice cream was Moose Tracks. She didn't like to shop. She snuck her school funds to her alcoholic father. I could have made a list a mile long of facts about Cordy.

I'd made a mistake, the biggest of my life, and I punished myself for it by watching her and knowing I couldn't touch her. That was then. Now, things were different. I'd finally taken the step I feared the most just so I could get the chance to make her happy.

Getting close to her was key, and I had no scruples about making it happen. Convincing the university president to make her the third-string kicker had been easy, especially with the cloud of the sexual discrimination lawsuit lingering over the athletics program. With her on the team, I could keep watch over her, and my foolish hope was that she would see I had changed. I wasn't the same selfish boy who left her that night. At least, I hoped I wasn't.

I leaned back under the cool spray and tried to clear my mind. It wasn't working. She was there with her soft skin and sultry eyes. I'd left her dorm with the stiffest hard-on of my life. The cold shower only helped marginally. I'd have to take care of it the old fashioned way.

I hit the knob, stopping the spray, and yanked my towel from the warming rack. Wrapping it around my waist, my erection problem jutted out in sharp relief against the white material. *Shit.*

I walked into my bedroom, the wide windows looking out onto the city park. Collapsing onto my bed, I whipped my towel onto the wood floor and gripped my shaft. *Cordy.* There was no one else I'd thought of for the past two years. Just her, her eyes, the sinful curve of her mouth, the taste of her lips.

Tonight, she'd given me something to hope for. That kiss. I stroked up and down slowly, thinking of how she'd felt in my arms—perfect. Her soft curves had molded to me, and she'd kissed me back with more passion than I'd ever experienced.

She'd stopped us, but my imagination kept going as I lay in my bed. I closed my eyes and pictured laying her down and kissing her neck as I pushed up the hem of her tank top. Would she squirm or moan? The thought of her trapped beneath me and enjoying my every touch had my hand speeding along my cock.

I kissed her tits, sucking a nipple into my mouth and licking the hard tip until she arched her back and spread her legs. Pulling her shorts and panties off, I finally got a look at what I'd been obsessing over for years. Pink and wet, glistening for me in the low light of her dorm room lamp. I licked her sweet taste, swallowing it down and going in for more as she ran her hands through my hair.

"Fuck." My hips rocked to the ceiling as I stroked myself.

I would climb on top of her, kiss her swollen mouth, and push inside. My hand tightened, and I imagined it was her tight pussy squeezing me. Her moans played in my mind, and her eyes were focused on nothing but me. I would fuck her hard, too hard, but I wouldn't be able to stop myself. I wanted to mark her, to claim her, to make her realize there was no other man who could fuck her like me.

She would scream and scratch. I'd make her come until she couldn't think straight. And then, once she was spent and panting, I'd coat her pussy with me.

I came with a grunt, hot come squirting onto my stomach as I smoothed my hand up and down my shaft. "Cordy, fuck."

When my cock stopped kicking, I relaxed and let out a breath.

The orgasm fog slowly lifted, but she was still in the forefront of my mind. The way she'd looked up at me after our kiss—I'd affected her. I could feel it in how she wanted me, how her body warmed under my touch. But then she'd gone cold. I couldn't blame her after what happened the last time we'd kissed. Even so, I wanted her to stay warm and yielding for me. If only I could erase the past and start over. But things didn't work that way.

She'd told me I couldn't touch her. Couldn't kiss her. I'd apologized to her, but I hadn't meant it. I'd never be sorry for tasting her lips or holding her close. Despite my need for her, I'd try and respect her wishes. That left me with one question. How in the hell was I supposed to spend three afternoons one-on-one with her, but not touch her? There was one perfect solution to the problem—convince her to trust me again so there could be touching, kissing, and much much more.

"Mark off your position." I crossed my arms over my chest as she backed away from the ball and took her steps to the left.

Once she was set, I walked up behind her and lined up her trajectory toward the ball. I stood too close for coaching, but I had to be near her. The light scent of her shampoo floated around me, and the fine sheen of sweat on her skin glimmered in the fading light.

Keeping my hands at my sides, I asked, "Why only two steps to the side?"

"A fifteen-yarder from the right hash doesn't need any more angle than this."

I smiled as goose bumps broke out along her neck and down her shoulder to her tank top. She clutched her hands in front of her, fingers wrestling with each other whenever I came too close. Her hair was tied up in a ponytail, and I had an excellent view of her tan skin and the tantalizing line of her tits. "Good."

Backing away, I kept in line with her to watch her movements. "Kick."

She dropped her hands to her sides and took a breath, let it out, then took her set up steps. She planted perfectly, her left heel in line with the ball as her right foot made contact. The ball soared through the uprights and slapped into the net.

"You were a yard off center." I snagged another ball from my gear bag and set it up for her.

"I split the uprights." She put her hands on her hips.

I forced myself to meet her eyes instead of staring at her hardening nipples. "You can do better."

"Better than three points?"

"Accuracy matters. It's only going to get harder the farther you get from the goal." I rose and towered over her.

She glared back at me with a defiant tilt of her chin. "Do I get more points if it's down the middle? No, I don't. So I don't see why—"

"Take a lap." I wanted to stop her mouth with a kiss and bend her backwards until she gave in to everything I wanted. One look at her told me that would end with me getting my eyes scratched out. Instead, I opted for run-of-the-mill sports discipline.

"What?" Her mouth dropped open in an 'O' that had my cock trying to rise to the occasion.

"Go on. One lap. Keep talking back and it'll be two."

She clamped her mouth shut, gave me a murderous stare, then turned and started jogging. I watched as her fine ass with the perfect amount of jiggle headed toward the visitors' side. Her long legs ate up the distance with ease. She turned and crossed the end zone, her ponytail swinging with her steady gait. My cock stirred even more, and I had to stop looking at her before things got out of control.

"Hey, douchebag. What are you doing out here?"

I turned to find Ethan walking up to me, a smug look on his face. As if I needed another reason to hate the asshole. He took every chance he could to nail me during practice, even when the coaches made it clear that for scrimmages, I wasn't to be touched. My arm was what kept the team moving forward, but Ethan didn't give a shit. He still went for me despite the coaches' threats to bench him. He knew, just like the coaches knew, that he was one of the best defensive players in school history. The chances of him sitting the bench were about the same as mine.

He scratched his balls through his athletic shorts. Any cliché about dumb or disgusting jocks fit Ethan perfectly. His dark hair was cut short against his shiny scalp, and his long chest hair was on full display in his v-neck tee.

"I'm busy. Fuck off, Ethan."

He glanced down to the holder and the sack of footballs. "Looking to try a new position?" He grinned and kicked the holder out of place.

I shook my head. "Wow. You really got me there, man." I faked a loud laugh. "Really stuck it to me with that move. What are you going to do next? Throw my footballs over there?" I pointed a few yards away. "So I can't get them?"

His grin turned to a scowl, and he stepped toward me. "I'm tired of your rich boy shit. Someone needs to knock you down a peg, and I'm just the guy to do it." He glanced up, and the stupid grin returned to his face. "Cordelia."

She jogged up behind me, her breaths coming faster from the run. "What does the brain damaged wildebeest want?"

Ethan focused on her like a dog staring at a T-bone steak. He tried to sidestep me.

I followed his movement and did my damnedest not to swing at him. The need to knock his teeth out was already insistent.

He ignored me. "It's not what I want, princess, it's what I can give you."

"I'm allergic to idiots, so whatever you want to give me would just make me break out in hives and vomit. So, no thanks." The sneer in her voice cheered my heart.

He grabbed his crotch. "You'll gag, for sure." He stopped trying to get at her. Instead, he let his gaze travel the length of her body.

She laughed. "We finally agree on something. Hurray."

I fisted my hands. I was ready to pummel him until he was unconscious. I didn't give a shit if it got me kicked off the team—or out of school, for that matter.

I felt a slight weight on my shoulder and saw movement from the corner of my eye.

Cordy was flipping him off, her wrist resting on me. "Now get out of here. I'm busy."

"Going to make first-string, huh?" He glanced back at the goalpost. "Good luck." He sneered. "You keep on splitting those uprights just like I'm going to split your legs."

That was it. He was going down. I started to raise my fists, but Cordy ran her hand down my right arm and held onto my wrist with a tight grip.

I could have pulled away from her, could have launched myself at him. But she didn't want me to, so I didn't. All the same, she couldn't stop my mouth. "I'm going to beat the ever-living shit out of—"

"Thanks for the well wishes." She talked over me. "Bye now. See ya. Go on. Get out of here and take your Axe body spray funk with you. Tell the other demented wildebeests I said hi."

Ethan stopped staring over my shoulder and glared at me instead. I burned to swing at him, to watch him go limp when I shattered his jaw. Cordy's fingers kept me from doing any damage.

He smirked at the rage in my eyes. "Later, princesses." He turned and walked back toward campus with an unearned swagger.

Once he was out of earshot, I pivoted around to Cordy. "What the hell was that? Has he touched you? And why did you stop me?"

She raised her hand to her forehead and shielded her eyes from the sun. "He's just an asshole. There's no point fighting him. He'll still be a douchebag when you're done."

My blood stayed at a simmer. "You didn't answer my question. Has he touched you?"

"One time he… Look, it doesn't matter—"

I ate up the distance between us, my shadow falling across her to the point that she lowered her hand. "Tell me."

She nibbled her lip, but didn't drop her eyes. "Before kickoff on Saturday, when we were in the tunnel, he…grabbed my ass."

"I'm going to rip him apart." I turned and started in the direction he'd gone.

"Trent!" Cordy ran beside me.

"He can't touch you like that." I gained on his retreating figure.

She wrapped her hands around my forearm and yanked. "Stop! Please. I need your help. Kicking help. Please?"

I kept barreling forward. "He needs to respect you."

"You beating him to a pulp won't earn me any respect!" She pulled again. "Please, Trent."

Fuck. Her begging did me in. I couldn't say no to her. The one time I'd said no had gutted me for the past two years. I slowed my pace and stopped. She walked around to my front and raised a hand to my chest. She hovered it over my shirt, not touching me for a long moment. Then she rested her palm over my heart. I wanted to cover her hand with mine, but I didn't move.

She'd touched me, which was more than I'd hoped for so soon in our time together. I wouldn't spook her.

"I'm not worried about him, okay?" She studied my eyes with her amber stunners. "I'm worried about getting that scholarship." She sighed and started to drop her hand.

I couldn't help it. I grabbed her and pressed her small palm to my chest.

She glanced to our hands and then back to my eyes. "Remember before? When I told you about my family. And my dad?"

Before I ran away and broke both of our hearts? Yes, I remembered. I nodded.

"It isn't any better. I still have to pay my way. I still send half my Pell grant home to my dad so he can live. If I walk away from this chance, it would be the second dumbest thing I've ever done. So, help me. I'm asking you to help me. I don't want to just be the Mav anymore."

I would have given her anything she'd asked for. Anything I had was hers. She wanted my help, and I would give it without reservation. The heat from her hand seeped into my heart, warming me all the way down to my toes.

I cocked my head to the side. "What's a Mav?"

"Oh, that. It's kind of what I call myself." She dropped her eyes. "Mascot with a vagina." Her mumble was almost inaudible.

I laughed as she blushed. "What about the W?"

"It's silent." She shook her head. "Forget about that. Will you help?"

"Of course. Whatever you need. But promise to tell me if he speaks to you again or touches you or does *anything*. Promise me."

She sighed. "I promise."

"So, what was the first dumbest thing you've ever done?"

"What?" She dropped her gaze again, and I knew she'd heard me.

"You said walking away from the scholarship would be the second dumbest thing you'd ever done." I put my fingertips under her chin and pulled her face up to mine. Though I dreaded the answer, I asked the question all the same. "So what was the first?"

She looked away, then stared me down and straightened her spine. "Two years ago. I kissed you."

CHAPTER NINE
CORDY

Two years earlier

"After I threw every sizeable oyster I could find into my net, I washed them off in the cold water running along the shore." Trent stood at the front of the classroom, his hands clasped in front of him and his eyes scanning the students as he spoke. He'd been talking for ten minutes, giving a detailed story about his time at the beach last summer.

"Then I took them home and gave them to our cook. That night, my family and I ate the oysters I'd found along the small reef near our beach house, and I've never had a better one since." Trent finished his speech and gave me a smile as the entire class clapped for him.

We'd practiced for weeks, and he'd gotten through the whole thing without so much as a missed word or a stutter. He smiled, but now he focused only on me. The butterflies went to war in my stomach, fluttering and fighting as Trent walked toward me and the professor called the next student.

Trent sat down beside me, his presence familiar but

also exciting.

I leaned over, aware of my breast pressing into his arm and the way he moved even closer to me. "You did it."

He turned to me, his green eyes sparkling, and smiled. "*We* did it."

After the final presenter told the class about his summer as a construction worker, our time was up. Class was over for the semester, and the last day of school was bittersweet. I wouldn't have another class with Trent. He would focus on business and math while I stayed in the humanities.

I gathered my notebook and stood as the classroom emptied.

The professor walked up. "Well done, Mr. Carrington. You've certainly come a long way this semester."

Trent grabbed my books and his. "Thanks. I'm not quite ready for the stage just yet. But you're right, I'm not so afraid of public speaking anymore."

Professor Lane looked at me over her glasses. "I think I know the reason for your improvement and, sad to say, it isn't my stellar teaching abilities. I'm proud of the both of you. You make a good team." She smiled and returned to the front of the classroom.

"We do, you know?" Trent walked at my elbow as we left the classroom and headed out into the muggy spring day.

My heart flipped at his admission. "I like to think so."

We had spent so much time together over the past few months—studying, practicing, and then just goofing off in-between. Sometimes I would catch him looking at me with a heat that made me blush. Then he'd glance away or crack a joke, and the delicious tension broke like water around a river rock.

I would deny to Landon that I'd fallen for Trent, but he was always in my thoughts. I'd think about him in the shower or at night when my roommate was asleep. I hadn't had time for boys when I was in high school.

Soccer, schoolwork, and my waitressing job took up every waking moment. But when I looked into Trent's mesmerizing green eyes, something combusted inside me until everything else was obliterated. Everything but him.

"I still can't believe we did it." He shook his head.

I yanked my backpack strap tighter as we walked toward the quad. "I knew you'd kill it. You didn't even blush that much. Maybe a little red, but that was it. You didn't do that splotch thing you used to do, where it looked like you were having an allergic reac—"

Before I could finish my thought, Trent picked me up and whirled me around. I grabbed onto his shoulders as he twirled me, and a laugh of pure joy escaped my lips. When he slowed and finally stopped, my feet hit the ground, but my head was in the clouds, spinning from his touch.

He put a warm hand to my cheek and leaned in. I closed my eyes and waited for my first kiss. His breath tickled my lips, and I panicked about whether I should have put on some gloss or chewed some gum.

"Cordy." His whispered word sent tingles along my skin as he pressed his forehead to mine. My heart stopped and waited for his kiss to bring it back to life.

"Hey, red shirt!" A loud yell broke through the stillness between us.

I opened my eyes and saw Jake Valley, the Bobcats quarterback, striding toward us.

"What are you two doing?" He gave a light-hearted laugh. "PDA on the quad?"

"We were just talking."

"Cool." Jake gave me a warm smile as he walked up. "I'm Jake. You are?"

"Cordelia Baxter."

"Nice to meet you, Cordelia. I was just about to tell the red-shirt here that me and some of the guys were going for pizza later tonight. You two want to join?" He kept his eyes on me.

"I, um—"

Trent slung his arm around my shoulder. "We have plans. Sorry, man. Next time?"

"No, it's cool. I wouldn't want to spend any time away from this one, either." He winked at me and kept walking toward the humanities building. "I'll hit you up next time," he called.

Trent's arm around me felt perfect, and I wanted to snuggle into his chest and just stand like that until the campus police came by and said, "Get off my lawn."

"Plans?" I asked and leaned my head against his shoulder.

Before I could make my snuggle dreams come true, he whipped me around to face him. "Yes, plans. I'm taking you out to dinner to thank you for your help this semester."

I could only offer a half smile. I wanted him to take me out because he was interested, not as some sort of thank-you. "You don't have to do that." I dropped my eyes to the green grass beneath us.

"I do. And not just as a thank-you."

I held my breath, hoping to hear more of what my heart craved. Was this it? Would I finally get a chance with the guy I'd been crushing on for four months straight?

I peeked at him through my lashes.

He smiled and tucked a lock of hair behind my ear. "I want to do this because I like you, Cordy. I want to take you on a date. Our first date."

CHAPTER TEN
TRENT

ON MONDAY, WE PRACTICED for two more hours until the sun got low enough to hide behind the oaks that ringed the campus.

Cordy absentmindedly rubbed her right thigh. I had the fleeting thought of offering a massage, but could already envision being shot down in a ball of flames.

She'd been avoiding my eyes ever since her statement that kissing me was the biggest mistake of her life. That had been a pretty big kick in the stomach, but I tried to play it off and keep coaching her. By the end of practice, she was nailing the center from as far back as forty yards. Anytime she missed one, we'd go over the problem area and she'd try again. She didn't miss twice in the same spot.

"Dinner?" I stuffed the last football into my equipment bag.

She stopped rubbing her thigh and twisted her hands in front of her. "I need to get back. There's some reading for class, and—"

"Just something real quick, okay? I don't want you to go back to your dorm and skip eating. That's a sure way to screw yourself over at tryouts." I wanted her company for as long as I could get it. If food was the proper bribe, then I would go all out. "SanPeggio's is not even a mile from here. Pizza okay?" I happened to know that pizza—with pepperoni, extra cheese, and fresh diced tomatoes—was her favorite food.

She looked toward Hope Hall, her dorm, and nibbled at her bottom lip some more. That one little movement drove me wild. I wanted to be the one with my teeth against her.

"I don't know—"

"Come on." I did my best to play it cool, but I was dying to get a yes out of her. "You worked hard today. It'll be my treat."

She narrowed her eyes, as if my last entreaty made the idea even less appealing. I was losing her. *Shit.*

Full desperation mode kicked in. "You can bring Landon if you want. You know, if you're afraid I might keep you in the back of my van and only let you out when it's time to lotion up or whatever."

That got a smile. She threw up her hands. "Come on. Let's go. I can't very well turn down free pizza."

"That's my gir—" *Oh, shit.* "My g-good friend." I recovered with a stutter. If that could be called a recovery. *Perfect.*

Her smile was quickly replaced with a pinched look. "Just because I accept free pizza doesn't mean I'm your girl." She turned on her heel and strode to my car.

I slung the equipment bag over my shoulder and followed. "I know. Sorry. Just an expression."

"I'm your kicker, nothing more." She walked to the passenger door and leaned against it.

"Right." I winced at her angry tone, and almost would have preferred a kick to the nuts rather than another protest about how we would never be more than teammates.

The car chirped and lit up when I hit the button. I stowed my bag in the trunk as she lowered into the passenger side. Once she closed the door, I leaned into the trunk and just breathed for a few moments. She was pissed now, but it would fade. This was my chance to explain.

Don't fuck it up. Don't fuck it up. With that mantra running on a treadmill in my mind, I slammed the trunk shut and prayed she'd let me make it all up to her.

My fingers shook as I reached for the door handle. The problem with my plan—one that I had yet to think of a way around—was that I'd have to start by telling her the cruel truth about that night two years ago. The truth about me.

CELIA AARON

CHAPTER ELEVEN
CORDY

TRENT CRANKED UP THE air conditioning, and I leaned forward as the cool air rushed over my skin.

I whipped my ponytail off my neck and stretched my back. "Mmm, this is heavenly."

"Glad you like it." He took University Drive, winding around the campus and out onto the main road in our college town.

My phone beeped with a text message. It was Landon.

Where are you? Feelin some tacos?

I tapped out a response.

Getting pizza with Trent. I'll call when I get back to the dorm.

My phone beeped again after only a few seconds.

Trent?

Then it went off in rapid succession.

Have you lost your mind?

Did you forget what he did?

Where are you?

I'm coming to get you.

"Popular, huh?" Trent quirked his lips up in a half smile and parked in front of SanPeggio's.

"Something like that."

I texted back as Trent got out.

Don't worry. It's just pizza. Calm down. I'll call after.

My door opened.

A slight thrill went through me as I glanced up at Trent. "You didn't have to open my door for me."

"I wanted to."

"This isn't a date."

"I think you said that." A smile tugged at the corner of his lips.

I stepped out, and he closed the door for me. Cars rolled down the darkening streets, and thunder rumbled in the distance. Billingsley was nestled in the foothills of the Appalachians, just far enough south to have hot, humid summers with stormy springs and falls.

Trent put his hand at the small of my back and led me up onto the sidewalk and to the front door, which he opened for me. I shot him a look, but he only smiled down at me and led me forward with the same steady hand.

The hostess seated us in the back near the busy kitchen, and the smell of fresh baked dough had my mouth watering. Students packed the tables and booths, and several upperclassmen hovered at the bar along the far wall. Trent sat across from me, but only after I gave him a death stare when he attempted to sit next to me on my side of the booth. Not happening.

The server walked up and introduced herself, giving Trent a too-bright smile before getting our drinks.

"What sort of pizza do you like?" He took his beer from the server as she set my lemonade in front of me.

"I'm not too picky. Just get what you like, and I'll live with it."

Tossing his head back, he took a swig of his beer. He wiped the foam from his upper lip with the back of his hand in a movement that was at once boyish and masculine. Why did he have to be so adorable?

"So, what are we having?" The server threw her long blonde hair over her shoulder and spoke only to Trent.

"Um." He ran a hand through his unruly hair. "I'm kind of feeling pepperoni, extra cheese, and diced tomatoes." He shot me a glance. "Is that okay with you?"

I wrinkled my brow. "Actually, that's perfect."

Trent winked at me. "Then I can't do any better than that. A large please, and some cheese sticks while we wait if that's cool with you."

Since when did he think he could wink at me? "Yeah, cheese sticks are good." I lifted my bare thighs off the vinyl material of the booth. I was still a little sweaty, and they were sticking.

"I'll get your order in." The blonde smiled and practically skipped off to the kitchen.

The restaurant buzzed around us as we settled into an awkward silence. Trent took another drink of beer as I unwrapped my straw and lowered it into my glass.

"So, are you still majoring in literature?" Trent leaned back, getting comfortable while we waited for our food.

"Yes. You're still in business?"

"Right. I'm pretty much done with my coursework. I did a study abroad for the first half of the summer, learning about international markets."

"Where was that?"

"Spain, Portugal, and then a week in Paris."

I dropped my eyes to my lemonade. That sort of "study abroad" took some serious cash—the kind I'd never even dreamed of having. Hearing him talk about it so nonchalantly reminded me we came from two separate worlds. It was well known on campus that he hailed from money, and I'd gleaned a bit of family information from him during our short time together two years ago. But I couldn't pretend to fathom a life where I could just go traveling the world on a whim. I'd barely made it out of West Virginia and was working hard not to land right back in my dried up coal town.

"That sounds amazing." It was all I could offer.

"It was. I just wanted to tell you what I did over the summer. How was my presentation this time?" He gave me a disarming smile.

I didn't return it, though I silently gave him points for wit.

He cocked his head to the side, trying another tack. "What about you? Do you still want to teach when you get out?"

"Yes." His question and my answer reinforced why I was spending time with him. If I could get that first-string scholarship, I would be able to teach wherever I wanted without fear of student loan bills. He was a means to an end. There was nothing more between us.

So why did my breath hitch whenever he touched me? Why was he all I could think about when I was in class this morning? We were two different people now, and our past was murky at best. I needed to calm down and think instead of falling under his spell again. The problem was, when he looked at me with those piercing eyes, I felt like it was the first time in my life that anyone truly *saw* me.

"Hey, Cordy." He reached across the table and took my hand. "Did I say something wrong?"

His palm was warm and engulfed mine. I didn't pull away. I knew I shouldn't have wanted his touch, but just the sensation of his skin against me thrilled and scared me at the same time.

I avoided his eyes, as if I could hide from him by looking elsewhere. "No, nothing wrong. It's just that, where I come from, we don't have the luxury of touring the world or..." I shrugged.

"Cordy, look at me." His soft voice was a caress. Our gazes clicked, and heat began to rise along my neck. Could he see my blush or feel the rapid beat of my heart?

He squeezed my fingers. "I know we have different backgrounds. I remember what you said about your family and where you're from." He drew his brows together, the center wrinkling. "I won't deny that there was a time when I cared about stuff like that." His eyes grew sad.

Embarrassment flooded me at the thought of him looking down on me. I tried to pull my hand away, but he maintained a firm, yet soft, grip.

"But I don't care about it now. None of that matters, okay? I don't care where you come from. And if where I come from bothers you, then I won't talk about it." He released my hand, and I pulled away from him, though it took an effort.

He was so open with me. Or at least he seemed open. Maybe he was fooling me again. I couldn't tell. His eyes were earnest, and his words had the ring of truth.

Even so, something about what he'd said rattled around in my mind, and I needed to know more. "When you said you used to care about—"

"Cheese sticks." The server slapped a basket of bread laden with mozzarella in the center of the table. "And your pizza will be out shortly."

Trent and I took the plates she offered. Thunder shook the building, and rain poured outside the plate glass window along the street. I was safe and warm with Trent, about to enjoy dinner like two normal people without a past.

He nudged the basket closer to me. "You first."

Cheese and bread were easily my favorite foods on the planet. He didn't have to tell me twice. I snagged an end piece, the cheese browned and still hot from the oven.

"Marinara?" He offered the little cup of red sauce to me.

I blew on the cheese stick and slowly shook my head. "I would never profane cheesy bread with marinara. Not happening."

"A purist." He grabbed a stick and dunked it in the sauce. "I can respect that."

I took a bite and forced myself not to moan around the salty deliciousness. I finished my stick in short order and followed it with a gulp of lemonade.

"Have another." Trent downed his beer and motioned for another from the server.

"I shouldn't." I reached for the basket.

"You should." Trent plucked another cheese-laden piece and took a bite, his eyes focused on me. "Live a little."

"How could I say no to that?" I snagged the next to last piece. "I'm going to be full before the pizza even gets here."

As I devoured half the cheese stick, he grabbed the beer from the server and took a long draw. When he set it down, I noticed his hand shook the slightest bit.

I placed the uneaten half of the cheese stick on my plate. "What?"

"It's just." He cleared his throat. "I've been waiting a while to tell you this."

I leaned back, a shock of cold flowing through my veins. "What?"

He squared his shoulders, as if waiting for someone to land a blow. "I think I'm ready to tell you what happened two years ago."

For just a moment, it seemed like maybe we could pretend two years ago never happened. We could have a pizza and a few drinks without giving a thought to that night. But from the shake in his hands and the anxiety in his voice, I could tell he'd intended to clear the air all along.

He reached across the table again and took my hand. All the noise of the restaurant faded into the background, and it was just the two of us.

His eyes softened as he stared at me, remorse crinkling the skin next to his eyes. "I made a mis—"

"Cordy!" Landon rushed up, his hair hanging in wet ropes and the rest of him soaked from head to toe. His gaze went to where my hand was encased by Trent's.

"Lan—"

Before I could say a word, he reared back and clocked Trent hard on the jaw.

CHAPTER TWELVE
Trent

Two years earlier

I SMOOTHED MY HANDS down my dress shirt for the third time since we'd gotten out of the car and into La Café Blanc.

Cordy smiled as the server unfolded her napkin and laid it across her lap for her. "I can say, without a doubt, I've never been somewhere this fancy in my life."

I stared at her, because I couldn't seem to see anything else. Her hair cascaded over her shoulder in a chestnut wave. The lavender dress she wore cut just under her collar bones, and the rest of the material clung to the curve of her waist. Her amber eyes glimmered in the low light of the restaurant.

"Trent?" She smiled, and my heart took off at a gallop.

"Yes, fancy." *Good one, you moron.*

She laughed, a small, delicate sound that I wanted to put on repeat. "Have you been here before?" Her eyes roved the fine linens, black tie servers, and the expansive chandeliers and candelabras that gave the restaurant its swanky reputation.

"A few times. Whenever my parents are in town."

"How often do they visit?" She smiled up at the server as he poured her water. "Thank you."

"Not too often, thank God. My dad's okay, but my mom can be a holy terror." I was putting it mildly.

My mother was hell bent on controlling every move I made and every detail of my future, including who I would marry, what career I would choose, all the way down to what pattern of china would be on display in my home. As the heir to the Carrington family fortune, I had been groomed since birth to carry on the family investment business and maintain a lifestyle befitting my station. What I wanted didn't matter, at least not to my mother. She believed my football aspirations were beneath me, and she made a point to bring her opinions to my attention every chance she got.

"She probably just wants what's best for you." Cordy glanced to the menu. "What's good here?"

"I always get the filet. But if you wanted something else, the game hen is pretty good, too."

She nibbled her lip. I rubbed my sweaty palms down my pants. That move of hers had gotten to me over the past few months. Whenever she was considering something, she would run her teeth along her bottom lip.

"I think I'll try the filet if that's what you like." She laid the menu down and gave me the full-on view of her glittering eyes again.

The server approached. I placed our orders as he deposited a small bread plate.

I passed the butter plate to her. "So, what about your parents? You've mentioned your dad a couple times, but I don't know much else."

She shifted in her seat and looked up at the closest chandelier. "He's back in West Virginia. He used to be a miner, but the company closed his mine, and he's been out of work ever since."

"What about your mom?"

"She left when I was a child." She shrugged, still keeping her gaze away from mine. "Long gone."

"So you're on your own?" My mom couldn't go a week without sending a passive-aggressive text, so I couldn't imagine a life without her.

"Something like that."

"Does it bother you?"

Cordy dropped her gaze to the candle flickering at the center of the table. "I have a scholarship that pays my tuition. Dad calls every so often. I'm able to study and get some soccer time in, so I'm happy as I can be, I guess."

It wasn't good enough. She deserved to be truly happy. I'd never met a woman like her. From the first moment I saw her in class, her head bowed shyly and her hands at war with each other, I'd wanted her. I'd had girlfriends in high school, dated a girl freshman year, had flings at parties. But none of them enthralled me like Cordy. Her quiet nature, the determination that burned in her heart, and her compassion drew me to her.

People like Cordy didn't exist in my world. The girls I grew up with either had enough money to be unrelenting bitches or they had an old money name with no actual money behind it, which turned them into schemers. Cordy was a breath of fresh air—one I didn't even realize I was desperate for until I found her.

"What about you?" She carefully buttered her bread with her knife.

"What about me?"

"Are you happy?"

"I am when I'm with y—" I coughed into my hand to stop myself. *Oh my God, Trent, too fast.*

She gave me a dazzling smile and her cheeks grew pink. Seeing that reaction made my chest warm and my heart race.

Reaching across the table, she took my hand. "I'm happy when I'm with you, too."

CHAPTER THIRTEEN
TRENT

LANDON'S SUCKER PUNCH STUNG just enough to enrage me. I rose and grabbed a handful of the front of his shirt, not sure if I wanted to show him what a real hit felt like or slam him on the ground.

"Don't fucking touch her!" He swung wildly, but I had fifty pounds of muscle on him, easy.

I shoved him back, and he fell over a table and skidded into another one. The nearest students yelled and backed away, their pizzas toppling to the floor. I stalked toward him as he struggled to his feet.

"Trent, stop!" Cordy pushed through the tables and stood between Landon and me.

"Get out of the way. I've got this." Landon brought his fists up and swiped his thumb across his nose.

She turned to him. "Have you lost your mind? He's the starting quarterback, all muscle, works out every day."

My chest puffed up a little more with each of her words, pride overcoming my anger.

"Move." Landon eyed me with no hint of fear.

I would have respected him if I didn't want to beat the shit out of him for trying to separate Cordy and me.

"I can take him." He advanced until Cordy was the only thing between us.

"You can try." I stepped closer, but Cordy put her hand to my chest.

"Stop it, both of you! You're being idi—"

"Hey!" Mr. Sanpeggio rushed from the kitchen and into the main dining area. "What's going on? Call the cops." He motioned to a server.

"We're leaving." Cordy's voice was strong and even.

"Outside! Go!" Mr. Sanpeggio waved his flour-covered hands at us.

"Come on." Cordy grabbed Landon's forearm and yanked him toward the door. I followed behind, ready to drop him if he tried anything else. Turning back, I called, "I'll stop by tomorrow and pay for any damage."

"Out!" Mr. Sanpeggio bent over and started righting the tables as the students finally relaxed. A couple had whipped out their cell phones after I'd sent Landon flying. Thankfully, they didn't capture anything other than the standoff. It might make campus news, but not much more than that.

The rain fell in sheets as all three of us stood under the awning across the front of the restaurant.

Cordy released Landon's arm and whirled on him. "What the hell was that?"

"He was touching you." Landon shrugged.

"Newsflash, Landon, it's okay for people to touch me!" She fisted her hands at her sides as the wind whipped droplets of water onto her bare calves.

She was wrong on that count, but I wasn't about to break this up. Landon needed to learn that he would never receive clearance to fly outside the friend zone.

"Not him." He pointed at me but kept his eyes on hers. "Have you forgotten what he did?"

"No." She crossed her arms over her chest.

"Then act like it. You're out to dinner with him like he's worth your time. He's not. He's the same spoiled rich boy who ran off and left you."

"I'm not having this conversation." She shook her head. "Not here and not in front of Trent."

"Let me take you home." He grabbed her elbow.

I'd heard enough. "Not a chance."

"I wasn't talking to you." Landon bristled and finally looked at me. "Go on back to your mansion and drown yourself in some Perrier or champagne or whatever the hell you got. This is between me and Cordy."

"Take your hand off her." I tried to keep my control, but every second he touched what was mine made a muscle tick in my jaw.

"You going to make me?"

"Stop!" Cordy stepped away from both of us and into the rain. "Trent, drive both of us back to campus. No talking from anyone. Just driving." She marched toward my car.

I fumbled in my pocket for the key fob and unlocked the doors right as she reached for the door handle.

She yanked it open. "Landon, get in the back."

"I'd rather walk." He turned.

"Landon Russell Garnet! Get your ass in this car!" Her shrill yell made the hairs on the back of my neck stand up.

That stopped him in his tracks. He stalked past me and muttered "motherfucker" under his breath. I followed and dropped into the driver's seat as he slammed my back door far harder than necessary.

"No talking. Just driving. Everyone cool off." She shivered as she spoke.

I turned the air to warm and tried to surreptitiously press the button to turn off the heat to the rear passenger seats, just to be a dick. She slapped my hand away and clicked it back on. *Busted.*

The rain didn't let up as I drove down the road back toward campus. Water rose along the edges of the pavement, and my tires sent up curtains of water with every puddle. Cordy stayed silent, and one glance into my rearview gave me a full view of Landon's scowl. I turned onto University Circle as lightning streaked the sky, followed by a crash of thunder.

"Where can I drop you, *Landon*?" I tried to keep the edge out of my voice. I failed.

"Hope Hall."

I shot him a death glare in the rearview mirror. There was absolutely zero chance I'd take him to Cordy's dorm.

"No." Cordy stared out the window, her face hidden. "He's in Rowen Hall."

My glare turned to a smirk. He flipped me off as I turned down the side street leading to his dorm.

He reached forward and put a hand on Cordy's shoulder. "I want to talk. We need to—"

My grip tightened on the steering wheel. His familiarity with her rankled.

"Not now. Not after that. I need a minute. We'll talk tomorrow." She shook her head.

He withdrew his hand and slumped into the seat.

I pulled up in front of Rowen Hall. "This is your stop."

Landon pulled the handle but didn't open the door. "Cordy, come inside with me."

"Not a chance." I glowered at him in the mirror. "Get out."

"Tomorrow, okay?" She glanced back at him, kindness in her eyes, but resolve in the set of her jaw. She definitely did not feel like talking.

"I don't want to leave you with him." Landon hesitated.

Every second he waited was one more second where I wanted to pummel him for even thinking he had a chance with Cordy.

"He's going to drop me at Hope Hall and then be on his way. It's fine."

I forced a chipper tone into my voice. "Yeah, Landon. I'll make sure she gets home safe and sound. Don't you worry, little man."

Cordy gave me a frown that had me rethinking my words. "Don't be an ass." She turned back to Landon. "I'll call you tomorrow."

He punched the back of my headrest and flung the door open before stepping out and slamming it shut. Tucking his chin to his chest against the rain, he walked up the front steps and turned to watch as we drove away.

"Stop taunting him like that." Cordy crossed her arms over her chest again.

I drove back up to University Circle and seriously considered leaving campus and taking her to my apartment, but her curt tone shut that thought down. I turned left and drove slowly toward her dorm. "He sucker punched me. I think I'm entitled to rattle his cage."

She shook her head. "And that's why he hates you. Because you think you're *entitled*."

"That's not what I meant." Why was she so good at cutting through my shit?

"It doesn't mean he should have hit you. Obviously, I'm pissed at him about it. It's not okay, and I'm sorry he did that. But Landon is my best friend. He's only trying to look out for me. Cut him some slack. He deserves it."

"What about me? Do I deserve any slack?" *No, I don't.* I swerved around a giant puddle on the roadway.

She didn't respond, just turned to stare out into the rain.

I took a deep breath and pushed Landon out of the equation. Repairing my relationship with Cordy was the real goal.

"I'm sorry, okay?" I turned into Hope Hall's parking lot and pulled into a spot near the doors. "I don't like him touching you or being close to you."

"He's important to me. He's always been there for me. Always." When she turned back to me, her eyes glistened with unshed tears. "You haven't. Remember? You don't get to bust into my life and push away the people who matter to me."

My heart thudded against my ribs, and I couldn't bear to see hurt in her eyes—more hurt caused by me. I clicked my seatbelt off and leaned closer to her. She didn't back away when I placed my hand on her damp cheek.

"I'm sorry." I wiped away an errant tear with my thumb. "Okay? I don't want to upset you. I'll do better with Landon. If he's important to you, he's important to me."

Her eyes widened in what seemed to be a mix of disbelief and confusion. "Why?"

"Because…" *Because I'm in love with you and have been for the past two years.* "Because I care about you."

"None of this makes sense. After all this time, why are you here? Why are you acting like two years ago never happened? It did." Her chest heaved, and she choked back a sob. "You're such an asshole."

"I know." I moved closer, our breaths mingling as the rain drummed on the car. "I had some things I needed to work out."

"For two years?" Her eyes flickered to my lips as another tear rolled down her face.

"Yes."

"What things?" She wrapped her fingers around my forearm but didn't pull my hand from her cheek.

"Things you won't like." I ghosted my lips over hers, and she sighed.

The sound traveled straight to my cock, and I needed her in my arms. But she wasn't there yet. The distrust in her voice and the hurt in her eyes was killing me, and I wanted nothing more than to take it all away. I smoothed my hand down to her neck, and her eyes closed for a moment. The urge to kiss her tried to overwhelm every bit of caution. *Wait.*

"I remember that night as if it were yesterday. The way you acted. The things you said." Her voice grew even quieter. "You said you weren't interested. You said…" She nibbled her bottom lip.

That was it. I couldn't stop myself. I claimed her mouth in a searing kiss. She dug her nails into my forearm as I pushed her back into the headrest. I wanted the pain; it was nothing to what I endured when I wasn't with her. She pushed against me with her other hand, but her lips parted the slightest bit. I took full advantage, sinking my tongue into her mouth and groaning with satisfaction as I did it.

Running my hand down her side, I clicked her seatbelt off. It retracted, and I pressed her to me, her breasts rubbing against my hard chest and her mouth under my control. When I gripped her hip and yanked her closer, she moaned. A swirl of desire blew through me like a tornado. My cock was painfully hard, and my hands were desperate to touch every inch of her. Instead of pushing me away, she clutched my shirt.

I tilted my head, angling our kiss, and grabbed her wet ponytail. When I pulled it back, she moaned as I left a hot trail of kisses down her throat.

"Trent, we can't." Her voice was breathy sex.

I bit her shoulder in response, and she gripped my hair as I continued tasting her.

Trent—" Her protest turned into a moan when I squeezed her breast. It was a handful, the nipple thick and hard against her damp white t-shirt. I raised my head, taking in the look on her beautiful face as I twisted her nipple between my thumb and forefinger.

Her lips parted, and her eyes were half-lidded. I twisted harder, and she bit down on her bottom lip. I leaned in and took it from her, running my teeth along it before giving her another hard kiss. I craved her, needed her to be skin to skin with me.

"Off." I yanked at the hem of her shirt.

"Someone might see. Wait—"

"No." I yanked it upward, and she lifted her arms for me. The windows had long since fogged up as the rain continued to pour. No one would see us, and I needed more of her.

I peeled her t-shirt off and tossed it in the back seat. Then I did the same with mine. Her gaze traced the line of my pecs and then ventured lower until she stared at the bulge in my shorts. When she licked her lips, I groaned and attacked her mouth again. She gave it right back, our tongues twisting and her hands running down my bare skin, setting me on fire.

A yellow sports bra was the only thing separating me from the stiff peaks of her tits. I kissed down her chest as her fingernails dug into my scalp. Licking the top of each swell, I enjoyed every tremble, every little tell from her that she enjoyed my touch.

Her skin tasted like rain with the slight hint of salt. I kissed between her breasts, her nipples teasing me through the yellow cotton. I took one in my mouth, sucking her through the material. Her harsh gasp sent a thrill down my spine as I sucked and bit at her. My other hand kneaded her right breast, pinching her nipple as I worked the other over with my tongue.

I bit down on her tight bud, and her back arched, her nails digging even harder into my scalp. I switched breasts, but wasn't content with the fabric between us. I shoved the cup of the bra down, revealing a deep rose nipple, the tip dark and hard.

"Fuck, you're beautiful." I took her into my mouth as she made an *mmm* sound.

Her flushed skin beneath my touch, her salt on my tongue, and her moans in my ears were hotter than anything I'd ever experienced. I sucked and nipped at her until she was writhing and shaking.

I slid the tip of my tongue up her throat and took her lips again. She opened readily, her arms wrapping around my neck as my hands roved her body. She trembled as I ran my fingers down her smooth skin, past her shorts, and to her legs. I slid my left hand up her thigh until I met fabric.

Her tongue warred with mine, and her heart pounded

against my chest as I slid my fingers up farther, until I grazed her wet panties.

"Fuck, Cordy. You're so wet for me."

"Trent." She grabbed my wrist and welded her knees together.

That wouldn't do. I pulled my fingers back the slightest bit and massaged her inner thigh while I sucked on the sweet spot where her neck and shoulder met. Her little moans floated around me until she relaxed enough for me to move my fingers back to where I wanted them. When I raked my thumb over her clit, she jolted and clung to me.

I glanced to the backseat, but there was no time. I didn't want her to cool off or come to her senses. I wanted her to come all over my fingers, my mouth, my cock— anything I could get, I'd take it.

I fastened my lips on her throat, sucking and biting at the sensitive skin while my fingers massaged her pussy through her panties. Focusing on her clit, I stroked faster and faster while still tasting her and biting her—leaving my mark. When I pushed her panties aside and delved my fingers into her wet folds, my cock kicked against my shorts.

"Trent. Oh my God." She made a keening sound, low and long when I squeezed her clit between my fingers and rubbed back and forth. Her knees fell open, and a song of triumph played in my heart.

"That's it." I slid my fingers lower and pushed one inside her tight entrance. Her hips bucked, and I covered her exposed nipple with my mouth.

I pulsed my finger in and out before sliding in a second. She was so tight, and I wanted to be inside her more with each passing second. But this wasn't about me. It was about her. I wanted to give her something for once, instead of taking.

She rocked her hips to my rhythm, her pussy hot, wet, and desperate—perfect. Sliding my fingers out, I focused on her clit again, rubbing in a circular motion as I sucked hard enough on her nipple to leave a bruise.

Her breaths came even quicker as she moaned and dug her nails into my back. I sped my fingers faster, giving her what she needed until her legs began to tremble. Releasing her nipple, I claimed her mouth, fucking her with my tongue as I stroked her sweet spot.

When she began to seize, I broke the kiss and pressed my forehead to hers. "Look at me. I want to see you when you come."

Her eyes flew open, and she moaned long and low as I pressed two fingers inside her, using my thumb to keep the pressure on her clit. Her pussy clamped down on me, clenching my fingers in tighter. She watched me as I thrust in and out of her as she came. Her heartbeat thrummed in her neck, and she pressed her lips together as her body ebbed and flowed with her orgasm. She was beautiful. When I'd wrung the last bit of pleasure from her, she relaxed, and her gorgeous eyes finally closed.

I eased out of her and drew my hand to my mouth. Her eyes fluttered open as I licked her delectable taste from my fingers.

"Oh my God." Her voice was half moan. "That's so hot. I can't even—"

I kissed her, sharing her taste as she melted into my arms. My cock demanded I do more than just kiss her, but he wouldn't be satisfied tonight. At least not until I got back to my apartment. Cordy deserved more, and she'd already given me so much.

Breaking the kiss despite the protest in my heart, I leaned back and pulled her bra into place. Her lips were redder, and I'd left a few calling cards along her neck and shoulder.

She put her hands to her face as I reached back between the seats and grabbed her t-shirt. "That was so... I've never done anything like that before."

"What?" My brain shorted out at the thought that Cordy was still a virgin. Of course, I hadn't seen her with anyone except friend-zoned Landon during the two years since we'd parted. It was a good thing, because I may have snapped any guy's neck who tried to get with her. But I assumed she'd fooled around in high school at some point. I certainly had.

I pulled her hands from her face and stared into her eyes. "What are you trying to say?"

She looked away as red rushed into her cheeks. "I didn't mean to say that out loud. Can we just drop it? I-I should go. I have homework to do and stuff."

"No." I gently grabbed her chin and pulled her face back around to me. "We can't drop it. Are you saying you're a virgin?"

She clenched her eyes shut. "This is up there with the most embarrassing moments of my entire life."

"Cordy, look at me. I need to know." *Because I want to fuck the ever-loving shit out of you, but I don't want to hurt you.* "So we're on the same page."

"Yes. Okay?" She covered her face again. "Yes."

CHAPTER FOURTEEN
CORDY

"WHAT DOES HE MEAN by the phrase 'confusions of a wasted youth'?" Professor Crane leaned against her desk at the head of the classroom. "More importantly, who was A.H.H., and why was Tennyson so touched by his passing as to write one of the greatest poems of all time? Ms. Baxter?"

I snapped my head up and fumbled with my pen. I'd been doodling the number nine all morning. "A.H.H. stands for Arthur Henry Hallam, one of Tennyson's friends from Cambridge. His untimely death changed Tennyson."

"How so?"

I put my pen down. "He brooded on the past. He complains about his 'wasted youth' because he could have spent his time with the man who mattered most to him instead of being engaged in other pursuits or holding onto grudges."

"Grudges?" Professor Crane cocked her head to the side.

Projecting much, Cordy? "I meant that he lamented about not focusing on A.H.H. before he lost him."

"Correct…"

Her voice faded as the class continued, and she called on other students. My thoughts were drawn back to Trent. He invaded every cell of my body, demanding my attention. I closed my eyes at the memory of his hot lips scorching a trail down my neck. He'd kissed me with an urgency that made my mind turn to mush.

His fingers had been magical, and I squirmed in my seat as heat rushed through me. Pressing my thighs together, I forced myself to open my eyes and focus. But when I remembered the look in his eyes as I came, pressing my legs together wasn't enough. I crossed my legs, but I'd moved too quickly. My knee hit my book at the edge of my desk and sent the book and my notes onto the floor with a clatter.

The professor stopped her lecture and gave me a piercing glare.

Sorry professor, I was daydreaming about being finger-banged in my dorm parking lot by a guy I hate.

She glanced down to my notes—a sheet of paper covered with various doodles of the number nine. My cheeks were already pink from the memories I couldn't keep at bay. Interrupting the class and getting stared at by twenty other students plus the professor only added to my mortification.

I bent over and gathered up my book and notes.

"Sorry," I mumbled and hoped my ridiculousness didn't affect my class participation grade.

"It's all right, Ms. Baxter." The professor gave me an amused smile. "I'm partial to the number seven, myself."

Kill me now.

She turned her attention to another student and continued her lecture. I quietly collected my things and hurried out of the door at the back of the class. There was no point in staying when I couldn't concentrate. Trent filled every corner of my mind. Lord Tennyson simply couldn't compete.

My cell buzzed in my pocket. I pulled it out and flicked across the screen. Dad was calling. That was odd. He never called when I was in class.

I swiped to answer. "Dad?"

"Hey honey." His words were barely slurred, which was practically sober for him.

My concern lessened a little. "What's going on? Are you okay?"

"Fine, fine. Don't worry. How are you doing in school?" He went into a coughing fit. Though years of working in the mines had ruined his lungs, he refused to file for black lung benefits. Too proud. Between the stubbornness and the drinking, my dad was a difficult man to love. But he was all I had.

"Everything is going well. I'm actually between classes right now. So I have to go in a minute."

"All right. I just wanted to call and let you know I appreciate the little extra you sent."

I cocked my head to the side. "What?"

"I made an arrangement with Stan's widow, you know, who lives two houses down and has really big, uh, really big—"

"Yeah, Dad, I know about Mrs. Trapper's assets. But what did you mean about extra?"

"The money." He coughed again, the sound dry and deep. "The extra money. Anyway, I made a deal with her to where she's going to fix my supper three nights a week."

"That's—" I shook my head in confusion. "That's great, actually. I'm glad. But I still don't know what—"

"Hang on!" He grumbled and the phone made a series of clicking noises as if he were juggling it. "Got it. Honey, someone's at the door. Might be the guy from the company. I heard some people were getting late severances or something. We'll talk later. Love you, honey."

"Love you too, Dad, but—"

The phone went silent.

I pulled it from my ear and stared at it like it was a

foreign thing. "What money?"

I walked across campus to the practice field, taking my time and trying to steel my nerves. A cold front had followed the rain, and wet leaves squished under my cleats as a chill wind blew through the trees. Dread settled in the pit of my stomach as my mind returned, yet again, to last night. Had I really told Trent Carrington that I was a virgin?

I shivered, embarrassment snaking around my spine and pulling tight until I felt awkward tingles in my brain. I'd kissed guys before, done the usual light petting, and even thought about going further. But that was before Trent. After Trent, I'd gone out a few times. I'd find myself comparing my dates to him. They weren't as tall, or smart, or didn't look at me the way he did. A litany of excuses from me would end our night, and then I'd never return their calls. Over the course of a single semester, Trent had managed to ruin other guys for me.

Still a virgin. *Ugh.* He'd seemed genuinely shocked when I'd told him, which only added to the awkwardness between us in the car. My humiliation had lit a fire under me, and I'd snatched my shirt and run into my dorm with it pressed against my chest.

He hadn't followed. Thank God. But the memory of his lips on mine and his fingers dancing along my skin still had me scissoring my legs at odd times.

Another cold gust blew by, and I pulled the sleeves of my long-sleeved t-shirt down so they covered my hands. I wanted to turn back to Hope Hall, to avoid practice and Trent altogether. But that would have been dumb. I wasn't ready to compete. Trent was the only thing that would give me a chance at tryouts the following day. So I soldiered on, passing a few students running along the track or hitting balls in the tennis courts next to the practice field.

My cheeks warmed as I approached, but my heart stuttered when I noticed Trent wasn't standing in his usual spot. I peered across the length of the empty field and into the bleachers on either side. No Trent. I stopped next to the goalpost and checked behind me, hoping to see him jogging up with his equipment bag. There was no one.

He'd ditched me. Every negative emotion converged inside my chest, and I had to lean against the goalpost to stay on my feet. I had never experienced humiliation in its fullest form as I did then. I'd let him back in, given him more of me than I'd ever given anyone, but once again he'd shown his true colors. Trent had walked away.

I tipped my head back and willed the tears to disappear. I wouldn't cry over him. I refused. He wasn't worth another tear or even another thought. I would practice without him. *You don't even have a ball.* I ignored that thought and sprinted out to the ten-yard line to start my stretches.

I bent over at the waist and reached for my toes. I focused on my breathing, keeping it smooth and steady as I tried not to come apart. My hamstrings began to hum as I maintained my stretch. I continued, going through each position until I was loose and ready to kick.

Straightening my back, I stared toward campus, foolishly hoping that Trent would show up. Nothing. I took a deep breath and let it out before lining up on the left hash and pretending a ball was sitting on the ground.

Marking off my steps was easy. Keeping my eyes on the imaginary ball wasn't. Pain warred with humiliation, but I wouldn't let either of them win. First-string had been my goal all along, not Trent. I let my arms hang loose at my sides and took my steps, ending with a kick that went nowhere.

"That would have definitely made it." Trent's voice made me whirl. He carried the ball bag, but wore street clothes instead of workout gear.

"Where have you been?" I wanted to hug him, but kicking him in the shin also seemed a decent option.

"I'm sorry." His gaze turned dark, and he rolled up the sleeves of his blue button-down. "My mom came into town for a surprise visit."

"Is everything okay?" My earlier resentment faded away into concern.

Something was off. He was tense, and it was as if he'd shuttered his feelings—none of which seemed good.

He knelt, his jeans sticking to his muscled ass just right, and set up the ball for me. "Line up again. You looked good, but your follow-through was lacking a bit."

I stepped to him as he straightened. "Do you want to talk about it?"

He sighed and met my gaze. Something fleeting passed across his eyes. Maybe reluctance or pain? "We'll talk about it." He put a warm palm to my cheek, and he leaned closer, his woodsy scent swirling around me in the cold air.

I held my breath, suddenly desperate for the indulgent feel of his lips against mine. My eyes fluttered closed.

He grazed his mouth against mine, and his voice lowered to a whisper. "But not until after practice." Placing his hands on my shoulders, he spun me around. "Set up."

I glared at him as he gave me a sexy smirk. *Asshole.* How did I manage to go from broken-hearted, to angry, to happy to see him, to wanting to kill him in the space of ten minutes? It was like emotional whiplash, and Trent was the sole cause.

We spent the next two hours setting up and kicking from various yardages. I made most of the kicks, only missing a couple from the thirty-yard left hash. Trent stalked around me the entire time, making small tweaks in my approach and coming down hard on my follow-through. By the time we were done, I'd run three laps and kicked countless footballs.

"That's enough for the day." He snagged the kicking holder from the ground as a particularly bitter blast of wind blew by. "I want you rested for tomorrow."

"All right." I watched as he tucked the last ball into his equipment bag.

I nibbled my lip, wishing I felt relieved that our time was over. Instead, disappointment pulsed through my veins.

"Come on. You need to eat a good dinner and sleep well tonight. Tryouts start at eight." He took my elbow and led me away from campus, toward the back of the practice field where his white car waited.

"I should probably just eat at the caf." Even as I spoke, I kept walking with him.

"Nah, I've got something better."

"What?"

He smiled and slid his hand across my lower back. Goosebumps broke out along my skin, and I couldn't pretend it was from the cold.

"You'll see."

The car chirped as we approached, and he strode ahead of me and opened my door.

A thump sounded from the trunk as he shoved the ball bag inside. After a few more moments, we were driving toward the center of town.

"Do you think I'm ready?" I rubbed my right thigh.

"As ready as you can be." He reached over and grabbed my hand. "And I'll be there the whole time."

My stomach swirled. Trent had me spinning again. He kept driving away from school, and I began to recognize the route we were taking. The architecture turned older and stuffier as we skirted the business district.

"Wait." I turned to him. "Are we going to La Café Blanc?"

"Yes." He squeezed my hand.

Panic rose inside me. My last visit was one of the worst nights of my life. "I'm not dressed for it. They won't let me in the door."

"They will." Certainty rang through his deep voice. "Don't worry."

"I need to shower. Can we just go somewhere else?"

"No." He took the final turn and eased into a parking spot alongside the ornate restaurant. Giving me just a glance from his sparkling eyes, he added, "I have a reservation."

"But—" Before I could make any more protests, he climbed out of the car and walked around to my side.

He opened the door, and I stepped out, my nerves balling into a knot in my stomach. The air grew colder by the minute as the sun set. I shivered, though I wasn't sure if it was because of the chill or the memories the restaurant evoked.

"Come on." He took my damp palm and walked me around to the front of the restaurant and up to the heavy wooden doors. A server swung them open and ushered us inside with a smile.

As Trent led me into what I thought was familiar territory, I gasped and squeezed his hand. He leaned down and whispered in my ear, "I told you I had a reservation."

CHAPTER FIFTEEN
TRENT

Two years earlier

DID SHE JUST SAY that she was happy whenever she was with me? The rest of the world continued around us, people eating and drinking as the servers bustled here and there. All I could hear was Cordy's voice. The only thing I could see, her amber eyes.

"Trent?" She smiled and took a sip of her water.

"Sorry." I shook myself inwardly. "But could you maybe say it again?"

She laughed and set her glass down. "I'm happy when I'm with you."

I let out a deep breath and locked her words deep inside me somewhere, like precious jewels. I'd take them out and inspect them later, turn them over in my hands again and again when I was alone. The pure emotion that radiated from her warmed me and had me smiling. I was buzzing as if I'd just shot-gunned two beers.

Our food arrived, and we chatted about classes as we ate. A normal conversation between two college students. But I couldn't keep my gaze from her lips. My heart kept galloping ahead, rushing too fast and falling too far. Each smile, each witty comment or intelligent thought only ensnared me more until I was hers. She kept talking, as if she hadn't noticed my heart in her hands.

When we were finished with our meal, the server cleared our plates and brought a chocolate lava cake with a scoop of vanilla ice cream. I got bold enough to where I changed seats so that I was sitting at her elbow.

We shared, each of us tasting the too-sweet dessert and moving closer and closer as we did so.

By the time only one bite remained, my left arm rested against hers, our shoulders almost touching. I scooped up the delectable bite and poised it in front of her lush lips. She opened them, and I slid the spoon inside. The quiet moan she let out had my cock locked in a desperate battle with my zipper.

Her eyes closed as she savored it. I leaned in and licked the chocolate off her bottom lip. Her eyes opened in surprise, then closed again as I pressed closer, my mouth on hers and my tongue dancing along the seam of her lips.

She opened for me, and I finally tasted her—sugary and perfect. She twisted her tongue with mine, sending waves of pleasure rushing over my skin. I'd kissed plenty of girls before, but none of them had been like this. Cordy was special, unexpected, and utterly intoxicating.

Someone cleared their throat. Cordy broke the kiss and dropped her head as embarrassment colored her cheeks. I glanced up to find Grandlin Daugherty giving me the nastiest look in his arsenal.

Fuck me.

"Trent, a word?" He spoke with his usual nasal intonation and motioned toward the back hallway of the restaurant. It wasn't a request.

"Mr. Daugherty, I didn't realize you were in town." I stood.

Cordy looked up at me. "Is everything all right?"

"I'll be back. Stay here, okay?" I squeezed her shoulder

and followed Grandlin.

He turned sideways to cut through the tables, though the move didn't help much given the width of his potbelly. I scanned the restaurant, and my worst fears were confirmed. A teary Carlotta and her mother sat at a table against a far window. The Daugherty clan had had an excellent sight line to the kiss Cordy and I had shared. A cold sweat broke out along my brow.

Once we reached the back hallway, Grandlin shoved me into the wall. I was a foot taller and made of muscle, but I was already in enough trouble without laying out Grandlin Daugherty.

"Are you trying to make a fool of my daughter?" His voice was rough, and anger boiled in his eyes.

"No."

A server rushed by and into the kitchen, giving us a worried glance as he passed.

"Then what are you doing with that tramp?" He pressed his forearm against my throat.

"Don't call her that." My anger at his words overtook my worry. I shoved him off me, but not hard enough to do any damage. "She's a friend from school."

"Lizzie is calling your mother as we speak." He stabbed his finger in my face. "And you have some explaining to do to Carlotta."

I rose to my full height and scowled at him. "I don't have to explain myself to anyone, especially not your spoiled brat of a daughter."

He stepped toward me, but seemed to think better of putting his hands on me again. "That *spoiled brat* isn't just my daughter, Trent. She's your fiancée!"

I sat in the formal sitting room at my parents' house.

The stuffy paintings of the last six generations of our family line hung along the walls, each of them haughty and puffed up with self-importance. I rubbed my temples and leaned back to wait for whatever scolding my mother intended to give.

After the scene at the restaurant, I'd taken Cordy back to her dorm and promised to call her later. She'd been confused, then hurt. The way she closed up and wouldn't even let me kiss her good night was like a razor along my heart, but I deserved it. I couldn't explain everything. She wouldn't understand about Carlotta and my family responsibilities. Cordy lived in the real world, not one created by tradition and set to spin on its axis by wealth.

I cradled my head in my hands as my father's shuffling gait and my mother's shrill voice sounded from the cavernous main hallway.

Grandlin strolled in first, anger in his huffs and puffs as he took a seat on the tufted leather couch across from me. "Carlotta is crying her eyes out at home. I hope your little side piece was worth it."

I glared at him. "Don't call her that. Don't even talk about her." My voice rose with each word. I'd been angry before, but the rage that boiled inside me at his insults to Cordy was something new.

"Trent. Don't speak to Grandlin in that manner." My mother walked in, her face drawn down in a familiar look of disappointment. My father held onto her arm as she led him to the couch and sat him next to Grandlin. She perched on a nearby chair, her beady eyes trained on me.

"What's all this about?" Dad gave me a curious stare as Grandlin launched into a diatribe about what he'd seen at the restaurant.

When the blowhard finally quieted down, Mom rose and began pacing, her heels whispering across the rug and then clacking on the herringbone oak floors. Her tall, willowy frame covered the distance back and forth. I'd seen this so many times. When I was a child, the pacing usually ended with a punishment for me. Now, I wasn't sure what she'd do. She couldn't exactly send me to my room.

She stopped in front of me. "What were you thinking, and who is this girl?"

"I just wanted to do something nice for her. She's no one, really." The lie stuck in my throat, but I continued, "She helped me in my speech class. I wanted to repay her."

"By mauling her in a restaurant in front of your fiancée?" Grandlin squawked.

"She isn't my fiancée!" I slammed my fist into the side table, and my mother started pacing again.

"Grand, can we have a moment with our son?" My father's quiet voice cut through the tension.

"Use it to talk some sense into him!" Grandlin rose and stalked out. His voice echoed into the room as he demanded a glass of scotch from our butler.

"Trent, let's discuss it." My father smiled and tried to lean forward, but he didn't have the strength. He gave up and fell back against the leather, fatigue already eating away at him.

The cancer was in the middle of its magic trick, making my father disappear right before my eyes. First it took the spring from his step, then his hair vanished, and now all that was left was his frail body and the sparkle that still lit his kind eyes.

He'd always been so strong, like an oak whose roots went to the center of the earth. But over the past year, his body had betrayed him. The hard worker, former college quarterback, and family man to his core was now looked after by a team of nurses day and night. It was still a shock to see how much he'd changed. Dad had always been so vibrant and sturdy that I'd been lulled into thinking he would always be that way.

Memories flitted through my mind—Dad lifting me onto his shoulders with ease after my peewee team won our super bowl, Dad throwing a particularly hard shoulder and laying me out during a "friendly" football game when I was in high school, Dad wiping away happy tears when I got accepted to his alma mater and recruited as a quarterback prospect. The memories should have been happy. Instead, they stung as I considered the pale reflection of the man my father used to be.

His brittle voice barely made it to my ears. "You know that our families have hoped for quite some time that you and Carlotta would grow on each other. Now that Zane is a senator, this would be the perfect time for you and Carlotta to solidify the union of our families."

Zane, Carlotta's brother, had won a U.S. Senate seat, made possible in large part by campaign money from my parents. A merger between our families would place the Daughertys and the Carringtons into the upper echelons of politics and power. I was interested in neither. And, most of all, I wasn't interested in Carlotta.

"I'm not getting engaged to that girl, Dad. She's a terror. My first memory of her is when she had her nanny fired for not giving her a Popsicle fast enough." I sat back in my chair as Mom continued her circuit of the room.

"Think about your future." Dad rubbed his left knee with bony fingers and winced. "Think how high you could climb with a senator for a brother-in-law and the Carrington family wealth in your pocket. Think of all the good you could do."

I scoffed. "As a politician? I can barely give a speech to my class of twenty people about what I did last summer. And I could only do that because of Cordy's help."

"Cordy?" My mom paused. "That's the bitch's name?"

I stood so fast my head swam. "Don't call her that."

"Geneva, please." My father held his hand up. "Maybe we should stop trying to force it."

"No!" My mother whirled and crossed her arms over her chest. "I haven't withstood the goddamn Daugherty family for the past eighteen years just so you could ruin it at the last minute with some girl you met at school. Your future is riding on this. You could be anything you want to be. Don't you see, Trent?" Her voice shook, but everything else about her was deathly still. She had always prided herself on perfection, and today was no different. "This is a small sacrifice on your way to wherever you want to go. Don't throw it away!"

"Come now, darling." My dad waved her over. He was the only one I'd ever seen who could gentle my mother.

She stopped her pacing and sat next to him, taking his hand. "I'm sorry. I don't want you to get excited. It's not good for you."

He kissed the back of her hand. "Maybe we should listen to what Trent has to say."

She turned to me, and her gaze hardened. "I've heard enough. Your dad wants to go easy on you, to let you find your own way in the vain hopes it would lead you back to reason. Clearly, that hasn't worked. So, here's what we're doing from now on. You will not see this Cordy person anymore. You will take Carlotta on at least two dates per month."

I shook my head and glared at her. "No—"

"I'm not finished." She narrowed her eyes. "If you choose to follow these instructions, everything will remain as it is. You'll go to college. You'll play on the football team. You'll have access to money, and all your needs will be met. If you choose to disobey, you will be cut off. No money, nowhere to live, nothing except the clothes on your back and the Carrington name."

My father gaped at her. "Geneva, let's not take this too far."

She softened the slightest bit as she glanced at my father, his eyes the same shade of green as mine. "Gordon, this is for his own good. He needs to learn how things are instead of living in some fantasy world."

I lowered myself into my chair and let her words sink in. Could I give everything up and try to make my own way? The thought of defying my mother set off fireworks in my mind. I could leave this house and never look back. But then my gaze moved to my father—the man who'd always been there for me. What sort of son was I to cause family strife during the small amount of time he had left? My heart was being ripped apart with competing emotions, thoughts of my father, and thoughts of Cordy.

Dad swallowed hard and turned his sunken eyes to me. "She's probably right." He sighed, as if unsure of his own words. "You have some growing up to do. The family needs you now that I…"

Mom leaned into him and rested her head on his shoulder. The same pain I felt at watching my father deteriorate showed in her eyes.

He cleared his throat and continued, "And, really, how much do you know about this girl? You've only just met her in the past few months. I think—" He fell into a coughing fit, his worn out body shaking from the effort. Once it abated, he wiped his face with one hand as my mom wrapped an arm around his narrowed shoulders. "Your mother is right. Give Carlotta a chance. Take her out on a few dates. See if this thing with the other girl is real. Time will tell. If you're still hung up on her after some time apart, we can revisit it. You don't have to decide on either of them today." He ended with a wheezing breath and put his palm on his chest, as if that could calm the life and death battle that raged in his lungs, his blood, even the marrow of his bones.

Mom glanced to Dad and then back to me as if to say, "Look, you're upsetting him." I couldn't bear the thought that she was right.

"Please, son?" Dad extended his hand to me.

I took it, his thin skin a ghostly reminder of the strong, healthy man he used to be. "All right. I'll give it a try, and"—I swallowed hard as the words burned like acid in my mouth—"I'll stop seeing Cordy."

CHAPTER SIXTEEN
TRENT

CORDY MAINTAINED A DEATH grip on my fingers as I led her to the same table we'd sat at two years ago. A few things were different this time around, including the fact that I'd rented the entire restaurant just for us.

The chandeliers glowed softly overhead, and overflowing arrangements of blue hydrangeas and yellow roses decorated the tables nearest to ours, encasing us in our own small world within the restaurant.

I pulled her chair out for her, and she sank down, her head on a swivel, taking in every detail I'd planned. "This is so..." She stared at the nearest floral arrangement, the large yellow roses in full bloom.

I lowered into my chair, sitting at her elbow so I could be close to her. A string quartet played softly in a back corner, and a candle flickered at the center of our table. Everything was as I'd requested, but the perfection of the venue didn't quell my nerves.

The server brought the wine I'd selected and filled our glasses. I couldn't take my eyes off Cordy. The shock and wonder on her face made me almost giddy.

She finally brought her gaze back to mine. "What is all

this?"

"It's for you."

"But why here?"

The server brought a bread basket and a plate of beef carpaccio.

"And why now?" She sipped her wine and kept her eyes on mine.

My mouth went dry.

My heart thumped in a rising rhythm as she peered at me with a mix of pleasure and confusion. How could I explain everything to her without sounding like a total jerk? I'd practiced my little speech a million times. Now that I was on the verge of giving it, the words stuck in my throat. I took a gulp of wine, set my glass down, and took her hand beneath the table.

My rehearsed explanation was gone, destroyed by the look in her eyes. "My father died," I blurted it and winced.

Her face fell and she squeezed my hand. "I'm sorry."

I shook my head. "No. I mean, thank you, but that's not—" I sighed and took a deep breath to start again. "That night with you two years ago was the best of my life."

Her eyes opened wide, and her lips parted.

"I wanted to see you again. The things I said on the phone about not being interested were lies. There was this other girl"—I kept speeding through my words even though her expression darkened when I mentioned Carlotta—"but I didn't want her. I wanted you. My parents, though, they had planned for a long time that I would be with Carlotta. That night at the restaurant, Carlotta was there with her family. Her father was the one who interrupted us. There were consequences for me. That night, I promised my parents I would stop seeing you." She leaned away from me, but I couldn't stop the words from spilling out. Not now. "And that's why I lied to you and said I wasn't interested. If I didn't, my parents would have cut me off. I wouldn't have any money or my trust fund." When she pulled her hand away from mine, a shard of anguish pierced my heart. "Cordy—"

"Let me get this straight." Her tone was cold. "You decided that having a nice car and a posh apartment were more important than breaking my heart?"

"No. I mean yes." Desperation laced my voice. "You don't understand. My family had certain expectations for me about the sort of girls I would date and eventually marry. You weren't what they'd hoped for. I felt like I was letting them down if I kept seeing you. And things were so confusing then. My father—"

"Please, just stop." She clenched her eyes shut, and the pain radiating from her was almost palpable. I wished I'd never started the explanation in the first place.

"I'm saying this wrong." The sinking feeling in my stomach had me gripping the white tablecloth. "All of it. I made a mistake that night. I should never have agreed to stop seeing you. You were all I could think about. For two years, it was only you. I'm sorry. If I could go back, I would choose differently, but I can't." I'd laid it all out, but I didn't feel any better. No weight had lifted from my shoulders.

She glanced around, her gaze critical where it had been admiring. "So you set all this up as some sort of do over?"

"Something like that. I wanted to explain and go back to where I messed up with you." I wiped my sweaty palms down my jeans.

She bowed her head, staring at her plate as I came apart next to her. Minutes ticked by, and I waved the server away when he came to take our entrée order. I wanted to give her a minute to process everything, but I also wanted to pull her into my arms and take away her hurt.

"Cordy?" My voice was drawn tight, like a piano wire about to snap.

She turned to me, but I couldn't read her expression.

"Please, say something. Anything. Hit me if you want. I don't care."

"What do you expect?" Her voice cut through the quiet violins. "You have the nerve to sit here and tell me you chose money over lo—" She pressed her lips into a thin line and tossed her napkin onto the table. "Over whatever we had between us. Then you go on about how I'm not good enough for you or your parents?"

"I'm sorry." It was all I could say, but it wasn't enough.

"So you thought you could go back in time and erase it all with flowers and music and a fancy restaurant? You can't buy me, Trent." She stood, her eyes glimmering in the low light. "You can't undo the hurt you caused then or now. I was dumb for believing you the first time. Even dumber for falling for it again. Now, if you're finished insulting me, I'm leaving."

I rose. When she shrank away from me and skirted the table, heading for the door, my insides twisted and cramped.

"At least let me drive you home."

"I'll get a cab." The frozen note in her voice stopped me in my tracks.

"Cordy, please." She didn't turn or even hesitate.

Like I had done two years ago, she just walked away.

CHAPTER SEVENTEEN
CORDY

I SNIFFLED INTO MY pillow while my roommate Ellie pretended not to notice. The distinct smell of nail polish filled the room as she painted her toes a garish pink.

Trent's words sifted through my mind like sand through a grate. The most hurtful ones were left behind as the rest poured away. He'd crushed the feelings we'd had for each other so he could keep his trust fund safe. My lungs seized at the thought, and I choked back a sob. Deep inside, I'd always hoped there was some good reason for him to do what he did. But there wasn't. He was a coward. He didn't stick up for us. Instead, he gave in for money.

I'd tried to put myself in his shoes, but I couldn't even fathom the idea of having a trust fund or being in a family that hand-selected the people I was allowed to spend time with. Surely, I would buck them and do what I wanted with my life. Right? I lay on my side and yanked my forest green blanket over my head. Ellie popped her gum.

"Want to, like, talk about it?" Her bored voice filtered through the cotton.

"No."

"Cool." Another pop of her gum.

Ellie and I had been randomly paired together when we were freshmen since I didn't have any friends coming to Billingsley with me. And, really, if I were being honest, I didn't make that many friends back home to start with.

We'd kept the same living arrangement since we got along for the most part. Ellie had been a decent roommate, except for the times she'd brought guys back to the room without any notice, or when she forgot her keys, or when she called me from random frats and asked me to be her designated driver. I was beginning to rethink my classification of Ellie as a decent roommate when a knock sounded at the door.

The last unannounced visitor had been Trent. The second knock sent a thrill of adrenaline through me, though I didn't like my response. I wanted to put him out of my mind, not get a rush at the thought of seeing him.

I heard her feet slap across the tiles to the door.

"Cordy here?" Landon's voice.

"Yep."

A moment later, the foot of my bed shifted. "Cordy?"

"How'd you get in here?"

"I know Brandy at the front desk." He rested his hand on my calf.

"Like from class?"

"No." He laughed and then cut it short. "From other things."

Brandy was likely turning out to be the worst desk attendant Hope Hall had ever seen.

"What happened to taco Tuesday?"

I groaned into my pillow. "I'm sorry. I forgot. Something happened."

"I figured that since you're hiding under your blanket. What's going on?"

"Trent."

His hand tightened on my calf. "What did he do?"

I shook my leg, and he let up. "He frickin' took me to La Café Blanc. And there were flowers, and music, and food, and the entire restaurant to ourselves."

"That doesn't sound like anything to cry about," Ellie chirped.

"Put a sock in it, Ellie." Landon's voice was low. "What else did he do?"

"I don't know." I wanted to flip the blanket down and get some cooler air, but I didn't want them to see what a mess I was. "He told me all this stuff. Like, bad stuff."

Landon scooted closer, his shadow falling over my face. "What did he say?"

I nibbled my bottom lip. I didn't want Landon to do anything to Trent. And the stupid part of me that I couldn't turn off—the part that still ached for Trent to be a good man—didn't want Landon to hate him, either.

"Cordy, tell me." He rested his hand on my arm.

The blanket started slipping, and I turned my face farther into the pillow as he pulled it all the way to my shoulder.

"Come on." He smoothed the wet strands of hair from my face. "Tell me."

I shrugged. "He just said that dating me would have displeased his parents."

"What else?" His voice was tight, his jaw clenched.

I glanced up at him, and he smoothed his palm over my cheek, though I could feel the anger roiling inside him. I decided to keep my response as vague as possible. "Just that he's a Carrington, you know? I guess that means a lot to people like him or something."

"You're over there crying about Trent Carrington?" Ellie blew on her fingernails.

I stared at her. It wasn't as if I could deny it.

"He's hot. My dad used to be the foreman at one of his dad's car parts factories before he retired. We went to Mr. Carrington's funeral a few months ago. Trent was smoking hot in a black suit and tie." She whistled for emphasis then popped her gum. "He was really broken up, though."

At the restaurant, Trent had started off with the news

that his father had died. I'd glossed over it once he told me the rest of his story, then forgotten about it completely as I nursed my newly injured heart.

I shifted to get a better look at Ellie. "What happened to him?"

"I don't know. I would have loved to comfort him. Damn, he was fine." She started painting a clear coat, her long blonde hair falling in a curtain on either side of her face.

I stifled my eye roll, barely. "Not Trent. His father. What happened to him?"

"Oh." She squinted her eyes, focusing on her polish task. "Cancer. Leukemia maybe?"

I settled back into my pillow. Had Trent's father objected to me? Had his death meant that Trent was free and clear of the trust fund threat? A queasy feeling slithered around my stomach at the thought of Trent coming back for me only *after* knowing his money was safe.

Landon scoffed. "I don't care about Trent or his father. All I want to know is where he lives."

"Why?" I grabbed his forearm.

"I'm going to kick his ass for thinking he's better than you."

"He doesn't think that." I closed my eyes and tried to go back through the things he said with a more objective approach. "He never said he agreed with his parents, only that he would stop seeing me so that his trust fund—"

Landon ripped his forearm from my grasp and rose. "You've got to be kidding me. He treated you like shit so he could keep his fucking trust fund?" His snarl verged on frightening.

Ellie made a purring sound in her throat. "You look good when you're angry."

I sat up, and Landon's gaze traced the line of my thin tank top down over my breasts. I yanked the blanket back up.

"Why don't you ever wear that to class?" His voice still carried anger, but his signature smirk hinted at making an appearance.

"All girls, Landon!" I huffed. "This is an all girls' dorm. You aren't supposed to be in here!"

"Glad I broke the rules." He turned back toward the door. "Now, if you'll excuse me, I have a preppy ass to beat."

"No!" I stood and pulled the blanket along with me. It wouldn't help if he saw the small pajama shorts that matched the top.

"Why not?" He placed his hand on the doorknob.

"I need him in one piece for tomorrow. He's my holder." That was the only reason. No other reason at all.

"Fuck!" He jiggled the door handle mercilessly, his frustration rising.

Ellie snorted and screwed her bottle of clear polish shut. "You break it; you buy it."

I walked to him. "I need you to support me here, okay? Trent is an asshole. I think even he knows that. But tomorrow is about me, about winning that scholarship. I'm going to need all the help I can get."

He leaned forward and rested his head on the door frame. "I can't stand him."

"I know." I ran my hand down his back, over the lettering of his vintage Megadeth t-shirt. "After tomorrow, I might even be rooting you on. But for now, I need to get some sleep and focus on kicking. Worrying about you and Trent getting into a fight isn't going to help me accomplish either of those goals."

He turned and pulled me into his arms. It was nice, but nothing even close to the way my blood turned to liquid fire whenever Trent touched me.

Resting his chin on my head, he sighed. "I won't touch him until after tryouts. Okay?"

"That's all I need. But I don't want you fighting at all. I can handle him." I thought it best not to add that it was obvious Trent was bigger and stronger, and that Landon would likely wind up on the losing end of any confrontation. No point in harming his pride.

"He's not good enough for you. You know that, right?" He squeezed me tighter.

I didn't have a response, so I just snuggled in closer.

"I could go for a hug," Ellie grumbled.

Landon laughed, some of the tension draining from him. "That can be arranged."

I backed up and waggled my finger at him. "No. I can't have things super awkward in my own dorm room. Do your dirt elsewhere."

He smiled, his dark eyes lighting up with mischief. "So as long as I don't do it here, we're good?"

"You know that's not what I meant." I lowered my voice. "Ellie is off limits."

"I can hear you, you know." Ellie clicked off the light on her side of the room and flounced down into her bed.

He put a hand on his hip and pointed to my bed with the other. "Get to bed. You need your rest."

I studied his face. "Promise you won't do anything?"

"The only thing I'm going to do is go back to my dorm and turn in. I'll be out bright and early to watch you kick. I haven't gotten up before eight o'clock in years." He rubbed a hand across the sandy stubble on his jaw. "This is going to be tough."

I walked backward to my bed and kept the blanket pulled around me. "You can do it."

"For you, I can." He gave me a wry smile before turning and opening the door. Stepping out into the hall, he glanced back. "It's cold out there. I need something to keep me warm on the walk. Can I just get one more peek at your pajamas?"

"Out!" I laughed and sank onto my bed as he closed the door.

Ellie turned her back to me in a huff as I arranged my blanket and clicked off my light. "You've got two guys in love with you. Both hot. And now you won't even let me borrow one of them?"

I snorted. "Landon is in love with no one but himself. He gets so many girls he's like a human speculum or something."

"One, eww. Two, you're an idiot if you can't tell he's all about you. Oh, and three, thanks a lot for the epic cock block."

I settled into my pillow and stared at Ellie's back in the dark. "It's not like that. He's like a brother to me."

"Like I said, you're an idiot."

"Sometimes." Especially whenever Trent Carrington was concerned. But Landon was far too much of a free spirit to ever be interested in a girl like me. Sure, he'd probably like to give me a go in the sex department, but that would ruin our friendship. He'd never tried anything, and I was glad, because I didn't think of him that way.

"Anyway, good luck tomorrow."

My eyes widened. "Are you going to come watch?"

"Hell no." She made a pfft noise. "And be quiet when you leave since I want to sleep in. My first class got canceled."

Such a bitch. "Thanks, Ellie." I shook my head and grinned.

"You're welcome. Now shut up. I need my beauty sleep."

I tried to quiet my mind as Ellie drifted off and started her familiar snoring pattern. Clenching my eyes shut, I mentally counted football field yardage to try and lull myself to sleep. It was almost working until Trent flashed through my mind like lightning, leaving a discordant rumble of thunder in his wake.

I flipped onto my back and tried to force him from my mind. But he wouldn't go. The sad tint to his voice at the restaurant still echoed inside me, and the remorse in his eyes made my mind wander back to the way his hands had felt on me. I fell asleep to the memory of his kiss.

CHAPTER EIGHTEEN
CORDY

THE DAY BROKE COOL and sunny as I marched into the stadium. A few team members were already sitting along the sidelines in front of the heaters, while the walk-on hopefuls stretched and practiced. The grass was soft beneath my feet, and the sun hadn't chased away the shadows on this side of the stadium yet.

"Well shit, if it isn't my favorite princess." Ethan rose from a bench and hustled over.

I crossed my arms over my chest and kept walking as he strode to my side. "Go away, Ethan."

"What, a teammate can't wish you good luck?" He leered and put an arm around my waist.

I jerked away from him. "Knock it off."

"Don't be such a bitch. Jeez." Undeterred, he kept walking next to me.

"Don't you have some puppies to kick or something?" I was already jittery enough without the wildebeest crowding me.

"You realize you'll never make first-string, right?" He laughed, the sound hollow and forced. "If we only needed someone to make chip shots, Coach could just use me as

119

the kicker. I can get it in from the one yard line every time just like you."

"Why are you always such a dick?" I stopped and looked up at him, my nerves completely disintegrating what little filter I had. "Is this one of those things where you are mean to me because you want to date me or something?"

He cocked his head to the side, his thick neck like a tree trunk. "Date you? No. I want to f—"

"Cordy." Trent walked up behind us, and I tried to ignore the relief his voice sent through me. "You ready?"

"We're talking, rich boy. Why don't you run along?" Ethan's sneer somehow managed to make him even more unattractive, something I didn't think possible.

"No, we're done. Stay away from me." I gave the wildebeest a too-sweet smile. "And thanks for your encouragement. It really got me fired up."

"I'll enjoy watching your chip shots." He grinned. "And go ahead and do your stretches. That's always my favorite part, princess." Ethan turned and headed back to the warm benches.

I hurried away from Trent and toward the large heaters that would block Ethan's line of sight to my warmups. Trent followed and dropped his ball and a tee to the ground. I wore a long-sleeved t-shirt and athletic pants, but goose bumps still broke out along my skin when he stood next to me and started stretching.

We remained silent, going through each position until I was as loose as I was going to get. I avoided his eyes the same way I'd trained myself to do for months, but my every sense was attuned to him. His steady breaths, the controlled strength in his movements, even the woodsy soap he used—all of it calmed me.

I rose to my full height and pulled my left arm across my body in unison with him. He went through each stretch with me, despite the fact he wasn't kicking.

"Cordy." Trent's voice was gentle. "I know we're not in

the best place right now, and I'm hoping you'll give me a shot at fixing it. But that's not what I'm here for. I'm here to help you, to be your holder. I'm going to watch and figure out which long kicker is the best. You've got this."

I gazed out at the fifty or so hopefuls—all of them male, all of them bigger than me. "We'll see."

"All right!" Coach Sterling shouted through his bullhorn, the sound far too loud in the stillness of a chilly morning. "Let's see what came out of the woodwork. First, I want every one of you who didn't play as a kicker in high school or community college to step forward."

Over half the kickers walked from the sideline and onto the field. "You boys go line up with Coach Carver. He's the kicking coach who will be beating your ass on a regular basis should you make the team."

The men did as requested. In the space of less than ten minutes, all of them were given chances to kick a chip shot. All but two missed them. Coach Carver sent those two back to the sidelines with the rest of us and dismissed the other hopefuls. Their dashed dreams didn't make a sound, but plenty of them left the stadium with their heads down.

"Poor guys." I rubbed my hands up and down my upper arms.

"Good riddance." Trent stood at my elbow and watched them leave with a slight quirk of his lips.

It was weird to be standing next to him as if everything were normal and I hadn't cried about him for hours the previous night. But there was nothing else I could do. He was the quarterback. I couldn't exactly escape him when I was at a team tryout.

Head Coach Sterling approached the remaining hopefuls. "All right. The rest of you are going to go in alphabetical order. We'll have you kick from different yardages on each hash, one at a time. You miss too many, you're out. Simple as that. Good luck."

"Thomas Allen, you're up." He handed the bullhorn

off to Coach Carver.

"Allen, line up on the right hash, ten-yard line, and show me what you got." Coach Carver strode out onto the field, his team windbreaker pulled up close around his neck. A ball boy hurried after him, pulling a pack laden with footballs and kicking tees.

The first kicker lined up. Allen was large, easily two hundred and twenty-five pounds. He was squat, and his beefy legs flexed with each stride.

I sank down on one of the benches near the heaters, but far from Ethan. Trent stood behind me and to my left, as if to further block the wildebeest from my view.

"Hey, I made it." Landon's voice rose over the hum of the heaters. He plopped down beside me.

My focus was entirely on Allen. The ball boy set up the football in the holding tee and scurried away. Allen measured his backward steps, then took three large steps to the right. I winced. He'd put far too much distance between himself and the ball for a twenty-yarder.

He dropped his shoulders and ran at the ball. I held my breath. He planted his left foot almost six inches behind the ball but still managed to swing hard enough with his right to get it airborne. The ball sailed like a wounded duck and nailed the left upright with a ping before falling to the ground. No good. My breath whooshed out of me.

Landon elbowed me. "I kind of want to cheer. Is that bad?"

I nodded as Allen lined up and tried again. "Yes, very bad."

Though Landon seemed to be pretending that Trent wasn't there, I could still sense him. His watchful eye vacillated between me and the other kickers.

Allen's second attempt split the uprights, but his form was still lacking. He moved to the opposite hash and tried from there. He made one out of three kicks. The rest of his performance remained mediocre at best, and I found myself critiquing everything from his stance to his follow-through. My three days with Trent taught me more than I'd thought.

The next kicker was dismal, and several after that fared almost as badly as Allen. One of them did better, only missing two kicks until he got to the thirty-yard line where his accuracy tanked. Three more mediocre ones tried their best. Then one of the few remaining men ran out onto the field. He had a head full of bright red hair, and when he dashed into the sun to line up, it blazed copper.

"Wow. That hair is gorgeous." I stared as he measured off his steps. He was a left-footed kicker. Rare.

Landon shrugged. "It's okay."

I smirked. "Please. If you saw a cute girl with hair like that, you'd be all over it."

"So?"

"I prefer brunettes." Trent broke his silence.

I glanced back, but his eyes remained fixed on the copper-headed kicker.

"Me too." Landon shifted closer to me.

"Hawthorne, get set!" Coach Carver had warmed in the sun, his voice rising in pitch and irritation.

Hawthorne made his first field goal from the ten, then his second. Coach Carver shouted for him to change to the left hash. He walked over and lined up his shot. The first sailed through. The second veered hard left and missed by two feet or so. I felt relieved, though I knew it wasn't a kind attitude on my part.

He backed up ten yards and made two of four kicks. At the thirty, something in his posture changed. He seemed to stand up straighter, as if his confidence increased with distance.

Trent stepped over the bench and stood beside me, his arms crossed over his chest. "You're next. Make sure you're still warmed up."

The redhead made two perfect kicks from the right hash, then moved to the left. I stood and walked a few steps away to go back over some of my stretches. I pulled my right heel up to my ass and held it there as Hawthorne sent another perfect kick between the uprights from the left hash of the thirty-yard line.

"Send him to the forty," Coach Sterling called.

Coach Carver obeyed and set Hawthorne up on the right hash. I dropped my right leg and pulled on my left. Hawthorne got set and took his long steps to the ball. It flew off his foot, straight down the middle of the field.

"Holy shit, that kid's good." Landon glanced over at me, his gaze tracing the line of my body as I bent over and put my hands flat on the turf. "You're flexible."

Trent stepped around him and sat on the bench, blocking Landon's view.

Another ball flew through the uprights from the forty-yard line. The few players who came to watch tryouts began talking amongst themselves, a slight buzz of excitement in the air.

Trent nodded and turned to me. "He's our long-distance guy."

Coach Carter pulled Hawthorne down the field and handed him a ball and pointed. The guy held the ball, ran, and kicked a perfect punt, the ball landing at the five-yard line and rolling one more yard closer to the end zone.

"He's *definitely* our guy."

"All right. Next!" Coach Sterling clapped his hand and motioned Hawthorne over to him.

"Come on." Trent ran out onto the field as Coach Carver started to call another name.

"Whoa, Coach. Cordy's ready to try."

I followed him out into the sun. Roping my hair up into a tight ponytail, I tried to settle my nerves as I approached the ten-yard line. My hands went cold like they always did, and my stomach roiled, as if displeased with my choice of cereal for breakfast.

Coach Carver put a hand on his hip and glared at Trent. "It's not her turn yet. I put her last since she's already on the team."

"She's ready now." Trent took a ball from the equipment bag and knelt at the ten.

"Come on, Coach." I gave what I hoped was a winning smile. I didn't know why Trent wanted me to go right then, but I suspected it had something to do with the redhead.

Coach waved his hand. "Fine, fine. Go ahead. You're lucky I like you, Baxter." He stepped back and took the same spot where he'd watched everyone else from. "Trent, we got a tee for that."

He smiled. "I know. I just wanted to see if she could handle the real deal."

Something about the way he said it pricked my pride. I stood tall, and walked to where he held the ball. "Try not to drop it."

"Never have." His eyes were warm despite his cocky tone. "You got this," he whispered where only I could hear.

I know.

CHAPTER NINETEEN
TRENT

THE FEISTY LOOK IN her eye was exactly what I wanted. Confidence was everything to a kicker, and just by the way she stood I could tell hers was where it needed to be.

"Whenever you're ready." Coach Carver tapped his foot on the grass.

Cordy let out a long breath and took her backwards steps. Then she counted off to the right just as we'd practiced. She let her arms go loose, then took off. *Step, step, step, plant, kick.* She nailed it, sending the smell of grass and earth into my nose as the ball split the uprights at perfect center.

Coach Carver whistled as the ball hit the net and rolled down to the field.

Cordy watched it with a look that verged on disbelief.

"Again." I motioned for the ball boy to toss me another.

I set up, and Cordy marked off her steps. She sent the second ball to the same spot as the first.

"Left hash!" Coach Carver yelled, a smile crinkling the brown skin around his mouth.

We set up, and she sent two more coasting into the net. I could almost feel her confidence growing with each kick. Her form was as close to perfect as I could get it, her foot planted just right and her follow-through strong.

She aced two thirty-yarders from the right hash. When we set up on the left, she shook her hands out, as if they were bothering her.

"What?"

"Nothing." She kept her eyes on the field goal. "When I get nervous they sort of freeze."

I had the urge to stand and warm her hands in mine, but one glance at the sideline nixed that idea. Coach Sterling had the redheaded kicker sitting next to him, both men watching Cordy with interest.

"Keep it up. You got this." I set up, and she gave another perfect kick.

She looked over at Coach Sterling and cursed under her breath.

"You okay?"

"Yeah." She shook her hands again. "They're just all looking at me."

"I know how you feel. Remember speech class?"

Her face fell the slightest bit. *Fuck.* I hurriedly continued, "I meant, I felt that same way, but you got me through it. Just concentrate. You could make these kicks in your sleep."

She backed away and got set. When she took her first step, I knew something was off in her approach. She kept coming and kicked. The ball flew to the right and missed by only a foot.

Laughter erupted from the sidelines. Ethan doubled over and guffawed as Cordy dropped her eyes to the turf.

"I think that's enough for her. We can move on to the next." Coach Carver lifted the bullhorn.

"Way to go, princess!" Ethan's yell had me on my feet. He was long overdue for a lesson in manners.

"No." Cordy popped her head up. "I want to try for a

forty-yarder."

Coach lowered the horn to his waist. "That's a long kick for most men, Cordelia. I don't think—"

"Let me try." She clasped her hands together. "You can at least give me a chance."

"She can do it, Coach." I stayed put, though Ethan's overdone laughter was like a nail in my temple.

The laughter stopped, and yells broke out along the sideline. We all looked over to see Ethan throw Landon to the ground and climb on top of him.

Cordy shrieked and took off toward them. I caught up and passed her as Ethan began raining blows down on Landon's face.

"Stop!" Cordy's scream spurred me forward.

I threw my shoulder into Ethan and ignored the pain radiating into my arm. He fell sideways, and I landed on my ass next to Landon, who tried to scramble up and go after Ethan.

"Landon!" Cordy dropped to her knees and grabbed his t-shirt with both hands, yanking him back around to her.

His nose was bleeding, and one eye was puffy, probably well on its way to a shiner.

A couple of other players held Ethan back as he scrambled to his feet. "Put your hands on me again, and I'll break your scrawny neck!" He surged forward, trying to get at Landon.

"Hold him back!" I thrust out my right hand, my shoulder stinging from the effort.

"What the hell is going on?" Coach Sterling shuffled up to the ruckus, his face turning into a wrathful mask. "We don't fight on my team. We are champions. Champions don't act like this!" He yelled into Ethan's face, then turned to look at Landon. "And who the hell are you?"

"I've got him, Coach. He was just leaving." I wedged my left shoulder under Landon's arm and got him to his feet. Cordy stood with me and pressed her fingertips to his nose.

He winced. "Jesus, that hurts."

"Get him out of here, and you"—Coach pointed a crooked finger at Ethan—"I know you think you're above the rules, but I'm here to tell you: you aren't. One more screw up and I'll bench your ass. I don't care what the administration says." He snugged his ball cap tighter on his head. "Carver, get the next kicker out there."

"Coach, wait. I wanted to try for a forty-yarder." Cordy's calm voice was a welcome note.

"No need. Next!" Coach waved an impatient hand toward the bench where only a few kickers remained.

"But Coach—"

"Cordelia Baxter! I am the coach of this team, and I said you're done!" The small spider veins along Coach's nose pulsed with anger, and he leaned down to get in her face. "Any more back talk and you'll be taking a lap."

"Cordy, come on." I grabbed her elbow.

She hesitated, but eventually walked around Coach and toward the field exit. Landon and I followed.

Coach grabbed my shirt before I could walk past. "I saw what you did. Never risk your throwing arm over a guy like Ethan, got me? Go see the trainers today. Tell them to check you over."

"Yes, sir."

"Good job all the same." He clapped me on the back and turned toward the field to watch the next kicker.

Landon threw his arm around Cordy's shoulders and pulled her close. "You did great."

Going caveman and ripping her away from him seemed like the most gratifying move, but I could imagine Cordy would be less than pleased with that idea.

"He wouldn't even let me kick the full distances." She lowered her head.

I caught up and walked on her other side. "He's right. You were amazing out there."

"She doesn't need you anymore, *Trent*." Landon glared at me over her head. "Go on your douchey way."

"Landon." She shook her head, her ponytail swinging with the movement.

"What?" He didn't take his eyes off me as we walked out of the stadium and into the parking lot.

"Let's just get you back to your dorm. We need to do something about your nose."

"My nose is fine. Wait—" His glare turned into a smile. "Actually, it kind of hurts. Your dorm is closer. Do you have anything to fix me up there?"

"Sure."

"I'll drive." My car was parked right at the front of the lot, and I wasn't about to let Landon go back to her dorm with her alone.

"We can walk." He turned her away from my car and toward the quad.

I couldn't let her go. "Come on, Landon. Ethan rang your bell. You need to take it easy for a minute. Let me drive you."

"He's right." Cordy stopped, forcing Landon to stop with her. "Just let him drive us."

"He's an asshole."

She whirled on him. "And you're an idiot for trying to jump a lineman twice your size! What were you thinking?"

"He was talking shit about you." He shrugged. "I couldn't let him do that."

"Ethan is an overgrown toddler. I don't care what he says. You shouldn't either."

"Well, I do. I care. A lot." He put more emotion into his words than I liked.

"And I appreciate it." She softened her stance and stepped closer to him. "But you didn't have to do that."

"I know. Come on. Help me back to your place and take care of me. It's the least you could do after ditching me for taco Tuesday and this." He pointed at his still-bloody nose.

She glanced back at me and then at Landon.

I willed her to choose me. She hesitated.

"Come on." Landon ran his hand around her elbow. He leaned down and whispered something in her ear.

Never in my life had I felt my blood turn as hot and as fast as it did then.

Cordy nodded. "I know."

Landon shot me a triumphant smirk as they walked toward her dorm.

Fuck. I'd really screwed things up with her. But I wouldn't give up. I would never give up.

I followed them.

Landon turned around. "Where are you going?"

"You wouldn't let me drive you, so I'll just have to walk with you." I took Cordy's other elbow.

She didn't shake me off, and a small smile played at the corner of her mouth.

It was enough to give me hope. At least Landon lost the skip in his step. Despite the fact that it looked like Landon and I were Stormtroopers escorting Princess Leia, I was happy to be near Cordy.

"I meant it when I said you did well." I guided her onto the sidewalk cutting across campus. The storm had knocked the leaves from the oaks, leaving the branches bare enough so the sun could filter down on us as we walked.

Cordy wrinkled her nose. "I don't want to talk about it. It's like doing post mortem on a test or something. Nothing good can come of it."

"That redhead, though." Landon shook his head. "His long-game was tight."

"Short-game was for shit." I peered down at Cordy. "No one kicked better than you."

"Yeah, but we didn't see everyone because *someone* decided to start a sideline brawl." She shoved her hip into Landon's.

Was I jealous of that little point of contact? Yes.

"I'm cautiously optimistic." Landon bumped her back.

"No one could touch you on the shorter distances," I said. "And the redhead had a hell of a lot of leg from the longer yardages. You plus the redhead are the perfect match." I hurried to add, "On the football field. Just for kicking."

"I followed." She smirked. "Thanks."

I needed to get her alone, to apologize and try again to explain everything. One look at Landon told me that wouldn't happen today.

"Don't fall for it. You know who he really is." Landon's harsh voice destroyed what little ground I'd just gained as Cordy stiffened, her smile long gone.

I didn't have a comeback. There wasn't one. He was right. Cordy did know the real me. The one who fell in love with her two years ago. I just had to remind her of who I was.

CHAPTER TWENTY
CORDY

THE SHARP KNOCK ON my door almost made me drop my laptop.

"Whoa, there." Landon rose from the end of my bed and stretched. The late afternoon sun filtered through my blinds and painted his upper body in orange stripes. He'd been playing on his phone for an hour and making eyes at Ellie. "I'll get it."

"No." I stood and darted past him. "How many times do I have to tell you it's an all-girls' dorm? Hide behind the door. If the RA sees you, we'll be in big trouble."

He sauntered behind the door and kept texting as I eased it open. A bouquet of flowers covered my entire field of vision. I swung the door open to find Trent smiling with his arms full of the largest bouquet I'd ever seen. White roses and blue hydrangeas—team colors—bloomed in a vivid display.

His smile brightened, his perfect dimples making my heart skip a few beats. "I just got word. You're our starting kicker."

I squealed and threw the door open. "Are you kidding?"

135

"Not even a little bit." He walked in and handed me the flowers. When he glanced to Landon, he tensed the slightest bit, but his smile was still there. "Congratulations!"

Excitement and disbelief churned inside me. I stared up at him, barely visible through the forest of flowers. "Are you sure?" My voice shook.

"I just left Coach's office." He stepped closer, the clean smell of his soap mixing with the sweetness from the flowers. "You're the first-string short kicker. Hawthorne, the redhead is the long-kicker, technically second-string."

"Oh my God!" I jumped up and down and ran around in a small circle like an idiot.

"You did it!" Landon scooped me up in a hug, my bare feet dangling off the floor. "I knew you could do it."

Even Ellie rose from her spot at the desk and walked over to inspect the flowers. "Wow."

Excitement thrilled through me, and I couldn't wipe the smile off my face as Landon released me. Had it really happened?

"I can't believe it." I turned back to Trent and took the flowers, hugging them gently to me. "They're beautiful."

"They're well-deserved." His voice and the look of pride in his eyes thrilled me more than they should have, especially after last night.

Ellie claimed the flowers from me. "I'll put them in some water. Or maybe the sink. We don't have anything big enough to hold them."

I looked up into Trent's kind eyes as he moved closer, his large frame perfectly dressed in a light blue button-down and well-fitting jeans. My emotions vacillated from ecstatic to still hurt, to unsure, and back to something warmer. "Thank you."

The tap in our small bathroom turned on as Ellie fussed with the flowers.

"Very welcome." He stuffed his hands into his

pockets and brought his chin down in a move that was boyishly cute. His gaze stayed locked on mine. "I'd also like to take you to dinner to celebrate—"

Landon chuckled, and twisted one of the spider bite piercings in his lower lip. "We'd love to go and celebrate, wouldn't we, Ellie?"

She poked her head out of our bathroom. "What?"

"Trent's going to buy all of us dinner to celebrate Cordy's success." Landon stood next to me and draped his arm across my shoulders. "We'd love to go."

"I'm not sure. I fell behind a little today because of tryouts, and I have some more reading for my Postmodern Poetry class." I nibbled my lip. I probably should have added *"and you broke my heart again last night,"* but I didn't.

Trent's voice, low and sure, caressed my ear. "You deserve a celebration."

"Rich boy is right on this one." Landon squeezed my upper arm. "I'll give him that. And you did mean all of us, right Trent old sport?" He added a little *Great Gatsby* accent to the last sentence.

Trent's eyes narrowed. It was clear he hadn't intended on taking anyone but me. Still, he relented. "Sure. All four of us can go out. Sounds like a plan. As long as Cordy agrees." He pulled his right hand from his pocket and held it out to me. "What do you say?"

My mind was a swirl of positive thoughts. The pain was there, too, beneath it all, sitting silently. I shook any dark thoughts away and took his hand. Trent's shoulders relaxed, and his large palm engulfed my small one. We shook as if we'd just completed a business deal, but his touch was far more than a simple gesture. Warmth snaked through me, and I grew hotter the longer I looked into his light green eyes. How could he still have this effect on me after all he'd done?

"Glad we're in agreement." Landon walked between us, and I dropped my hand. "You girls change clothes and get ready. I'll wait here. Keep watch and all that."

I cocked an eyebrow. "Not a chance. Both of you go outside and wait for us. We'll be down in fifteen."

Landon scrunched up one side of his face in disgust. "I have to wait with him? Why can't I stay in here?"

"You know why, perv. Don't play dumb. It doesn't suit you."

"I don't care if he stays," Ellie called from the bathroom, and the oversized t-shirt she had been wearing flew out the door and onto her bed.

"See?" Landon grinned and tried to lean over and get a look at Ellie.

"Out! Now!" I pushed him toward the door as Trent opened it.

Landon walked out first. Trent hesitated, and all the air seemed to evaporate from the room. The look in his eyes was fire, and my lips tingled when his gaze settled on them.

He bent down so his mouth was close to my ear. "I'll see you downstairs."

"Okay." Was that my breathy voice?

He closed the door, and I backed away and sat on my bed, my head still spinning. Pulling out my phone, I dialed my dad.

He answered on the fourth ring. "Hey, sugar!"

I winced at how badly he was slurring. "Hi Dad. I've got some news."

"Wha-what you got?"

"You know how I'm the kicker, right?"

"Soccer. You always loved soccer." He laughed and I could hear him swallowing, liquor no doubt.

"Football, Dad. Remember?"

"Sorry, right."

"Well, they had tryouts because our first-string kicker got hurt last—"

"I saw it, Cordy baby. I sure did. You tried your best. It's okay. Don't worry."

I sighed, though my exasperation had never

overcome his drunkenness and likely never would. "I know, Daddy. That's not what I'm talking about. They had tryouts, and I made first-string. I'll have a full scholarship for the rest of this year and next."

"First-string? You're the starting kicker?" He laughed, pleasure in the notes until it turned into a gut-wrenching cough. Once he had it under control, he continued, "I'm so goddamn proud of you, I don't even know if I'm coming or going!"

"Hey, hey Bonnie. My daughter is the starting kicker at Billingsley. You hear that?"

I heard a woman reply, but couldn't make out her words. It had to have been Bonnie Trapper, the widow from down the street.

"Thanks, babe." A sloppy kiss sounded from his end of the line, and I held the phone far away from my ear. After a moment, I put it back. "Yeah Cordy, I'm just proud as all hell. So glad you got out. So glad you're making more of yourself. I don't know what I'd do without you to hold on—" He choked up, and tears welled in my eyes at the emotion in his words. "You're the best thing I've ever done. The best thing."

"Thanks, Dad."

"I mean it, Cordy." He sniffled. "You make me so proud."

"Thanks." I wiped at the tear that rolled down my cheek. "My friends are taking me to celebrate."

"Perfect!" He coughed. "Get to it. Have a good time, and be safe. Maybe I can make it down to watch a game sometime soon."

"I hope so."

"Me too. Love you, Cordy."

"Love you too, Dad."

We hung up, and I sat in a daze for a few minutes. Had so much really happened in the space of ten minutes?

Ellie puttered around in the bathroom. "You think Trent will take us somewhere fancy? Like maybe La Café

Blanc? I've always wanted to go."

My stomach twisted at the thought of going back there. "No, I doubt it."

"What are you wearing?"

I wiped the last tear and stored my father's praise somewhere deep inside me to use when I needed it. "Jeans, I guess. Maybe a sweater?"

"No." She popped her head out, one of her eyes ringed with eyeliner. "Dress nice. He's a Carrington, and," she shrugged, "you deserve to celebrate, I guess. But your clothes are shit." She ducked back into the bathroom. "Pick something out of my side of the closet."

I muttered under my breath and went to the closet. My clothes were the basics—t-shirts, jeans, sweaters, some hoodies. I had one dress. I'd worn it to my high school graduation three years prior, and it was covered in garish pink flowers. Ellie may have had a point this one time.

I scanned over to her side of the closet, which was always bursting. Digging through, I found a pretty blue dress. I held it up to my front and realized my boobs would be spilling out the front. "Definitely not." I put it back and kept looking. Another, lighter blue dress caught my eye. It, too, suffered from a scoop neckline that was far lower than I'd ever worn.

"Move." Ellie padded up, wearing only her panties, and pushed me to the side. Her fingers expertly maneuvered through the multitude of hangers and seized on one in particular. She pulled it out and hung it over her back. "This one."

It was a deep crimson sweater dress with a cute brown belt around the middle.

"It looks kind of short."

She bent over and tossed a pair of brown knee-high boots onto our rug. "What size shoe do you wear?"

"Seven," I said and held the dress up to me. It would fit.

"I'm eight, but it's just for tonight. You'll be fine."

"I have boots."

She turned around, her perky tits on full display. I turned my head so fast I worried I might have pulled something.

"Your boots are made for mucking out horse stalls, not a night on the town. Trust me. Go put some makeup on, and take your hair down. I'll come and fix it once I'm dressed."

Over the next fifteen minutes, Ellie dressed me and did my makeup. By the time she finished, I was wearing her dress, her heeled boots, and only as much makeup as I could stand.

"Voila!" She smiled at me in the mirror, her big blue eyes looking at me instead of herself for a change. "Much better than the tomboy crap you usually wear."

It felt strange, but not necessarily bad. I was just so used to being on the soccer field, or the football field, or sitting in my spot in the library, that I didn't spend much time on my looks. Ellie had enough makeup to paint me a hundred times over, but she'd been sparing at my request. My light brown eyes almost glowed, even in the stark bathroom lighting, and the dress hugged my curves.

Ellie wore the blue dress I'd originally snagged from her closet, the neckline cutting low across her tan chest. "Let's blow this joint. Come on."

The night was cold, an icy wind blowing through the holly bushes and oak trees around the dorm. Trent's car was out front, the headlights shining and the engine nearly silent. We hurried down the steps. I slid into the passenger seat while Ellie climbed in the back.

"Where's Landon?" I fastened my seatbelt.

"He said he needed to have a quick chat with Brandy." The look on Trent's face told me he believed they were "chatting" just as much as I did.

"Oh. I guess we'll wait then." I sank into the smooth leather.

Ellie pulled out her phone and started texting.

Trent cleared his throat. "You look amazing."

"Thanks." My fingers itched to pull the top of the dress closed more, but Trent's eyes weren't on my chest. I met his gaze and slowly began to melt.

"I'd wanted to talk." He glanced back at Ellie. "It'll have to wait, I guess. But there's more to what I was trying to tell you. I said everything wrong. I didn't mean—"

My phone rang, the sound a rising series of chimes. Dad was calling.

"Hang on." I dug my phone out and swiped to answer it. "Dad?"

"Cordy?" A woman's voice, worry in her tone.

"Yes." I sat straighter. "Mrs. Trapper? Is something wrong?"

"Yeah, honey. A little while after you got off the phone with your dad, he had some kind of fit. We called the ambulance. They're taking him out now."

All the blood drained from my face. "Is he going to be okay?"

Trent took my left hand, but all I could focus on was Mrs. Trapper and muted voices in the background.

"They don't know. One of them said some kind of toxins maybe led to a seizure, but they don't know."

"I'm coming home. Tell Dad I'm on my way." My mouth was moving, and I was saying words, but my heart was in a vise.

"He's not conscious—oh, okay. We're leaving. I'm riding with him to the hospital. I'll call if anything changes. I have to go."

"Wait, Mrs. Trapper—"

The line went silent.

CHAPTER TWENTY-ONE
TRENT

I KNEW IT WAS bad when her tan skin paled and she clutched the phone with a death grip.

When the call was over, she stared at the phone, disbelief in her eyes. "I have to go."

"What is it?"

"My dad. Something's wrong. They're taking him to the hospital."

"Shit." Ellie patted her shoulder. "Sorry."

Cordy reached for the door handle.

I squeezed her hand. "Wait. How long does it take to get to Gray Valley?"

"Five hours. Maybe a little more. I-I have to go."

"I'll drive." I wasn't about to let her face this alone. Her father was the only family she had left. I caught Ellie's eye in the rearview mirror. "I'm sorry. I'll buy you dinner another time."

"No, it's cool." She squeezed Cordy's shoulder one last time before opening the door and climbing out. "Call if I can help."

"We will." I shifted to reverse as she closed the door.

"I can drive." Cordy's voice was thin, quiet.

"You're in no shape to drive." I reached across her and re-fastened her seatbelt, then pulled out onto University Drive.

She leaned back in the seat, tears silently running down her cheeks. "But we have practice in the morning."

"Fuck practice." I took her hand and kissed the back of it. "Everything will be okay."

"I just talked to him. I called to tell him about making first-string. He was fine." The pain in her voice tore at me.

I tried to think clearly even though I wanted nothing more than to stop the car and pull her into my arms. She needed me, and I wasn't going to let her down. "Is there anyone else we can call? A friend of your dad's or someone else you know in Gray Valley?"

"Charlie, my dad's best friend." She dialed him and gave him the news as I took the highways leading to the interstate.

When she hung up, I programmed in her home address and settled in for the trip.

"Everything will be all right." I held her hand as we flew down the dark road.

We drove for five hours, only speaking here and there as she made calls to Mrs. Trapper and Charlie. Her father was awake, but not alert enough to talk. They'd given him some pain medication and run tests to figure out what had happened.

By the time we made it to the hospital in the rolling hills of West Virginia, it was midnight.

I parked out front and hurried inside with Cordy. After checking with the front desk, we followed the attendant's directions deeper into the hospital and up a few floors.

Cordy was almost at a run when we reached her father's room. It was small with a window that looked out onto some woods. A stout woman sat at his bedside, and an older man rose and hugged Cordy.

"Charlie, how is he?"

"We don't know. They think it's his liver."

Her father was asleep. He looked about sixty with a faded gray beard and a head full of silver hair. Deep wrinkles along his forehead hinted at a lifetime of worry, and he looked thin.

Cordy sat down on the bed and took his hand in hers.

"You are?" Charlie, a tall, wide man with an even larger beard than Cordy's father, put out his hand.

I took it and shook. "Trent Carrington. A friend of Cordy's from school."

He narrowed his light eyes. "Come a long way just for a friend."

I nodded. "I think any true friend would have done the same."

"Heh." He grinned, two of his front bottom teeth missing. "Good man. This here is Mrs. Trapper."

She took my hand in hers and gave me a warm smile. Even at her age, she was a looker with a killer figure.

"You can call me Bonnie. I'm so glad you came. I hated to worry Cordy like this, but I couldn't tell how serious it would be." She withdrew her hand and tucked a dark lock of hair, shot through with silver, behind her ear. "I'm glad you're both here."

"Daddy?" Cordy leaned over, getting a better look at her father. "Why is he asleep?"

Mrs. Trapper gave her a quick hug. "He got to hurting, so the doctors gave him something to help him sleep through the night."

I stood behind Cordy and put my hand on her shoulder, giving what comfort I could. "Where's the doctor?"

"They called in a specialist from Charleston. He's supposed to be here first thing in the morning." Charlie shrugged. "The on-duty doc thinks it's his liver. That maybe he's got a liver problem, and the fluid built up and caused toxic shock or some such."

"Oh God." A sob caught in Cordy's throat.

I rubbed her shoulder, letting her know I was there but not crowding her.

"He likes his whiskey. We all know that." Charlie sank back down into the chair. "I do, too." He reached into his pocket and pulled out a small flask.

"Charlie!" Mrs. Trapper put her hands on her hips. "Not at a time like this."

"Ain't no time better." He took a quick swig and stowed the flask as Mrs. Trapper glared at him.

"We should be going." Mrs. Trapper moved around the bed and dropped a kiss on Mr. Baxter's forehead. "I have second shift at the diner tomorrow, and I want to be here first thing when the doctor from Charleston shows up." She gave Cordy a matching kiss. "He'll be okay. He's tougher than a buckeye nut."

"Thank you."

"Anytime." She turned to me. "Very nice to meet you, Trent. Take care of Cordy, and I'll see you both bright and early."

"Yes, ma'am."

She reached up and patted my cheek, a warm smile on her face. "Charmer."

Charlie rose from his seat. "I'm charming too, you know."

Mrs. Trapper laughed and shooed him out the door ahead of her. The room fell silent except for the steady breaths of Cordy's father and the noise from the nurse's station.

"He's so stupid." She looked up at me, tears suspended at the corners of her eyes. "I told him. His doctor told him. Everyone told him to stop drinking. He never listened."

I sat behind her, perching on the foot of the bed, and wrapped my arms around her. She let me pull her against my chest, giving me a trust I didn't deserve.

We sat silently for a long while. I'd never felt content, not since the day when I'd let her go. But when she was in my arms, my heart was at ease.

Eventually, a nurse walked in and checked on his IV. "You two should get some sleep. We're monitoring him just fine. That sofa over there pulls out into a bed, and this chair is far more comfortable than it looks." She took his blood pressure and vitals while giving me instructions on how the pull-out bed worked.

I got it all set up and motioned for Cordy to lie down. The nurse brought some pillows and a blanket.

Cordy gave her father's hand one more squeeze before walking to the makeshift bed. "I can sleep in the chair. I don't mind." Her voice was quiet, fatigue and fear dragging her words down.

"It's not a problem." I put my hand at her lower back and guided her to the couch. "Go ahead and get settled."

She sank down and kicked her boots off.

"I'll try not to come in too much." The nurse made a few notes on her clipboard. "But call if you need me." She hit the light on the way out, leaving only the soft glow from the heart rate monitor.

I unbuttoned my shirt and stripped down to the white t-shirt underneath. Setting my shoes to the side, I lowered into the chair Charlie had occupied. The vinyl seat was cracked along the edges—showing wear like a lot of the items in the small hospital—but it was bearable. I fidgeted around until I got comfortable and could still keep an eye on Cordy across the room.

She rolled to her side. Then, after only a few moments, she rolled to her other side and faced me. I couldn't see her well in the dark, but I could sense her eyes on me.

"Trent?" Her voice was thick with tears.

I sat forward to get a better look at her. "Yeah?"

"Do you really think he'll be okay?"

I stood and walked around the bed to her. Kneeling next to her, I stroked the soft strands of hair away from her face. "I don't know, but I'm going to hope for the best."

She trembled as she searched my eyes, looking for reassurance.

I ran my thumb along her soft cheek. "But I can promise you that I'll be here for you. No matter what. Whatever it takes. Okay?"

She nodded, never breaking eye contact.

"Get some sleep." I kissed her forehead, lingering for a moment as I took in the scent of her hair. When I rose, she took my hand.

"Stay?"

I stilled.

"I mean, could you, um, sleep here with me?"

She already possessed my heart, and I would never deny her any comfort I could give.

"Sure."

She scooted all the way to the back of the small bed, giving me just enough room to lie down beside her. It wasn't the most comfortable spot, but I would have lain on a bed of hot coals just to be close to her.

"You have enough space?" I put one hand over my heart and the other behind my head.

"Yeah." She tossed the blanket over me.

She shifted next to me, her body grazing mine. I wanted to pull her against me, but it wasn't the time or the place. She seemed to find a comfortable spot and let out a sigh, her breath tickling the hair on my arm.

"Good night."

"Night." I glanced at her, but her face was shadowed.

"And, thank you." She placed her hand on my bicep and gave me a soft squeeze. "For staying. It means a lot."

"I'm happy to do it."

She let her hand fall so that it only just touched my arm. After a few deep breaths, she began to relax. Fifteen minutes later, she was asleep.

I finally spoke the words I'd wanted to say when she'd thanked me. "I love you, Cordy. I'd do anything for you."

It had been a long morning of doctors, tests, and bad results. Cordy's father had been awake and lucid the entire time, though his mood soured more each hour he went without a drink.

"I just want to go home." He sat up and pulled the heart rate monitor off his finger.

"That's not a good idea, Mr. Baxter." Dr. Edgars shook his head. "Your liver function is so low that any further alcohol is only going to cause more permanent damage."

"I won't drink. I just don't want to be here." He put his feet on the floor, but paused before standing. "Where are my pants?"

"Dad." Cordy put her fists on her hips. "You aren't going anywhere until the doctor says so. Lie down and listen to what he has to say."

"But Cordy, I don't need him to tell me to quit drinking. I get it. I'll quit."

She shook her head, clearly not believing a single word he said. "No, you need help. Real help."

He gave a harsh laugh. "From where? I can hardly afford to eat, much less go to some goddamn rehab or whatever you and that doctor have been cooking up all morning."

"Dad—"

"I need my pants." He was just as stubborn as his daughter.

"Lie down right this minute!" Cordy's voice had changed from cajoling to commanding in a second.

"You'd better listen to her, Frank." Mrs. Trapper had been sitting in the comfortable chair, watching the scene just like I had.

He scowled, but when faced with the brunt of Cordy's anger, he caved and sat back in the bed. "Women always telling me my business," he grumbled and snapped the heart rate monitor back onto his finger.

Cordy sighed and sat next to him. "What am I going to do with you?"

I leaned closer to Dr. Edgars. "Doctor, can I have a word?"

He clicked his pen and placed it in the pocket of his white jacket. "Sure."

"Hey, Cordy, I'm going to get some snacks. Want anything?"

"Cheetos." Her answer was decisive.

"Puffy or crunchy?"

She smiled. "Surprise me."

The doctor and I walked into the hall as Cordy and her dad talked.

"What can you do for him?"

He shook his head. "Nothing if he's unwilling. The cirrhosis will eventually kill him, and quickly, if he doesn't stop drinking."

"Is there a rehab you know of that would work?"

"There is one I've had some success with, but what he said was pretty much true." He adjusted his glasses and frowned. "It costs money. Mr. Baxter doesn't have any insurance, and I suspect he doesn't have the income to cover it."

"But if he did have the money, you know a good place, right?"

"Well, sure. There's a place about an hour from here. It's in the woods on a lake. Serene, isolated. A perfect place to kick any habit. They specialize in drugs and alcohol, but take all kinds."

"Get the paperwork going. Do whatever you need. I'll cover the costs. But don't tell him or Cordy, okay? Just make something up like"—I tapped my foot—"like it's a scholarship or something like that. I don't know."

He quirked a smile. "You've won an all-expense-paid scholarship to rehab. Like that?"

"Sure. Just make it believable."

"I can do that. At least, I think I can." He put his hands in his jacket pockets. "But why can't I tell them you're paying?"

"They wouldn't accept it, and I'm not doing it for me. I'm doing it for her."

"Right." He nodded. "For love. I can certainly tell a lie about a rehab scholarship for that cause."

"Thanks, Doc."

"No, thank you. Anytime someone saves a life around here, I appreciate it."

CHAPTER TWENTY-TWO
CORDY

TRENT DROVE US BACK to Billingsley late that afternoon. I tried to convince him to let me handle the drive back so he could rest, but he wouldn't have it. I dozed as we left the hill country, the sun setting behind the treetops.

Dad had managed to luck up on a spot at a local rehab. He wasn't too happy about it, but agreed to go and at least give it a try. I would be able to visit him in a month, and Trent had volunteered to come with me. As the world darkened, my sleepy thoughts focused on the man next to me.

He was so different than what I'd thought for so long. I believed him to be selfish and heartless. But the way he cared for me over the past day showed a depth of kindness and warmth that rocked my assumptions off their foundations. Maybe I'd been wrong about him.

His words at the restaurant flitted around my mind— about how he'd stopped seeing me because of his family. It hurt, but now that I was looking at it from a distance, I realized he'd never said that *he* believed I was beneath him. I'd stormed out before giving him a chance to explain. I reached over and took his hand.

He shot me a smile and laced our fingers together. My heavy lids closed again, and the stress of the day pulled me down into sleep.

"Cordy?"

I turned over and buried my head under a pillow.

Deep laughter and his voice again. "Cordy? We're going to miss practice."

Practice? Something was off. My dorm room bed didn't have enough space for me to roll over and stretch out. I pulled my head from beneath the pillow and blinked against the sun streaming into the room. *Not my room.*

"Shit!" I clutched the blanket to me and blinked the sleep away.

Trent stood at the foot of the bed, his hair wet as if freshly showered. And, sweet baby Jesus, he wasn't wearing a shirt. Dark hair dusted his broad chest, ran down the center of his hard abs, and disappeared into his athletic shorts.

I swallowed hard.

"Want me to take you back to your dorm so you can get ready?"

"I, uh." I looked around at the room—dark wood floors, high ceilings, and a wall of windows looking out onto the city park. Elegant and understated, it was easily the nicest bedroom I'd ever been in. I still wore the sweater dress, but my boots were sitting by the door, and my belt was draped over a dresser. "How did I get here?"

"You were out by the time we got back. I figured it would be easier if you slept here."

I glanced to the other side of the bed. It was still made.

He followed my gaze. "I slept in the guest room next

door."

"Oh." Was that disappointment in my voice?

He walked around and sat next to me, his golden skin and light eyes making tension swirl in my stomach. "I called the doctor first thing. Your dad is doing better and is set to be released this afternoon. He'll be transported straight to the rehab. It's all taken care of."

"Thank you."

He took my hand. "You're welcome." He stared down at me for a few beats, and something in his look had my body buzzing. His gaze darted to my lips, and he stilled. The longer he looked, the more it seemed my lungs couldn't get enough air. But he pulled his hand away and stood. "I, um, I've already set out some breakfast we can grab and go." He walked into a large closet next to what looked like an en suite bathroom. He snagged a team t-shirt and pulled it over his head as he walked out of the bedroom. "I'll wait in the living room."

All the heat he'd stoked inside me dissipated and left me on edge.

I rose and took a tour of his marble bathroom with clear glass shower and soaking tub, then walked out the door and into the sunny living room. He leaned on the granite bar in the kitchen. A bagel, already slathered with cream cheese, sat at the ready along with a travel cup of orange juice.

"You can eat on the way." He finished his coffee and placed the cup in the sink.

I snagged the food and the juice. "I love bagels."

"Yeah?" He dropped his gaze.

I took a big bite as I followed him to his front door. "And this is my favorite flavor of cream cheese."

"Good to know." He walked around the kitchen island and toward the front door.

I took in his spacious apartment. The living room was full of leather furniture, a big-screen TV, and a plush rug that I wanted to run my hand across.

He opened the door and led me out, then closed it behind him and locked it. We rode the elevator down to his car, and the drive to my dorm was less than ten minutes. I ate my bagel and downed the last of my juice as he parked.

"I'll wait here for you and drive you to practice. It's faster that way."

I opened the door, a blast of cool air whipping into the warm car, then turned to him. "Come on up. I don't mind."

The corner of his mouth twitched into a smile, and he killed the engine. "Sure."

Brandy waved us through and gave Trent a wink. I pretended I didn't see it and climbed the two flights of stairs to my floor. Trent walked behind me, his presence making my skin warm and my mind wander. I fumbled with the keys, but managed to make it into my room without dropping them.

Trent followed and closed the door behind him. Ellie was out, but had left a half-eaten piece of peanut butter toast on her bed, crumbs and all.

I walked to my closet and picked out a t-shirt, athletic pants, and fresh underwear. Ellie's dress had served me well over the last day and a half, but I was ready to be rid of it.

"Just make yourself at home." I turned as Trent sat at the foot of my bed. He watched me, never taking his eyes from me as I strode to the bathroom. "I'll shower and dress right quick."

"I'll be here. We're making good time. Practice doesn't start for another forty-five minutes." He lay back and tucked his hands under his head, his broad back taking up almost all my double bed.

A shock of need shot through between my thighs, and I scissored my legs to fight the sensation. He followed the movement and licked his lips.

"I'm just going to shower. Yeah." I hurried into the

bathroom and closed the door behind me.

"What are you doing?" I whispered to myself, though the scolding did nothing to chill my need for Trent. He'd looked like a jungle cat lounging on my bed.

After peeling off the dress, I took a short shower to wash off the stress of the past few days. Halfway through, my fingers dipped to my pussy as I thought of Trent laid out on my bed. God, why did he have to be so gorgeous? I stroked myself a few times before forcing my fingers to stop. He might hear, and I couldn't bear the thought of him busting me touching myself in the shower.

I dried off, put on fresh clothes, and wrapped my towel around my wet hair. When I opened the door, he was in the same position, but his eyes were trained on me.

"Better?" He let his gaze travel the length of my body.

"Much. Thanks." My nipples tingled and hardened. "I just need to get some socks."

I walked past Trent to my bedside table and opened the bottom drawer. He shifted on the bed, and when I turned around, he was sitting up.

My heart raced at his nearness, but I tried to play it off by sitting next to him and pulling on my socks. I could sense how focused he was on me, and the knowledge sent a tingle over my skin. I finished and pulled the towel from my hair.

"I think I'm ready." I met his eyes, our arms lightly touching as we sat beside each other.

"Are you?" He leaned in and kissed me.

I trembled as he put one palm on my cheek. His mouth was hot, and he used his tongue on my lips, seeking entry. I closed my eyes as he snaked an arm around my waist and pulled me close.

He took my breath, and I clutched at his shoulders as he slanted his mouth over mine. When I opened for him, he groaned and sank his tongue inside, licking and tasting me as he slowly lowered me to the bed. So many thoughts tried to barge their way to the forefront of my mind—what had happened two years ago, what he'd said two nights ago, and everything in-between. I pushed them all away and focused on him.

He broke our kiss and stared down at me. "Cordy." His voice was drawn tight, and his pupils dilated until only a sliver of light green remained. "I don't think I can stop if we start this. Understand? I want you so bad it hurts. But I don't want to do anything you don't want me to."

My heartbeat thundered in my ears, and I made a decision. It was foolish, reckless—especially given our past and my inexperience. I didn't care. I leaned up and kissed him. It was a light caress of my lips against his, but it set off a tidal wave of need from him. He crashed down on top of me, pinning me beneath him as he settled between my legs.

I wrapped my arms around his neck as he kissed me hard, his tongue demanding, and his hands roving down my sides. I shivered beneath his touch. He claimed me with each swirl of his tongue, each delicious taste. I had never been kissed like this. He didn't hold back; there was no tentative opening salvo, only pure possession. I reveled in it and ran my hand through his hair, tangling my fingers and tugging softly as he deepened our kiss. My blood was on fire, and my core tightened as his big body pressed down against mine.

He broke our kiss, and I gasped for air when he trailed his mouth down my neck. I squirmed as he licked and sucked along my throat. It verged on a tickling feeling until he sucked my skin between his teeth and bit lightly. The sensation jolted down my body and landed between my thighs.

When he grabbed the hem of my shirt, I froze. What if he didn't like my body? He'd seen my breasts, but not the rest of me.

"I want to feel you. All of you." His voice was gravelly. "Here. I'll go first." He stripped his shirt off, showing me the golden expanse of skin and rippling muscles that made my mouth water. "Your turn."

I gripped his wrists as he tugged at my shirt. He stared down at me with a heated look, his face flushed and his eyes fixed on me.

"Do you trust me?" He ran his fingertips along my stomach, my flesh quivering at his touch.

Everything in our past screamed at me to say no. Instead, I told the truth. "Yes." I relaxed my grip and lay my hands to the side.

He swallowed hard, his Adam's apple bobbing, and lifted my shirt. He peeled it off, then hitched his fingers beneath my sports bra. Without taking my eyes from his, I lifted my arms, and with a swift tug, he pulled it free. I lay beneath him, my breasts on full display, my nipples hard and jutting to the ceiling.

"Fuck me." He stared. "Perfect. So fucking perfect."

My cheeks heated, and my hands itched to cover my bare skin. I forced myself to stay still. And the longer he stared, the more erotic the moment became. The look in his eyes was predatory, dark, and full of a desire I was desperate to taste.

He eased his hands up my stomach and cupped each of my breasts. When he squeezed, a moan lofted from my throat.

"Jesus, Cordy." He ran his thumbs across my nipples. Back and forth several times, each swipe was a new flame added to the fire raging between my thighs.

He bent his head to my left breast. When his tongue hit my stiff peak, my back arched, and I gripped his shoulders. He wrapped his lips around my nipple and sucked while squeezing both breasts with his hands.

"Trent, oh my God." I writhed as he sucked and nipped at first one breast and then the other. His tongue was wicked, flicking and licking until the tension between my thighs had me writhing.

When he relented and kissed to my mouth, I sighed

and ran my hands down his chiseled back. He settled his hips against me for the first time, his hard length pressing against my thigh. Fear erupted in my mind, but it was quickly quelled by the passion of his mouth, the all-encompassing pleasure of his kiss. My breasts pressed against his chest, the skin-on-skin contact sizzling every nerve ending.

He kissed down my chest, between my breasts, along my shuddering stomach, and stopped at the edge of my pants. I gripped my blanket and closed my eyes as he tucked his fingers in my waistband.

"Look at me. I want you to watch." His low voice was like velvet.

I bit my bottom lip and forced my eyes open. He had a devilish look in his eyes as he pulled my pants down my legs, then stripped my socks and tossed it all on the floor. He kissed my ankle and ran his lips up my calf, lingered on my knee, and kissed up my thigh. It tickled at first, but the closer he came to my panties, the sensation fermented into something far more intoxicating. He repeated it with my other leg until he knelt between my legs and ran his fingertips up and down my hips, plucking at my panties.

He licked his lips. "I've dreamed about this for so long." The tremble in his voice raised goosebumps along my skin.

"Me too." My voice was barely a whisper.

He closed his eyes, as if he were savoring the flavor of my words. Giving the cotton a tug, he dropped his gaze to my pussy. I took a deep breath and lifted my hips. He eased my panties down, and I bent my knees and put my legs together so he could pull them off.

"Show me." He ran his hands up my legs and put gentle pressure on my knees, pushing them apart. "Slowly."

I opened for him, my heart in my throat and my body on fire.

He groaned as I let my legs fall open, then smoothed

his palms down the insides of my thighs. He rested his hands in the crease where my legs met my hips, as if framing my most intimate parts.

"So fucking sexy." He leaned down, and when his breath swept across my hot, wet skin, I dug my nails into the sheets.

He scooted down in the bed, his face hovering over my dark curls. "Has anyone ever tasted you?"

"No." My legs shook as he wrapped his palms around my thighs and stared up at me.

"I'm the only one." When his tongue connected, I cried out from the overwhelming rush of pleasure. He licked again, the broad side of his tongue lapping at me. "The only one who will ever know what you taste like."

I stared down at him, almost disbelieving that Trent Carrington was between my thighs. But when he sucked my clit, I became a believer.

"Trent!" I gripped his hair, and he smiled up at me before diving back down, burying his face in my pussy.

He licked and sucked, his tongue doing things I didn't even know were possible. A chain reaction of tiny explosions worked their way from my clit to deep inside me. Trent didn't stop, only pulled my thighs apart farther and covered me with his mouth.

I began rocking my hips, grinding my pussy on his face as my breath caught in my throat. He focused his tongue at just the right spot. I could feel the excitement cresting, the wave ready to break. He sank two fingers inside me, and I bit my arm to cover the low moan that escaped me as I came. The pleasure broke me into a million pieces, all of them shooting skyward and turning to ash under the heat of his tongue.

When my hips finally found the bed again, I was covered with sweat. Trent kept pulsing his fingers in and out of me, his tongue licking my too-sensitive nub in a leisurely caress.

"Trent!" I tried to shy away from him, but he licked

harder. "Please, oh my God." I gasped in breath after breath.

He grinned and rose onto his knees.

The door handle jiggled, and Trent tensed.

"Shit, it's Ellie." I reached for the blanket to cover myself.

I yanked it to my neck just as the door swung open. Ellie walked in and stopped, her eyebrows raised in shock.

The door almost closed behind her, then opened again. Landon froze in the doorway, and then the shouting began.

CHAPTER TWENTY-THREE
CORDY

LANDON PUSHED PAST A stunned Ellie. "You motherfucker!"

Trent put a steadying hand on my hip as Landon stood over us, his hands clenched into fists.

"Please don't tell me you gave it to him." Landon's voice was soft but lethal. He smelled like a keg, his hair was mussed, and some obvious hickeys dotted his neck.

Trent straightened his back. "That's none of your busines—"

"I wasn't talking to you!" Landon's yell ricocheted off the walls of the room. He stared down at me, the awkwardness growing with each second. "Did you?"

"Landon, please leave." I tried to keep my tone even, but the hurt and anger in his eyes constricted my heart.

"You did." His face fell. "He didn't deserve it. He's just going to use you and throw you away."

"That's your M.O., not mine." Trent made sure the blanket was tucked around me, then stood. "She's asked you to leave." He stepped toward Landon until both men were nose to nose.

Ellie leaned against the door frame and fanned herself

with her hand.

"I know who you are, Trent." Landon seethed with anger. "You aren't fooling me."

"Either you walk out of here, or I'll drag you out. Your choice."

I sat up and clutched the blanket to my chest. "Landon, go." I put as much authority into my voice as I could.

"You're choosing him over me?" Landon's voice shook.

"It's not like that. You and I are friends. Trent and I—"

"Are fuck buddies now?" Landon kept his eyes on Trent.

I glanced at Ellie, then back to Landon. "What are you even doing here? Why are you with Ellie?"

"Don't try and turn this around on me!"

I focused on Ellie. "Were you with Landon last night?"

She didn't look at me, but answered slowly. "We went to a party at the KA house and fell asleep in one of the rooms there."

"Together? You slept together?" I pointed a finger at her. "And you know what I'm asking."

"Yeah." She shrugged.

I flicked my gaze back to Landon, his hypocrisy raising my blood to a steady boil. "Get out."

He finally broke his staring match with Trent and looked at me. "That's not the same—"

"Go!"

He flinched at the anger in my voice. I couldn't remember a time when I'd been this livid with him. His whoring ways and over-the-top antics had never bothered me before. But I wasn't about to let him stand in judgment of my choices, especially not after all the women he'd been through.

"You heard her." Trent's voice was low, the threat

more tangible than a raised fist.

Landon scowled and shook his head. "Fine. But I warned you, Cordy. Don't come crying to me when he breaks your heart again. I won't be waiting. Not this time."

His shoulders drooped, and he strode to the door and into the hallway, his head down and his steps heavy.

I stared at the open doorway, my heart angry and aching at the same time. Trent sat next to me and took my hand.

Ellie let the door close and threw herself on her bed. "That went well." Then she turned over and began snoring in less than ten seconds.

Practice went well. Coach Carver was impressed with my technique and even more pleased with my accuracy. I was the Mav no longer. Maybe I could be Ice Man?

Between kicks, my thoughts strayed to what I'd done with Trent earlier that morning or, sometimes, to the hurt on Landon's face as I'd ordered him out of my room. So much had happened that I felt as if I were spinning, not sure when I'd stop or who I'd be when I did.

I spent my classes that day in the same fog. I found myself blushing during my Beat Poets class, and again as I was walking across campus back to my dorm for the night. Trent had already texted and asked if he could take me to dinner.

Despite what we'd done, there was more left unsaid. We needed to clear the air. I'd seen enough teen dating shows to know that it wasn't yet time to DTR (define the relationship), but I needed some sort of assurance from him that this was real. More than that, I wanted to know what he was trying to tell me about his father's death. The niggling suspicion that he was only seeing me because his trust fund was safe haunted my thoughts.

"Princess." Ethan's gruff voice startled me.

I looked over my shoulder to see him catching up with me. "Go away, Ethan."

"What?" He grinned and slowed to walk at my elbow. "I can't have a chat with our star kicker?"

I pulled my jacket closer to me and sped my pace. The air had warmed over the day, but another line of storms was expected to hit overnight.

"I feel like you need to read the part of the student handbook that talks about sexual harassment." I kept him in my peripheral vision.

"I'm not harassing." His leer didn't match his words. "Promise."

"Then go back to your wildebeest clan. I'm busy."

"I will. But first I wanted to talk about your friend Landon."

I swiveled my head around to him. "What?"

He shrugged, his bulky shoulders flexing. "I heard him crying to some hot piece of ass in the caf at lunch. Something about you and Trent?"

I stiffened and focused on the lights gleaming in Hope Hall's windows. "It's rude to eavesdrop."

"He thought so, too. He's got a smart mouth."

"Leave him alone."

"I'm more interested in Trent. So, you're giving it up to the QB?" He moved closer, his arm pressing into mine as we walked.

I didn't respond.

"It's okay." He leaned closer. "I'll take rich boy's sloppy seconds."

I drew my arm back and shoved it out beside me, nailing him in the ribs with my elbow. "Touch me, and I'll do much worse."

He grunted and his steps faltered. "Don't be a bitch, princess."

I hurried until I was nearly running up the sidewalk

beneath the oaks, passing students as the twilight turned into full-on night. Ethan didn't follow, and by the time I reached Hope Hall, I was trembling. Whether it was from Ethan or the cold, I couldn't tell.

I swung the door open and darted inside.

Trent leaned against the reception window, chatting with Brandy, but when he saw me, he rushed over. "What is it?"

I snuggled into his chest as he threw his arms around me. If I told him, he might start a fight with Ethan. *Hard pass.*

"Just cold."

He placed his lips next to my ear and whispered, "Want to go upstairs and warm up before dinner?"

I giggled, a thrill running through me and an ache growing between my thighs. "No. I'm hungry." Pulling back, I stared up into his eyes. "And I want you to finish what you started at La Café Blanc."

He took my hands and kissed my forehead. "Whatever you want."

"Dinner."

He led me out the front door and down to his car. "Any requests?"

"Pita Stop."

He opened my car door, his eyes following my every move. "Excellent choice."

It took about ten minutes to get to the south side of town. We chatted about classes and practice. Beneath it all, tension grew inside him. I felt it in his movements, in the quiet spaces he would usually fill with words.

The Pita Stop was located on the bottom floor of a three-story building. The exterior was faded, but a bright blue sign promised the best hummus in town. We walked in and claimed a booth near the front window. A TV was set to a broadcast about the coming storm, and the air was filled with the delicious scents of grilled seafood and Mediterranean spices. Only a few tables were occupied, most people in town already bunkered down for the bad weather.

A waiter walked up and handed me a menu, then turned to Trent. "Usual?"

"Yeah."

"I'll have the same."

The waiter smiled and retrieved my menu. "Very well. It'll be right out."

Trent kept eyeing the window behind me, the wind rattling the thin pane of glass.

I reached across the table and took his hand. "Tell me the rest. I didn't give you a chance, and I want to." Doubt welled inside me—what if my fears about the trust fund were true? I couldn't be with someone who only wanted me when it was convenient. But I had to give him an opportunity to explain it, all of it, before I made any decisions.

He scrubbed a hand down his rough cheek and leaned forward. "I'm going to do my best to say it right this time, but I don't entirely trust myself. So, if I say something that hurts you, please bear with me. I don't mean to." The boy from two years ago—timid despite his size, and with his heart on his sleeve—reappeared in his sincere gaze.

I nodded and squeezed his hand. "Go on."

"My family is sort of… Let's say set in their ways. My mother, especially. Two years ago, I wasn't strong enough to stand up to them, to stand up for us. I told you about Carlotta. My mother has been set on that match for years. Her brother is a senator. Mom thought that marrying Carlotta would, you know, give me the right connections."

He squeezed my hand. "At the time, my dad was sick. The cancer had destroyed him from the inside out." His voice thickened with tears, and I wanted to take the pain away. He continued, "Anyway, he cautioned patience, too. God." He leaned his head back and swallowed hard. "My mother threatened my trust fund. My dad was sick. My mom said that I was making his last days harder. I was just a stupid kid. I gave in. I let you go. Even though you were the best thing that had ever happened to me. To make them happy, I let you go."

He fell silent, but kept my hand in his. When he brought his gaze back to mine, his eyes were clear. "My dad died last summer."

"I'm sorry." I ignored the emotions twisting inside me and forced myself to be present for him.

"Thank you. He was the beating heart of our family. When he stopped, it turned my mother even colder than she was before. It did something else to me, though. It made me see how stupid I was to think I could walk away from you. I never did. Not really. I watched you. I did some things…"

I cocked my head to the side. "What things?"

He ran a hand through his hair, tousling the brown locks, and darted his gaze away before coming back to me. "I maybe, um, I…"

His tan cheeks turned a cute shade of red.

"That bad, huh?" I smiled, wondering what he could have possibly done.

"I got you the third-string spot on the team. I sent money to your father. I have a copy of every one of your class schedules. I'm the one who set him up with that rehab." The confession came in a torrent. "I *know you*, Cordy. I spent two years getting to know you, and it only made me love you more. It sounds crazy, but I swear I didn't mean any harm by it. Even though I tried to let you go, to forget about you, to take Carlotta on dates like my mother demanded, you are all I've thought about."

I couldn't seem to get enough air, mainly because I'd been holding my breath. He covered my hand with his, his fingers trembling. I tried to process his words, my brain telling me he was a stalker, my heart melting into a puddle. Did he say he loved me?

"You paid for my dad's rehab?" I repeated his words,

as if testing their weight. "Sent him money?"

He nodded as the waiter appeared and slid our plates onto the table. Trent leaned back, and the warmth that had cocooned my hand dissipated.

"Thanks." He nodded as the waiter backed away, then refocused on me. "So, what do you think? Is this the part where you scream and get a restraining order?"

I took a deep breath and tried to settle the runaway beat of my heart. "That can wait until after you pay for the food."

He snorted and gave me a half-smile.

"But can I ask you a question?"

"Okay." He nodded hard, as if I'd asked him if he could throw me a perfect pass. "I can deal with that. Hit me."

"When your father died, did that mean that your trust fund was safe?"

He winced. "I deserve that."

"I'm sorry. This is a lot, and I don't know—"

"No. You're right to ask. It makes sense. But no, I didn't come back into your life because my money is safe. My dad's death did the opposite, really. Mom has become even more insistent that I propose to Carlotta. She's promised that I won't see another cent if I don't fall in line."

I sat still, hoping for him to tell me what I wanted to hear. I didn't have to wait long.

"I didn't come back to you because my money's safe. It's the opposite, Cordy. She'll cut me off. But"—he laid his hand on the table next to our plates—"I don't care. I couldn't wait any longer. You are everything. She can never give me another dime. I don't care. You're more important than any of it. We'll make our own way." He pierced me with his emerald stare. "If you can forgive me for the past two years. If you'll have me."

I glanced to his outstretched hand. Could I forgive him? I'd hated him for so long, my heart nursing the wound he'd inflicted.

He watched me, his body tense, as if he were bracing himself for the worst. I could shatter him the same way he did me. But it would leave me in ruins right along with him.

I pressed my hand into his, and a smile that rivalled the sun spread across his face. Warmth rushed over my skin and heated every spot in my body and soul. He rose and scooted into the booth next to me, crowding me against the wall.

His lips met mine, and I was suddenly ravenous for him. I wrapped my arms around his neck as he smoothed his hands to my waist. His nimble tongue left me breathless, and when I came up for air, he ran his hot mouth along my throat.

A low roar began to overtake the sound of the weather broadcast. I gasped as Trent nipped at my neck. Glancing to the window, I discovered the reason for the sound. Rain poured in unforgiving sheets, giving the street lights a white halo and pounding on the cars outside.

"Trent." He stopped kissing me long enough to follow my stare, then called to the waiter. "Hey, we'll need this to go." Settling back into the booth, he nuzzled next to my ear. "You're coming home with me."

The second his apartment door closed, he pinned me against it. He owned my body, caging me in with a wall of muscle and desire. Gripping the lapel of my jacket, he shucked it off me and tossed it to the floor. I ran my fingers along the hem of his pullover and yanked. He stepped back and stripped off his pullover and the t-shirt beneath it. I let my gaze wander the hard planes of his body, the roping muscles, the strong line of his jaw, the hot look in his eyes.

He pinned me again, his lips owning me. I let my fingers rove along his back as he gripped my hair with one hand, pulling until he was able to slant his mouth over mine. His tongue knew just how to stroke mine, to sink and tease until I was wet and desperate for more.

I arched when he cupped my breast through my sweater and squeezed. His cock pressed against my stomach. Fear and desire burned inside me, because I knew tonight was the night. I would finally give myself to Trent the way I'd been dreaming about for years.

He broke our kiss and backed off a fraction of an inch. "I need to go slow with you. I *have* to."

"Who are you trying to convince?" I moaned when he tweaked my nipple.

"I don't want to hurt you." His thin veil of control was slowly ripping apart.

Running my hand down his hard stomach, I stroked his cock through his jeans. I may as well have flashed a red cape in front of a bull.

He crushed me against the door again, his hands roving me. "Fuck going slow."

He gripped my ass and lifted me so I straddled him, his cock pressing against my hot core through my jeans, then carried me to his bed and lay me on his navy comforter.

His bronze skin was flushed as he grabbed my sweater. I lifted my arms, and he pulled it over my head, then tossed it to the floor. He groaned and grazed his palms over the white lace of my bra.

"Innocent, sexy." He scrubbed a hand down the stubble along his jaw. "Take it off." His voice was full of a command that sent a thrill down to my pussy.

I did as he said, releasing the clasp and sliding the lace off. He licked his lips as my breasts were revealed, and a tremble shot through me. The way he stared melted away any of my shyness and made me feel sexy.

He claimed one of my hard nipples, sucking as his tongue flicked across it. I squealed and ran my fingers through his hair, my body on fire. He gripped the front of my jeans, and with a yank, undid the button. Kissing down my stomach, he pulled the zipper and hooked his fingers in my jeans and panties.

"Off." He tugged, and I lifted my hips as he removed every stitch of clothing I wore.

He stood above me, studying my body like a map that would lead to his heart's desire.

"Slow, go slow," he repeated, though the look in his eyes said anything but "slow."

Easing his hands to his waistband, he undid his jeans and pushed them and his boxers to the floor. When he stood, his cock pointed straight up toward his belly button, the shaft thick and the head damp. An *mmm* sound escaped my lips. I'd never seen one up close like this. The fact that it belonged to Trent had my thighs on fire, and I wanted to touch him, to taste him.

"Spread your legs." The predatory look in his eyes had my heart beating faster than if I'd run a race.

I eased my knees open a little, nerves trying to overtake the heat he'd stoked in me.

"Wider." He gripped his shaft and pumped it in one long, slow movement. "All the way, Cordy."

"Trent." The word sprang from my lips as I opened my legs wider, bending at the knees and placing my feet flat on the bed.

"Look what you do to me." He held my gaze as he worked himself in long strokes. Then he climbed between my legs, kneeling there as he devoured me with his searing gaze. "Give me your hand."

I leaned up, anxiety filling the synapses where my endorphins had been. What if I wasn't good at it? What if it hurt? What if I hated it?

He took my hand and guided it to his shaft. It felt velvety, and I gripped it, testing how much I could squeeze.

He groaned and braced himself with one arm on the bed. "Are you trying to make me come?"

I kept moving up and down the length of him, pleased that my touch had such an effect on him. He started thrusting his hips in time with my rhythm. I was getting the hang of it when he put his hand on my shoulders and pushed me down on my back.

His weight settled on top of me, though he kept most of it on his elbows. He kissed my neck, all the way up to my ear as the head of his cock slid down my wet folds. "So fucking wet for me."

I shivered as he centered his small thrusts on my clit, each stroke of his cock more pleasurable than my fingers had ever been.

"I'm going to bury myself inside you." His muscles shook as he kept making the measured movements that drove me wild. "Are you on the pill?"

"Y-yes."

"Good." He let the head of his cock slide to my entrance. With a small push, he nudged inside the slightest bit.

I squeaked at the intrusion and felt a minor burning sensation. It subsided until the only thing left was the promise of pleasure.

"Are you okay?" His voice was strained.

"Yes. I think." He pushed a little farther, and my toes curled at the sting mixed with the sensation of being filled. "I think I'm ready."

He rested his forehead on mine. "It's going to hurt, Cordy. I can't help that. But I promise I'll make it feel so good you won't care. Do you still trust me?"

I stared up into his eyes. They were filled with passion, but also a gentleness that erased any of my doubts.

I took a breath and grazed his lips with mine, my decision made. "Yes."

CHAPTER TWENTY-FOUR
TRENT

I FORCED MYSELF TO go slow. She looked up at me, her amber eyes full of trust and a hint of something else, something I'd wanted to see there from the first moment I saw her. I kissed her again, realizing I would never get enough of her lips or her sweet taste. She pressed her palms against my back, clinging to me as I began to move inside her.

Her pussy was hot, wet, and incredibly tight, and it took everything I had to keep my movements controlled. I eased my head farther inside her and groaned my pleasure into her mouth. She tensed for a moment, then relaxed again as I massaged her tongue with mine. I pushed in a little deeper, her slick walls bearing down on me in the most exquisite vise.

She ran a hand to my ass and dug her nails in as I embedded myself. She tensed again, and I kissed down to her neck, biting lightly at the juncture of her shoulder. I slid a hand to her breast and pinched her nipple. Her moan told me I could continue, and I pushed the rest of the way with slow, smooth, unrelenting pressure. My cock was ready to explode from the sheer deliciousness of her body, but I would make it last.

She shook, and I popped up to check on her. She bit her lip, and her eyes were half-lidded. The sexiest thing I'd ever seen, and far better than the many hot scenarios I'd imagined over the years.

"Are you okay?" I nipped at her jaw and reveled in the feeling of being fully inside her.

"I—yes."

"Does it hurt?"

"I-I, well it did, but now it just feels...good. Like, full and good." She fidgeted a little, and I bit back a groan.

Slow, slow, slow. I dropped another kiss on her mouth and slid out to my tip. She squirmed and let out a breath. I gave her a moment, then pushed slowly back into her, even farther than before.

"Mmm." She dug her nails into my side.

"Fuck." I dropped my head onto the pillow next to her, trying to keep myself together. My balls were already drawn up tight, but I wasn't coming until she got off on my cock. I'd taken her virginity, but I wanted to give her so much more.

She pumped her hips tentatively, just enough for her clit to grind on me. A surprised sound left her lips, and she did it again, making my cock throb from the friction.

She purred. "Oh, that feels so—"

I moved my hips with hers, and she dug her nails deeper.

"Together." I licked her earlobe and kissed the spot beneath it. I surged forward, and she met my stroke with one of her own. "That's it, Cordy."

I set a slow pace, and she met me each time, grinding on my cock and taking a little piece of my sanity each time, until I was fucking her harder than I'd intended, but not as hard as I wanted to. Our skin was slicked with sweat as we moved against each other, my lips always on her delicious neck as she moaned and moved beneath me.

I pulled back and sucked one of her tight nipples into

my mouth, a slight hint of salt on my tongue as I sucked and kept pumping in and out of her. She arched her back, giving me all of her. I took it and wanted more. I feared I would never get enough.

Sitting back, I pulled her hips off the bed and gripped around her thighs, fucking her in steady strokes. Our skin slapped together, echoing around the room.

"Look." I directed her attention to where her tight pussy took every inch of me.

She watched transfixed, the weight of her gaze driving my load up my shaft.

I licked my thumb and pressed it to her swollen clit. She bucked, but I kept her hips locked in place with my other hand.

"Touch your tits."

She panted, her lips open as she watched me fuck her, and cupped her breasts as I'd instructed. I increased the pressure on her clit, rubbing her as I impaled her on my cock.

"Pinch your nipples."

"Oh my God." Her moan lit up pleasure sensors in my brain that I didn't even know existed.

She was a wet dream come to life, her hands pinching her pink nipples while my cock disappeared inside her. She kept her eyes on where we were joined. She was easily the sexiest woman I'd ever seen. And she was mine. Just watching her pussy take me again and again had my mouth watering.

I sped my strokes, my cock hardening with each thrust. I wouldn't last much longer, and I needed to feel her come, to experience the height of her pleasure while buried inside her. Drawing up some of her own wetness, I swirled my thumb around her clit, and she bit her lip.

"Oh my God. It feels so…" Her voice faded as her hips began to lose their rhythm.

She stilled and held her breath. Then she arched so hard that only her shoulders remained on the mattress. She came, her pussy squeezing me as she moaned loud enough for my neighbors to hear. I didn't give a shit.

I slammed into her a few more times as she began to come down, then pulled out. I didn't even have to stroke myself. Rubbing my cock on her curls, I came hard, thick ropes of come marking her pussy as mine. I groaned and thrust against her, emptying everything I had as she panted beneath me.

When my cock stopped kicking, I sat back and stared at her, a masterpiece of sex and perfection. Her brown hair curled slightly around her neck, and her skin glowed luminous in the low light. I couldn't stop the pride that welled in my breast as I surveyed my come on her pussy. I didn't care if it made me a cave man. I wanted her to feel my possession the same way I felt hers over me.

She placed her palm on her forehead and left it there, her fingers in her hair. "Wow."

My heart leapt and was far more gratified by her response than was modest. Leaning down, I brushed my mouth against hers. "Are you okay?"

She smiled against my lips. "Better than okay."

"Hang on." I darted to my bathroom, then came back and cleaned her up with a warm washcloth.

Lying next to her, I couldn't stop touching her, my fingertips greedy to feel every bit of her skin, sift through every strand of her hair.

She giggled when I skirted my hands along her ribs.

"Ticklish?"

"A little."

The wind howled outside, the steady thrumming sound of rain against my windows reaching my ears. Every sense in my body had been so focused on Cordy that I forgot all about the storm. She was finally here in my bed, in my arms where she belonged. The thunder and rain were only background noise.

I kissed her forehead. "Thank you."

She stared up at me as I pulled her to my chest and

whipped the sheet over us. "For what?"

"Giving me something no one else will ever have."

She buried her face in my neck. "I should have done this sooner."

I frowned and tugged on her hair. "With *me*. Sooner with me, right?"

"Of course." She ran her teeth along my neck, and my cock began to thicken again. "I've never even thought of anyone else. Not since we first met." She sighed. "I probably shouldn't have told you that."

"Yes, you should have." I pulled her chin up and kissed her. "It's the same for me. Only you. Besides, I told you everything earlier. Every sordid detail."

"You did, stalker." She smiled, her warm breath tickling my lips. "I can't believe we did it."

"You're not too sore, are you?" I hugged her close.

"I'll live. I might be kicking sideways a bit at practice." She laughed again and let out a contented sigh that I locked deep in my heart.

"That won't do." I kissed the crown of her head.

We lay silent for a while until I heard a distinct rumble that wasn't thunder.

She laughed and rubbed her stomach. "We skipped dinner."

"Come on." I sat up and pulled her with me.

She reached for her sweater.

"Wait." I walked to my closet, pulled a t-shirt off a hanger, and tossed it to her before donning some boxers. I watched as she slid my shirt over her head. It fell to her upper thighs, and fuck me if she didn't look hot as hell wearing my clothes.

"Mmm." She hugged herself. "Smells like you."

She likes the way I smell? My ego and my cock began to swell at the same time. I took her hand and pulled her from the bed, then bent her back and claimed her mouth again.

She made a high-pitched sound and wrapped her

arms around my neck. I could kiss her for days. Her stomach rumbled again, so I reluctantly broke our kiss and led her toward the kitchen, then sat her down at the bar.

"This apartment is really nice." She looked around and tapped her nails on the granite.

"Thanks. My dad lived in this same building when he was at Billingsley. He had such great memories here that he bought it and had it renovated." Just another Carrington perk. I studied her, wondering what she must think of me. The phrase "spoiled little rich boy" definitely came to mind, and she wouldn't be wrong.

I'd dropped the boxes of food from Pita Stop on the entry table when we'd walked in. I retrieved them and set us up at the bar. We ate in silence for a while, listening to the ongoing roll of thunder. The food was room temperature, but still delicious.

She wiped her mouth and turned to me. "Thanks."

"You're welcome."

She put her hand on my forearm. "Not just for the food. For helping with my father. I'll repay you somehow."

"No, you won't." I smiled. "Don't be fooled. Money is easy for me. I can pay for things all day long, but I want you to know that if there's anything I can do to help you, or to make you happy, I'll do it."

"Like getting me the kicker position?" She took a sip of her water.

I nodded. "Like that, yeah."

She set her glass down and frowned. "Wait. Did you get me first-string?"

"No." I took her hand and kissed the back of it. "That was all you. I promise. Nothing to do with me."

Her smile returned. "Thank God. I didn't want to start off with a confidence problem. But it had a lot to do with you. Don't kid yourself." She ran her hand down my cheek, and I leaned into her palm. "And I hear what you're saying about money being easy for you. But you've done more for me than anyone else ever has. Thank you."

I toyed with a lock of her hair and grinned. "It wasn't completely altruistic."

"No?" She took a bite of baklava.

I gripped her waist and pulled her closer to me. "Not at all. I had my sights set on a very particular goal."

She batted her lashes. "Oh, my dear Mr. Carrington. What sort of girl do you think I am? You can't buy my affection."

I kissed her, the honey on her lips only enhancing her taste. "I know exactly what sort of girl you are. Mine."

CHAPTER TWENTY-FIVE
CORDY

THE BEAT OF THE drums behind me reverberated through my chest. The offense was on the field, Trent leading the charge toward the Gators' end zone. I stood along the sideline, mixing in with the players as Coach Sterling stalked past us.

We were already up by fourteen, and I'd kicked each point after the touchdowns.

Hawthorne stood at my elbow. "Looks like you're about to be up again."

I glanced up at him, his red hair glowing under the stadium lights. "Don't jinx it!"

"Whoa." He held his hands up, a wry smile on his lips. "Don't even say the J-word around me."

"You started it."

"And I take it back."

"Then I take back the J-word. Though, I must say, your kickoffs have been epic this whole game." I shook my head as Trent ran the ball up the middle to the two-yard line. "And I couldn't believe the punt you kicked to the five that rolled to the one. That was crazy."

He shrugged, modesty written in the movement. "I

just get lucky sometimes."

"I'd like to get lucky with the princess here." Ethan hovered behind me.

I rolled my eyes. "Go drink some Gatorade. I think all that running around and sweating has fried your wildebeest brain."

"Keep insulting me." He moved closer, his hot breath flowing down my neck. "It's just going to make it that much sweeter when I've got you on your back."

"Hey, asshole." Hawthorne turned and scowled. "Back the fuck off her."

"I'm not talking to you, copper top."

Hawthorne laughed far too vehemently to be believed. "Oh, good one. I've never heard that one before." He guffawed. "Tell me another."

Before Ethan could spew any more bullshit, the crowd came alive. Trent had thrown a perfect pass to the back of the end zone. The offense ran off the field, bringing the smell of grass and earth with them. I snugged my helmet into place as Coach walked up.

"Bring it on home, Cordy."

"Yes, sir." I trotted onto the field.

Trent followed. "You're doing great."

I grinned and fidgeted with my mouth piece. "So are you."

The crowd grew louder as an image of Trent and me lit up the huge screens on each end. We were standing close, and my smile was on full display. My cheeks heated, but I trained my eyes on the field. I needed to keep my head in the game.

"You got this." Trent tapped my helmet, then knelt.

The crowd was quiet, many of them to help me concentrate, the rest because defeat was at hand. I lined up, took my steps, then signaled for the center to hike the ball.

I took my steps, connected with the pigskin, and the ball flew through the uprights. The crowd cheered, and for the first time, I was actually glad I was on a football field instead of a soccer pitch.

Trent stood and smacked my helmet again. "Perfect."

"Thanks." I ran off the field as Hawthorne prepared for his final kickoff of the game.

Trent walked to Coach and had a brief conference before coming to stand at my side. His brown hair stuck up every which way, and his eye black was smeared on one side, but he smiled down at me.

"You did it. Your first game as the starting kicker."

Pride swelled in my chest, and I couldn't stop my smile. "*We* did it."

Hawthorne kicked to the Gators, who ran two plays, then took a knee to end the game. The crowd roared with approval as the teams took off to their locker rooms.

Trent patted my ass once we were in the tunnel. "I'll have to do the press conference, but I'll see you after."

"Baxter!" Coach Sterling's yell cut through the click of cleats and the high spirits of the team.

Trent and I stopped and turned.

"I'll want you at the table for the conference. Be ready in half an hour."

"Me?"

Coach Sterling stared down his bulbous nose at me as the rest of the team filtered past. "Is there another Baxter on the team I don't know about?"

"Um, no?"

"No. So have your ass showered and ready to talk in thirty. Same goes for you, Trent. You know the drill. Get to it."

"Yes, Coach."

Once Coach Sterling was out of sight, Trent dropped a quick kiss on my lips. "See you at the table."

A press conference? I strode to the women's locker room and pushed inside. We were at the Gators' field, so the room wasn't familiar, but it had everything I needed to wash the game off me. I showered and dried my hair as fast as possible. I didn't have time for any makeup other than some mascara, but it would have to do.

I walked through the stadium's inner hallway and joined the team milling around outside the men's locker room. Coach Carver tapped Coach Sterling on the shoulder and jerked his chin at me.

Coach Sterling waved me to him. "Come on, Baxter. Hotfoot it over to the press room."

Pulling my bag behind me, I navigated through the players, several of them smiling and clapping me on the back. It felt good, and I found myself returning their grins and even doing a fist bump with a wide receiver.

"I'll take that and see it to the bus." Coach Carver snagged my carry-on luggage.

"Thanks." I let it go and continued down the corridor.

Gabrielle Younce, the head of school media, stood in the hall, her well-coiffed blonde hair done in beachy waves and her skirt suit fitting her trim form perfectly. I'd become well acquainted with her when I was initially picked to be the Mav. She'd given a press conference about Billingsley inclusivity while I smiled and waved next to her.

"You ready?" She looked me up and down, then undid the last button on my team polo.

"Hey." I wanted to slap her hand away.

"Trust me." She pulled a lock of hair over my shoulder and backed away so I could continue toward the media room.

"We good?" Trent jogged up, though he looked paler than usual.

Did he still get nervous talking in front of people?

"I think so. I don't know." I clasped my hands in front of me as I walked, my fingers at war with each other. "I've never done a press conference before."

"It's easy." Coach Sterling clapped me on the back. "I'll handle most of the questions. You two just sit there and look pretty."

We came to a set of green double doors, and Gabrielle whipped around in front of us. "Just be your best selves." She smiled and turned the handle.

Trent took my hand, his palm clammy, and gave it a quick squeeze.

I followed Coach, Trent at my back, as we filed into the media room. About a dozen reporters sat in chairs or chit-chatted with each other. TV cameras were set up in the aisle, and a couple more recorded from the back of the room. Coach took two steps onto a podium and claimed the center seat where a bank of microphones was already waiting. I scooted past and sat on the far end. Trent sat on Coach's other side.

The reporters took their seats. I recognized a couple at the front from ESPN and the local sports channel. Gabrielle stood off to the side, her arms crossed over her chest.

"Let's get started." Coach Sterling gave a play by play of how he felt the game went. He praised Trent's leadership and mentioned the strength of our defensive line. After a long spiel about how we have to work on avoiding penalties that cost yardage, he opened the floor for questions.

"Is there any truth to the rumors that lineman Ethan Granger and your QB have a long-running feud of some sort?"

Coach waved his hand as if he were swatting an annoying fly. "None whatsoever. This is a competitive sport. Even on the same team, players want to be the best. That can lead to gossip, but nothing more. Both men are trying to be the best this team has to offer."

Two reporters started asking questions at the same time, but the one in the front row won out. "Trent, how has team morale been since the kicking fiasco last Saturday?"

Some photographers moved around, taking my

picture from different angles.

Trent cleared his throat. "Well, I wouldn't call it a fiasco. That's pretty harsh. We lost one of our best guys to injury, and Cordy did her best to fill that spot and win the game. What happened couldn't have been foreseen. We got past it as a team, and now Cordy's our starting kicker. We're all behind her one hundred percent. So I think that tells you how the team's morale is."

I forced myself not to smile, though I wanted to burst with happiness from his vote of confidence.

"Cordy," One of the men farther back called. "What's it like being the only starting female college kicker in the country?"

I glanced at Coach. He nodded at me in the "go ahead" motion.

"It's great. I couldn't wish for a better team or a better set of coaches."

The reporter leaned forward, his elbows on his thighs. "How did you go from missing so badly last weekend to knocking it through with ease during this game?"

"Practice. Trent helped me work on my form." I winced as the reporter smirked, but continued, "Since he's the holder, he knows a lot about kicking. We practiced together for a few days, and then I went to walk-on tryouts. I was the most accurate for shorter distances. And that's how I got the first-string position."

"Are you and Trent still *practicing*?" The inflection in his word and the smirk on his face had me fisting my hands beneath the table.

"The team practices every day of the week." Trent's voice boomed out. "Next question."

But the reporter wouldn't give up. "We saw an interesting display of affection out on the field during the game. Coach, are you okay with your players dating?"

Gabrielle stepped forward. "If you don't have any football-related questions, we'll call an end to the conference. The private lives of Billingsley's students are not up for debate or questions."

Relief coursed through me as the rude reporter held a hand up and leaned back, though he still kept looking at me, then to Trent, then back to me.

The rest of the conference was taken up by questions for Coach and Trent. I was able to relax as they went over every bit of minutiae from the game. By the time the reporters began asking about our next game, our time was up. Gabrielle ushered us back into the hallway where Trent took a deep breath and leaned against the wall.

I rubbed his arm. "You did great in there."

Gabrielle raised an eyebrow at the contact. "Cordy, a word?"

I stared up at Trent, not leaving until I was sure he was all right. "You okay?"

Trent smiled. "Yeah, I just have to decompress for a second, let my nerves calm down. Go on. I'll see you on the bus."

"Okay." I followed Gabrielle, who turned into the nearby ladies' room.

She bent over, checking for feet in the stalls. Apparently satisfied, she leaned against the nearest sink and sighed. "How long have you two been seeing each other?"

I couldn't deny it, and I didn't want to. "We've known each other a long time, but we only started dating a few days ago. Why?"

"The team doesn't need any distractions." She turned and perused her face in the mirror. "We already have a loss. It will take a miracle for us to make it to the playoffs this year. And we'll likely have to face the Eagles again to do it."

"I don't care about facing the Eagles. They're just another team."

She peered at my reflection. "Do you have any idea how much pressure will be on the team, on you, if we go up against the same team who beat us solely because of your disastrous kick?"

Her tone grated on me. "Look, I intend to kick the best I can. That's all I can do. My relationship with Trent has nothing to do with what happens on field."

"If you two have a falling out, it will affect the entire team. It will affect how he plays and how you play." She turned and faced me, her eyes narrowed. "Kickers are a dime a dozen. Quarterbacks aren't. Bear that in mind if you want to keep your spot and your scholarship."

I couldn't believe what I was hearing. "Are you threatening me?"

"No." She strode to the door and pulled it open before affixing a fake smile on her face and responding brightly, "I'm educating you."

CHAPTER TWENTY-SIX
TRENT

MY PHONE RANG AS soon as I climbed onto the team charter bus. I already knew it was my mother. I ignored the call and pushed past my celebrating teammates to my seat. Cordy had saved a spot for me and smiled as soon as I came into view. I moved a little faster, the need to be close to her overwhelming my senses.

Sliding down next to her, I got a whiff of her shampoo. *Would it be creepy for me to lean in and smell her hair? Yeah, probably.* I did it anyway.

She laughed and punched my arm. "Weirdo. You're going to get kicked off the bus."

"I'm surprised they let you ride with us." I glanced around. Cordy was the only woman I could recall being allowed on the team bus. The cheerleaders and the band always rode separately, and so did Cordy—until today.

"I think it was Gabrielle's doing." A frown tugged at one corner of her mouth. "Wanting to make the whole 'she's a real team member' thing more effective for the press."

I was just happy I got to sit next to her for the three-hour ride. "I guess your Mav days truly are over."

"Well." She glanced around as if she were about to tell me a highly classified secret, then leaned over and whispered. "I still have the vagina, so I can always reprise the role if I feel like it."

"How's my princess doing?" Ethan's voice sounded from the aisle. I looked up to find him grinning at Cordy.

I bristled. "Move along, asshole."

"I would, but you're in my seat."

"Wildebeests have reserved seating at the rear." Cordy grabbed my elbow. "Google it if you don't believe me."

I rose, ignoring Cordy's strengthening grip on my arm. "Don't talk to her."

"Who's going to stop me?" He was about four inches shorter than me, but a whole hell of a lot wider.

I'd take my chances. "I think you know who." I flexed my fists. The fact that he thought he could even look at Cordy made my blood boil. Guys like him had to be taught a lesson about the right way to treat women, and I was more than happy to be his instructor.

"Hey, guys." Hawthorne stood in the aisle behind Ethan. "Knock it off."

Ethan pointed a finger in my face. "One day soon, I'm going to put you in your place, rich boy."

I stepped closer, until we were almost nose to nose. "That's reassuring, since my place is always far above yours."

Some of the closer players whistled. Cordy rose behind me and gripped my elbow. "Stop it. If either of you get hurt, it hurts the team."

Ethan ignored her. He didn't give two shits about the team. And my need to hurt him overcame Cordy's sound logic. His comments about her couldn't go unanswered any longer.

"What in the hell!" Coach Sterling's voice cut through the chatter as he barreled down the aisle. "Ethan, sit the fuck down. Hawthorne, what are you doing just standing here?"

"Coach, I was uh—"

"You were putting your ass in a seat, is what you're doing. Go on. We're ready to get out of this shit hole, and we won't be back until a couple years from now when we kick their asses again!"

The team whooped and yelled at Coach's words, and Ethan continued down the aisle with lumbering footsteps. Hawthorne followed and patted my shoulder as he walked past. He was a good guy, and I could tell he would have had my back against Ethan.

I sank down in my seat.

Cordy grabbed my hand. "Don't let him bait you. Ignore him. That's what I do."

"It's not working. He's obsessed with you." I considered getting up and following him to kick his ass and be done with it.

"I seem to have that effect." She rested her head on my shoulder as the bus began to move. The interior lights dimmed until only a soft glow from the floor lights illuminated us.

I kissed her hair. "He's not going to stop being a problem."

"I don't want to talk about him. I want to talk about us."

I threw my arm over her shoulder as we settled in for the ride. "What about us?"

A movie started playing on the back of each seat, but I focused on Cordy. Her polo was unbuttoned, and I could see the swell of her breast. My cock went from fight mode to fuck mode in the time it took me to shift closer to her.

"Are we…" She nibbled her lip.

I grabbed her chin and turned her to face me. "What?"

"Are we like, together?" She stumbled over her next words, as if she couldn't get them out fast enough. "I know it's too early to DTR—"

"DTR?" I grinned.

"Define the relationship." She furrowed her brow.

"Right. Well, I define it as you're mine and I'm yours. How's that?"

Her gaze brightened. My phone buzzed again, but I ignored it.

"Someone's calling you." She glanced to my pants.

"It's my mother."

"Oh."

I'd told Cordy about the difficulties I had with my mom, but I didn't go into the details of how much acrimony our relationship would stir up. Mom had no doubt seen the press conference. She would know. Mom always knew. She was waiting for me to pick up the phone so she could load me down with Carlotta's tears, my family's legacy, and the bright future she thought I was throwing away. Future Trent could deal with it later.

I leaned close to Cordy's ear. "Put your jacket on your lap."

She turned to me, a wary look on her heart-shaped face. "Why?"

"It's cold."

"Not really."

"You're trembling."

She arched a brow. "Not because I'm cold."

"Then why?"

"Because you—" She seemed to rethink her answer and, instead of responding, pulled her jacket into her lap as I'd requested.

"Good. My hands are cold." I slid my palm along her thigh beneath the jacket.

She jumped and looked at me with a scandalized expression. "Trent!" She hissed through clenched teeth.

"What?" I pressed my fingers higher until I reached the top of her thighs, then I eased my hand between her legs.

"We can't do this here." She glanced around, but no

one could see any details in the dark, and if anyone was looking, all they'd see was us sitting together and Cordy's jacket in her lap.

I rubbed my index finger along the seam of her jeans over her clit. "We can."

She gripped my wrist, but I didn't stop. Her breathing grew faster as I stroked her. My cock demanded reciprocity, but it would have to wait. I wanted to pleasure her more than anything. When her lips parted, I knew I had her.

I pressed my lips to her ear. "Unbutton your jeans and unzip them."

She tilted her hips forward and did as I'd said.

"You'll have to be quiet." I ran my fingers along her quivering stomach and she let out a small sound.

"Shhh." I slid my hand into her panties and through her slick folds. "So wet."

She pressed her lips into a small line as I circled her clit in slow strokes. I nuzzled closer and licked along the shell of her ear. She let out a breath and then placed one hand over her mouth.

The bus hit the interstate, the sound of the engine a constant background hum. I stroked faster, my fingers playing her clit as she worked her hips against me in small movements. Delving lower, I pushed a finger inside her tight pussy, and she moaned into her hand. I added a second finger and curled them to find her spot. Her hips moved faster as I massaged the little ridge inside her.

I slid my fingers out and went back to her clit while I kissed her neck. My back was broad enough to block the view, and the bus had grown even darker once we'd gotten past the city lights. Squeezing her clit between my index and middle finger, I rubbed up and down. Her eyes rolled back, and she came, her body quaking. She caught her quiet moans in her hand as I sucked her neck and kept pleasuring her with my fingers.

When she relaxed into the seat, I pulled my hand

from her panties and licked her taste from my fingers. My cock was hard enough to fuck a hole through a sheet of plywood as I settled back into my chair. Cordy let her hand fall from her mouth and panted, her gaze fixed on me.

"You're bad. That was bad. You are bad." She kept whisper-babbling, and it was the cutest thing I'd ever seen.

I claimed her mouth with a kiss, sharing her own taste with her, then rested my forehead against hers. "Baby, I'm just getting started."

CHAPTER TWENTY-SEVEN
CORDY

ELLIE TRIED TO SNEAK in while I was asleep. She'd been absent from our room more and more frequently. Then again, so had I. Over the month since I started seeing Trent, I'd spent the night at his place at least half the time.

Landon hadn't returned my calls or my texts. When I'd gone to visit his dorm, no one came to the door. I even tried waiting outside his classes for him, but he wasn't much for attendance, so that was a bust. He'd ghosted on me.

I missed him and wished he'd at least talk to me. I still went to brunch at the caf every Sunday morning and waited for him to show up. He never did, and I sat alone and full to bursting with all sorts of things I wanted to talk with him about—how well my father was doing, how we hadn't lost a game since I'd become first-string, how Trent wasn't the bad guy we thought he was.

Asking Ellie about Landon was a lost cause, and I suspected she was sleeping at his place when she wasn't at the dorm. She'd remained tight-lipped during our few interactions since they'd caught Trent in bed with me.

That night, she eased into our room at about one in the morning. After creeping around in the bathroom, she climbed into her bed.

"Ellie."

"You're awake." I heard her turning over to face me.

"Yeah. Can we please talk?"

"About what?"

"Landon."

She sighed. "Look, I'm tired. I want to sleep."

"Please? I just want to know if he's okay." I wanted more, but I'd settle for that if I had to.

"He's fine. Just nursing a broken heart." Bitterness laced her words.

"I didn't break his heart."

"Could have fooled me." She huffed and flopped down on her back.

"Why are you mad at me?"

"I'm not mad at you." She yanked her blanket up. "I take that back. I'm mad, but it's not all at you."

I propped up on my elbow. "Why?"

"Landon. I thought I just had a stupid crush on him, but then when we started getting together…"

I knew the feeling. "There was more than you bargained for?"

"Yeah. I didn't expect it. It just sort of hit me. But I can't do anything about it because he won't shut up about you. And, no offense, but I'm so fucking tired of hearing how perfect you are. I mean, he clearly doesn't have to live with you. Otherwise, he'd know that you leave toothpaste gobs in the sink and haven't cleaned out your hairbrush in months."

"You got me on the toothpaste, but I do clean my hairbrush."

"Then you shed like a sasquatch."

"Accurate." I stared at her in the dark, trying to figure out a way forward with Landon for both of us.

"I don't understand it. He's known you for years,

never made a move, and now he just *has* to have you. It makes zero sense." She pummeled her mattress with her fist. "It sucks."

"If you could get him to talk to me—"

"No way. I'm not wading into this any further than I already am."

"Please, Ellie. It's the only way for me to fix it. If you want a chance with Landon, I have to talk to him first. We need to solve the problem between us. And more than that, I miss my best friend, okay? I need him." I sank down onto my pillow and fell silent as Ellie shook her head.

"I don't know how well that would go."

"I don't care. I have to talk to him. Trent isn't a bad guy. We thought he was, but we were wrong. Maybe if I can explain that, things will be better."

She let out an exasperated sigh. "You aren't listening to me. He doesn't care what sort of man Trent is. He won't be happy as long as Trent is in the picture. Landon isn't going to stop wanting you just because you say, 'Oh, hey, Trent's great and here is a detailed list of why.' Hearts don't work like that." Her voice thickened toward the end, as if tears threatened.

"Just tell him I need to talk to him, and ask him to honor our brunch on Sunday. After that, if he doesn't want to see me again, he doesn't have to. But I think I deserve at least a chance to talk to him. Ask him, please."

She rolled over, faced away from me, and sniffled. "I'll tell him. But I'm not making any promises."

"That's all I ask. Thank you." I wanted to hug her, but I learned long ago that Ellie wasn't the hugging sort. She was like a cat. If she wanted you to touch her, she'd let you know.

Instead, I pulled my phone out and texted Trent.

You asleep?

My phone blinked with a response in record time.

No. You're not here, so it's hard to fall asleep.

I smiled in the dark.

I just don't want to rush us into anything. You know I love spending the night.

I'll come get you.

My smile grew bigger.

No. Go to sleep. We need to rest. It's going to be cold at practice tomorrow.

I'll warm you up after.

Promise?

Always. I want you here.

I sighed.

Tomorrow night.

And every night after that.

I shook my head.

Go to sleep. I'll see you bright and early. Have my seat warmer on.

Of course. What am I? A barbarian?

I stifled my giggle.

Good night.

I love you. Sleep well.

My fingers hovered over the keys. I wanted to tell him I loved him, but I held back. When he would say it to me, I felt it. I wanted to return the words to him, but I ended up hugging him or kissing him instead. He would sigh, and I hated the thought of causing him pain.

Even so, I wasn't ready. My heart had healed from two years ago. But now that he was so entwined with me, taking up my thoughts and all my spare time... If things went bad again, my heart couldn't take it. Saying those three words would somehow leave me open to that sort of pain, and I shied away from it. It was probably foolish. Just because I didn't say it didn't erase the fact that I *felt* it. All the same, I set my phone back on my bedside table, and left his last text unanswered.

"This is my favorite Saturday of the season so far." Trent ran his fingers through my hair and smiled down at me.

I lay in his lap as we watched football on the big-screen TV in his living room. The Eagles were playing our in-state rivals, the Bears, and beating the crap out of them. It was the Bobcats' bye-week, so we didn't have a game. We were scheduled to play the Bears the following Saturday, then we had a creampuff team to close the season. After that, we were through. Unless we made it to the playoffs.

He flipped to another game, checking the score. "If the Tigers win this one, they'll be undefeated. They'll control their own destiny and get into the playoffs."

"We'll get there."

"I hope so." He flipped it back to the Eagles game.

The playoffs weren't a guarantee, but if the Eagles kept bulldozing through their season, they'd be ranked number one. The Tigers and the Rangers would vie for second and third place as long as they kept winning. And if we didn't suffer any more losses, we'd have a decent shot to be the fourth and final team with a playoff berth. Our schedule was grueling, and our in-conference games were consistently against top-ranked teams. We had a shot.

Trent played with my hair. "I've been thinking."

My eyes opened wider. That was never a good opener. "Yeah?"

"Why don't you just move in here?"

Holy shit. I sat up and scooted next to him. "That's kind of a huge thing."

"I know." He took my hand and laced our fingers together. "But it feels right. You being here makes me happier than I've ever been in my life."

"We've only been dating a little over a month." I shook my head. "What if you get tired of me? What if—"

He placed both hands on my cheeks and pulled me into a kiss that verged on angry. "I'll never get tired of you. You're a smart girl, Cordy. Don't say dumb things."

I smiled and nuzzled against his stubbly cheek. "It's just kind of sudden."

"Not for me." He pressed his forehead to mine. "I've been waiting for you."

I couldn't respond, because he stole my breath with a passionate kiss, his tongue teasing mine as his hands roamed down my tank top. He yanked the hem, and I lifted my arms so he could strip it off me. I pulled his t-shirt over his head and tossed it on the coffee table as he pressed my back into the couch.

"I need you here." He kissed my neck, his tongue leaving a trail of fire down to my breasts. "Please say you'll stay." His mouth around my nipple made me squirm, and when he bit down gently, I gasped.

"I don't know."

He bit harder and squeezed my other breast, sending a highway of heat to my pussy. "Say you'll stay." His voice grew more insistent as his tongue did wicked things to first one nipple, and then the next. He smiled against my breast. "I know what will make you say yes."

My stomach quivered as he kissed down it and ran his tongue along the waistband of my shorts. I definitely wasn't agreeing to anything until he used every persuasion tactic he had. He nibbled at my stomach.

"Trent—"

In a rough move, he yanked my shorts and panties down, leaving them dangling around one ankle as he spread my legs and placed an open-mouthed kiss on my pussy.

I bucked, and he splayed his fingers on the insides of my thighs, then teased me with his amazing tongue. He kept his gaze on mine as he licked and sucked, making me moan as my body became a furnace. Sliding his hands up my thighs, he stroked the creases of my legs, sending more tension pooling in my core.

He took no prisoners, focusing on my clit and driving me toward my orgasm. I raised my hips to him, fucking his face as he groaned into my wet skin, his eyes always on me. When I reached the edge, my breath coming in short bursts, he backed off.

I groaned and tried to yank his mouth back to me.

He grinned and licked his lips. "Say you'll move in with me." He lapped at my clit, then stopped. "Tell me yes." Another quick flick had me writhing.

"This is cheating!" I panted.

He ran the broadside of his tongue from my entrance to my clit. "So?"

"Please." He'd reduced me to begging.

"Just say yes, and I'll let you come." He stroked down my pussy and sank two fingers inside me, applying steady pressure as he hovered his sinful mouth over me. "Just say yes."

He circled my clit with the tip of his tongue.

"You are bad."

He grinned and kissed my pussy, his fingers working me in a slow rhythm. "I know."

His swirling tongue erased any rational thought from my mind. My body hovered at the edge, and I had to get there. I considered finishing myself, but he would never let me do that. And was moving in with him really so bad? The soft caress of his tongue told me it wasn't. The steady stroke of his fingers told me it was a good idea. Us living together, sharing everything.

He curled his fingers up and hit my spot.

"Oh my God. Yes. Yes, I'll move in."

"Good." He dove down, his tongue lashing my clit as my hips rocked and then froze. I came on a long moan as he pumped his fingers in and out. He kept licking, pushing me further as my orgasm rolled until the last spasm ebbed, and I lay flat on the couch, panting. Kissing up my body, he seized a nipple, sending a jolt of pleasure to my over-sensitive pussy.

His hard cock rested against my leg, and I closed my eyes as he kneaded and sucked my breasts. The urge to taste him overcame all other concerns, and I gripped him through his shorts.

He jerked in my hand and threw his head back. I pushed him off me, one hand on his cock and one on his chest. He sat, and I wedged myself between his legs, my knees on the fluffy rug. Keeping my eyes on his, I pulled down the waistband of his shorts, and his cock sprang free. He lifted his hips, and I took his shorts all the way to the floor, then pulled his cock toward me.

"Fuck." He gritted his teeth as I grazed his wet tip with my breath.

A hard lick gave me the taste of salt and him, and he ran his hands in my hair. I licked again, then gripped his shaft and licked the length of him. His muscles drew tight, and he stared down at me with an intensity that verged on primal. I kissed the head of his cock and then slid it into my mouth.

His grip tightened in my hair, and his hips surged forward. I gagged when his head touched the back of my throat. He backed off, but didn't relax his grip. I was still new at giving head, but I'd learned a lot during my first few times. One move in particular always seemed to draw Trent tight as a wire. I glanced at him, then tilted my chin up and bobbed my mouth on his thick length, pressing the tip against the roof of my mouth in a steady rhythm.

He thrust his hips, the head of his cock rubbing deeper, but not deep enough to make me gag. I used my hand on his shaft and worked him in tandem with my mouth. My fingers couldn't quite reach my thumb when I slid to the base of his shaft, so I squeezed. He groaned and began pulling me forward, using my hair as a handhold to direct me. Playing my tongue along the base of his cock, I moaned as he kept his eyes on me, watching every move I made to please him.

His muscles were rigid, and a fine sheen of sweat broke out on his chest as I worked him. I slid him out and sucked on his head, darting my tongue to the slit at the end. He pulled me back onto him, filling my mouth with his cock as I licked and sucked any way I could. He grunted and shoved his hips up farther and faster, fucking my mouth. He was close, his cock hardening even more as I stroked him.

A knock at the door had me trying to pull back. He gripped my hair harder. A second set of knocks didn't stop him. He surged upward, then pulled out, bent me back by my hair and came all over my tits. Each splash had me moaning and wishing he'd come in my mouth.

Another knock came at the door, this time accompanied by a woman's voice. "Trent McKinley Carrington, if you don't open this door right this minute, I'll use my key!"

Only one sort of person used a middle name in a threat. A parent.

My heart sank, and embarrassment churned in my stomach.

He released me and snatched his shirt up to wipe me off. "I'm coming. Give me a minute, Mom."

CHAPTER TWENTY-EIGHT
TRENT

I HURRIED CORDY INTO my bedroom and closed the door behind her, then strode to greet my mother. She was already turning her key in the lock when I pulled the front door open.

Her eyes narrowed as she tried to look past me. "I know she's here."

"Okay." I shrugged. "What do you want?"

"That is no way to greet your mother!" She pushed past me and into the apartment.

I sighed as she stalked into the kitchen. Her eyes missed nothing—likely noting the double dishes in the sink and the few touches Cordy's presence added to the apartment.

She whirled, her silky scarf flying out a bit as she did so. "And where is she?"

Irritation welled inside me. "This isn't an inquisition. You can't come barging in here—"

"I own this building. I can come in whenever I like." She dropped her key into her handbag and gave me the same glare that would have instilled fear in the younger version of me.

The adult version, though, was livid. "It's easy enough to have the locks changed."

"She's here, isn't she?" She glanced to my closed bedroom door.

"Did you come to talk to her or me?"

She strode into the living room and sat in a side chair. "You, since you've been ignoring Carlotta and me for the past month. I got a particularly angry visit from her father this morning." She wrinkled her nose with distaste at my rug. "So here I am to fix your mistake yet again."

"Cordy's not a mistake." I'd wanted to spend some more time with her before the reality of my mother came crashing down on both of us. But it appeared my time was up.

"Put on a shirt." She trained her eyes on my bedroom door.

I knew what she was doing, trying to verify her suspicions that I wasn't alone. Not that I cared.

"Sure." I strode to the door and cracked it open.

Cordy, dressed in a t-shirt and jeans, paced the floor, but stopped and looked at me, her amber eyes filled with worry.

I entered and pulled on a t-shirt. "Come on. She wants to meet you." I took her hands and kissed her. "You're everything to me. Understand?"

She gave me a weak smile and nodded. "I trust you."

Her hand shook as I took it and pulled her behind me into the living room.

"Mom, this is Cordy. Cordy, this is my mother, Geneva."

Mom gave Cordy an appraising look. "You may call me Mrs. Carrington."

I prickled, but tried to keep my cool as Cordy and I sat down on the couch. Pulling her hand into my lap, I laced our fingers together. My mother's face wrinkled even more, disdain creating an unappealing web of crows' feet next to her eyes.

"It's nice to meet you." Cordy's voice was even, no fear in her tone. "Trent has told me so much about you."

"Oh, I'm sure he has." Mom smoothed her hands over her light gray pants. "And I'm sure you know all about his trust fund and the rest of his money?"

Cordy's grip tightened on mine. "From what he's told me, yes."

"Mom, say what you came to say. Stop playing games."

She leaned back, her eyes never leaving Cordy's face. "I'd rather discuss family business without an audience."

"She's staying. You may as well spit it out." I hadn't come this far with Cordy to turn my back on her. Either my mother would accept both of us or neither.

Mom huffed. "Trent, you are already treading on thin ice. I suggest you don't push me any farther than—"

"Mom, I'm never going to marry Carlotta." My voice was devoid of the usual anger I carried over this subject. Instead, it was matter of fact. "I don't want to see her, much less take her on a date. I choose Cordy. I should have chosen her two years ago, but you got your way then. You aren't getting it now."

"I don't think you understand your situation." She propped her elbow on the arm of the chair and rested her chin on her fist. "If you decide to take up with this coal town girl, this apartment?" She looked around with a dramatic sweep of her head. "Gone. Your trust fund? Gone. Your connections from the Carrington family name? Gone."

Cordy shifted, discomfort in every move. "I don't think I should stay—"

"Yes, you should." I stood and pulled her up with me. "I want you to hear this."

Staring down at my mother, I realized how much she'd changed in just a few short years. Her hair was whiter and her body thinner. Despite her age, she still had the same iron in her spine. She never bent for anyone, and

I didn't expect her to change for me. Problem was, I was my mother's son. The same iron running through her was also part of my makeup. I hadn't realized it until my father died, but I was just as strong as she was. "This is it, Mom. Either you accept us and make an effort to get to know Cordy, or you and I are done."

Mom stood, too, hell in her dark eyes. "I don't need to get to know her, Trent. I already do! How many women do you think chased after your father? Plenty, I can tell you. And they weren't after him. They were after his name, his money." She pointed a bony finger at Cordy. "This girl is no different. She comes from nothing. You're a golden ticket to her. Your name, your future, your chance at the NFL, all the money—don't be stupid." Her voice rose with each venomous word. "A climber, an opportunist, that's all she is. Why can't you see that?"

"It's time for you to go." I walked to the front door, Cordy at my side.

"Trent, I'm warning you. If you do this, there is no going back. I won't stand for this kind of disobedience. If your father was alive—"

"Don't you dare bring him into this!" I snapped. "He actually cared about what I wanted. The only reason he went along with you two years ago was because the cancer had made him too sick to fight. You took advantage of that." I hurled the most hurtful words I could find. "He was the only thing that ever made you bearable. I don't know how he stood you for as long as he did. He was warm and vibrant, but even he couldn't survive you."

"Trent." Cordy squeezed my arm and shook her head. "Don't."

It was too late. I'd already said what I wanted.

Mom gave me a look so wounded—her dark eyes open wide, showing me both her shock and grief—that regret washed over me.

But the damage was done. I thought if I finally stood up to her and got back at her for making me choose

Carlotta two years ago, I'd feel lighter, as if I'd put the past to rights. Instead, the weight of what I'd said crushed me. I'd gone too far.

"Mom, look—"

"No." She tilted her chin up, though I'd seen the rare sparkle of tears in her eyes. "You've said quite enough. You can keep the apartment until you graduate. Other than that, we're finished."

She snatched her bag and left, slamming the door behind her.

CHAPTER TWENTY-NINE
CORDY

MY STOMACH TWISTED INTO knots as I stared at my brunch. Last night had been a mess, and given that Landon was nowhere to be seen in the caf, this morning didn't look to be much better. I put my elbows on the table and cradled my head in my hands.

Trent had been quiet after the scene with his mother. I could tell he was hurting, but he kept trying to put on a brave front about it. We sat and watched football for the rest of the day, but his gaze kept wandering. He was lost in his thoughts, and I couldn't do anything to bring him back.

His mother had been just as unpleasant as I'd expected. What I hadn't expected was Trent's reaction. She'd snubbed me, sure. But Trent took his response a lot further. Though his mom and I weren't on a good footing, I pitied her. The sorrow in her eyes at his words was almost palpable. Something was broken between them, and I hoped there was some way it could be repaired.

I scrubbed my temples with my palms, fatigue washing over me. Trent had tossed and turned most of the night, keeping me awake. The familiar sounds of the caf were some comfort, at least. Friendly voices, laughter, and chatter wafted to me from the cliques scattered around the dining area.

The loneliness at my table made me realize I should have tried harder to get to Landon. A month without him felt like a piece of me was missing.

I sighed and looked up, hoping to find him sitting across from me with his signature smirk. He wasn't there, and my food had grown cold as I waited. Either Ellie hadn't asked him to meet me, or he refused to show. I pulled my phone out and texted him—another in a long list of unanswered missives.

Landon, please come and meet me. I miss you.

My phone remained silent as I stared at it, willing Landon to reply. I picked at my waffle for a few more minutes, then downed my orange juice. My phone beeped. I grabbed it so fast I fumbled it.

Are you a family member?

I gawked at the phone, beyond confused. Had Landon changed his number and not told me? I texted back.

What? This is Cordy Baxter.

A few moments after I hit "send," my phone rang. Landon was calling.

"Hello?"

"Ms. Baxter?" A man's voice, and definitely not Landon's.

Fear trickled down my spine like ice water. "Yes, who is this? Why do you have Landon's phone?"

"This is Detective Monroe from Billingsley PD. Are you friends with Landon Garnet?"

Panic rose inside me like floodwaters. "Why do you have his phone? Is he okay? What's going on?"

"He's okay. A runner found him near his dorm. He'd been beaten pretty badly. He's still out, under sedation until he recovers a bit. I'm here with him at Mother of Mercy."

All the blood drained from my face. "Oh my God.

What happened?" I rose and snatched my bag before darting out of the caf.

"We don't know. Someone jumped him, it seems. Does he have any enemies you know of?"

I ran across the quad, heading for Hope Hall and my car. "I can't think of anyone, no. He's a nice guy. Everyone likes him."

"His parents said the same. They're getting on a plane and heading down right now. Do you know of anyone else I could ask?"

"Ellie maybe. She's my roommate. They've been dating, I think." My lungs hurt and my eyes watered, but I ran as fast as I could, not caring that I was panting into the phone.

"I'll call her next. I was going through his contacts when you texted."

"What room is he in?"

"Three twenty-three."

"I'll be there in ten minutes." I hung up, topped the hill, and started the downward stride to my car. Then I hit Trent's speed dial. I explained everything to him as I made it to my car.

"Come to my apartment. We'll go together."

"I have to get to him." I couldn't think for the icy grip of fear on my heart.

"Cordy, with the way you sound, you might get into a wreck driving there. I'll come get you."

"No time." I cranked the engine.

"Then come here first. It's on the way."

"I—"

"I'll be downstairs waiting. Be careful."

"Okay." I gunned it down University and made it to Trent's place in under five minutes.

He was waiting outside as promised. I got out and ran around to the passenger side as he slid into the driver's seat. He drove even faster than I did, but I wasn't afraid.

Wiping a tear from my cheek, he asked, "They have

any suspects?"

"No. When he wakes up—" I choked on a sob.

"Baby." He grabbed my hand and squeezed. "He's going to be fine."

I took a deep calming breath as Trent blew through a red light when there was no cross traffic. "He'll wake up, and then he can tell us who."

My phone rang, and I jumped. It was Ellie.

"Have you heard?" Her voice had the same edge of panic as mine.

"I'm on the way there now."

"Me too. I'm just leaving campus."

"Shit." I could've picked her up at Hope Hall, but I wasn't thinking straight.

"What?"

"Nothing. Do you know who it was?"

"No idea. He had beef with his last roommate, I think, but he's gone."

"Yeah, he's in California now." I shook my head and tried to focus on suspects. "Maybe a boyfriend of one of his girls?"

"He's only been seeing me the last few weeks." She sniffled.

"Maybe one of them found out about a past hookup or something?"

"Cordy, I have to concentrate. My eyes keep watering, and driving is hard."

"Okay. Be safe. I'll see you there." We hung up, and I chewed my lip as Trent raced into the hospital parking lot.

I jumped out and hurried through the front door. He led me to the elevator, and I felt like I was back in West Virginia, waiting on bad news about my father. This time it was Landon. My legs felt weak, and I leaned on Trent. He wrapped a strong arm around me and held me as we rode the elevator to Landon's floor.

My steps quickened as we approached his room. My breath caught in my throat, and I would have fallen if

Trent hadn't pulled me to him. Landon's face was covered in purple and dark gray bruises. Both eyes were swollen shut. Gauze was wrapped around his chest, black and blue skin peeking out from beneath the white fabric.

A man stood at the foot of the bed, his hair salt and pepper and his demeanor no-nonsense.

"Ms. Baxter?"

"Y-yes." I walked to Landon and took his limp hand.

"I'm Detective Monroe. We spoke on the phone. And this is?" He must have been speaking to Trent. All I could see was Landon's battered face.

"Trent Carrington. I'm Cordy's boyfriend."

"Quarterback, right?"

"Yes, sir."

"Mind if I take a look at your hands?"

"Sure, I guess." Trent didn't sound so sure.

I heard the shuffle of feet as I stroked Landon's sandy hair off his forehead. His breathing was even and steady. I cried silent tears and clasped his hand between mine.

Trent held his hands out for the detective. "What are you looking for?"

"These look fine." Detective Monroe cleared his throat. "Whoever did this to Landon will have some signs on them. Busted knuckles, for starters. Yours are clean."

"Wait, you thought I—"

"I've heard you and Landon had a little dustup over Ms. Baxter. I had to check. I'm sure you understand."

"I guess." Trent stood behind me, his hand on my shoulder.

"It's fine." I didn't look at them. "Trent would never do something like that." But I knew someone who would. Nausea washed over me. "You need to talk to Ethan Granger. He and Landon got into a scuffle at the field a few weeks ago."

"Over what?"

"Me." I couldn't look away from his battered face.

Guilt covered me like a fine layer of soot. If Ethan had done this, I had no doubt it was to get at me somehow.

"I'll check in with him. Thanks."

"No other suspects?" Trent asked.

"I was hoping Landon would wake up and give me a name. Problem is, he doesn't have any defensive wounds. His knuckles are fine. I suspect he was jumped from behind and didn't have a chance to fight off his attacker. They took his wallet. Left his phone. We'll know more as the day goes along. I've sent some uniforms over to his dorm to ask if anyone saw or heard anything." His phone chirped. "Excuse me for a moment." He stepped out, and we were left with Landon.

"He's going to be all right." Trent rubbed my upper arms. "He's a tough guy."

"You don't know him."

"I know enough." He kissed the crown of my head.

We sat in silence for a while, the sound of Landon's breathing and random words from Detective Monroe's conversation in the hall, the only sounds.

"What's he saying?" I tried to cock my ear to listen.

"Not sure. I think it's on another case."

"Oh." I stroked Landon's hand. "Hey, Landon. Can you hear me?" I kept my words soft, though I was desperate for him to wake. An irrational fear that he wouldn't settled in my stomach. "Landon?"

He stirred, his eyelashes fluttering until his eyes opened into swollen slits, then closed again. He tried to shift in the bed. A groan rasped from his throat, and he opened his eyes as far as he could again.

"Fuhyoulookat?" His words slurred from his busted lips.

Relief washed over me. "Landon, you're in the hospital. Someone hurt you. Do you remember?" I leaned closer, trying to find the color of his eyes beneath the dark, swollen skin.

"Water."

"I'm on it." Trent hustled from the room.

Landon closed his eyes and gave my fingers a weak squeeze.

"I'm so sorry." I kissed the back of his hand. "But there's a detective here. He's going to arrest whoever did this to you."

Trent returned with a pitcher and a small white Styrofoam cup. "Here." He poured a cup and slid a straw into it before handing it to me.

I put the straw to Landon's lips. He managed to get a few good draws before coughing. Water dribbled to his chin. I wiped it with my sleeve and gave him more until he signaled he was finished. Trent took the cup, and I scooted closer to my friend.

He winced as he turned toward me.

"Who?" I burned with the need for retribution against whoever had done this to him.

"I didn't see him." His voice was barely a whisper. "Tackled me from behind, then everything went black. Woke up here."

"Any clue who would do it? You piss anyone off lately?"

He tried to smirk, but his swollen lips wouldn't cooperate. "Always."

"Anyone bad enough to want to hurt you?"

"I don't know." His eyes closed. "I'm tired."

"It's the drugs." I squeezed his fingers.

Loud footsteps in the hallway had us both turning toward the door. Ellie burst in and rushed to Landon's bedside.

She covered her mouth with her hand. "Oh my God."

Trent backed up so she had room to sit with Landon. "The detective said he's going to be okay."

Ellie sank down on the other side of the bed and carefully took Landon's left hand. The one with the IV in it. She leaned up and kissed his mottled forehead. The movement was almost too intimate, and I felt as if I was intruding.

"Landon." Ellie's voice was soft.

He turned toward her, his face wrenching into a pained mask as he did so. She ghosted her lips across his and settled back at his side as he fell into a peaceful sleep.

Ellie wiped her eyes. "Do they know who did it?"

"No. Landon woke up for a few minutes and talked, but he didn't see who hit him. He just remembers being tackled and then waking up here."

"Why?" The question caught in her throat.

"They don't know."

She ran her hand down his chest and inspected the bruises on both sets of ribs. "Jesus Christ. They could have killed him."

"He's going to be okay." I said it mechanically, because I didn't feel it. Looking at him in the bed, so weak and helpless, made worry creep into my veins and rage at whoever had hurt him bubble in my mind.

Trent gently tugged me to my feet. "Let's give them a minute."

I resisted his attempt to pull me from the room. I couldn't leave Landon like this.

Ellie didn't look up. "I've got him. I'll call when he wakes up again."

I stared at him, willing him to recover. Ellie ran her fingertips across his forehead, an intimate touch that reassured me. He was in good hands.

"I'll stay with him." Her voice was soft.

"Come on." Trent steadied me with a strong arm and walked me from the room.

In the hallway, Detective Monroe leaned against the wall and texted furiously.

"Ethan?" I hugged myself.

He paused and shook his head. "I spoke to him briefly. He has an alibi for last night. His roommate vouched for him. But I've got a uniform checking into it all the same. I'll be in touch if I hear anything."

"Thanks, Detective." Trent led me away and out of the hospital.

I was in a daze as I got into the car. If it wasn't Ethan, then I was out of ideas. Did the theft of Landon's wallet mean it was just a random act of violence? If so, why had the thief beaten him so badly? I had no answers, just a sick feeling in the pit of my stomach.

I hadn't realized we'd parked in front of Trent's apartment until he opened his door. Then he walked around and opened mine. I climbed out.

"Come upstairs and decompress."

"I'm okay."

"You're shivering." He took my hand and led me to the elevator. "And this plus dealing with my mother would put anyone on edge."

I snuggled into his side, breathing in his familiar scent as we rode up to his floor. He scooped me up into his arms.

"I can walk." Even as I said it, I threw my arms around his neck.

"I know. I want you to depend on me. Tell me what you're feeling, what you're thinking. I want to be here for you."

"How do you always say things that speak to my heart? 'Hear my soul speak. Of the very instant that I saw you, did my heart fly at your service'."

He laughed and swung open his front door. "Are all lit majors romantics at heart? And what was that?"

"Yes, and Shakespeare. *The Tempest*."

He kicked the door shut behind him and sat on the couch, cradling me in his lap. "I promise it'll be okay." Hugging me close, he kissed my cheeks, my forehead, the tip of my nose—each caress gentle.

"I hope so." I relaxed even more into him, letting his strength surround me. "You didn't sleep last night."

"Yeah. I had too much going on in my head, I guess."

CELIA AARON

"I'm sorry." I rested my head in the crook of his neck.

"Don't be."

"She'll forgive you. Just give her some time."

He rested his chin on me. "Now who's the one who just knows the right thing to say?"

"Thank you."

"For what?"

"For picking me this time."

"Every time from now on. It's only you and me." He hugged me so tight I squeaked. "And now that I've got you, I'll never let you go."

CHAPTER THIRTY
CORDY

I LAY MY CELL phone on the bench. Detective Monroe had called during practice. It was the Friday before our game against the Bears, and I'd been nailing every short kick. Hawthorne was also crazy accurate, and we seemed to feed off each other, trying to be the best from our respective distances.

I ran back onto the field, my heart heavy. No one had come forward with any information, and without any suspects, the case had gone cold. Landon had been released from the hospital, but he was too busted up to navigate the stairs in his dorm. Trent had offered to let him stay at his apartment. Landon had, of course, vehemently declined. After more than a little convincing from me, and the promise of endless blowies from Ellie, he grudgingly agreed.

"Let's try the fake." Coach Carver blew his whistle and motioned for the kicking team to line up at the ten.

I trotted out and took position next to Trent. "Monroe called. No leads."

"Damn. Sorry." He shook his head.

"He's going to stay on it, though."

"He'll find something. He has to." He glanced to my cheeks. "You're getting wind-chapped."

"I'm fine." The weather had turned even colder since November had arrived.

"I should take better care of you. You definitely need my attention."

His words were benign, but the look in his eyes was anything but.

"Trent." I glanced around at our teammates and lowered my voice. "Ixnay on the sex talk."

"Are you going to hike the ball or are we taking a break? Get set, ladies!" Coach Carver blew his whistle, but the sound died toward the end as he looked at me and his eyes widened. "I didn't mean that as an insult. I-I mean, I wasn't saying women are less than…" He swallowed hard, then pointed at me. "Just run the damn ball."

I grinned. "Yes, sir."

Trent knelt and I took my steps back, going through the exact same setup as if I were truly going to kick. I motioned for the hike and immediately went in motion toward the left hash. Trent caught the ball, then tossed it over his head to a predetermined spot. I was there, just as planned, caught the ball and ran toward the end zone. I would have made it, too, except Ethan crashed into me out of nowhere.

I landed on my back, the wind gone from my lungs as I struggled to take in a breath. Two suns shone above me, and my ears rang. Even with the high-pitched tune, I could hear shouting and the thud of feet.

Hawthorne appeared. "Jesus, are you okay?"

I blinked and finally got my breath back. "I-I think so."

He glanced up, then covered me with his body as the thumps of heavy feet grew louder.

I turned to look, but only saw a mass of legs. "What the?"

"Ethan and Trent are going at each other."

The thuds stopped, but the yelling didn't.

He raised off me. "Sorry. I didn't want them to step on you."

I smiled. "That's sweet."

"Can you get up?"

"I think so." I took his hand and sat, looking around for Trent. Three linemen held him back, and another set of players held a smirking Ethan while Coach Carver yelled bloody murder at both of them.

"You know you aren't allowed to hit like that in practice. And on her? Have you lost your fucking mind?"

"She needs to learn—"

"I'm doing the talking!" Coach bellowed. "And you"—he pointed at Trent—"you can't get in a fight on the field. I don't care who you're dating! Is that understood?"

"Yes, Coach."

"Let them go." Coach shook his head in disgust.

Trent shrugged off the guys and jogged to me. "Are you all right?"

"I think so."

Coach stabbed a finger in Ethan's face. "Get your sorry ass over there and help her up."

I shook my head, though it made it ache. "I can get up."

Ethan walked up and held out his beefy mitt. The tape across his fingers had come undone during the struggle, and I noticed a series of scratches and marks along his knuckles.

"Walk the fuck away, or I'll lay you out." Trent bit out the words, each one soaked with loathing.

"Wait." I stared up at Ethan, the grin on his face turning my stomach. "It *was* you."

"It was me that put you on your back where you belong? Yeah."

"You hurt Landon. It was you." Rage warmed my blood, and I scrambled to my feet. "It was you!" I flew at him, gouging my nails into his neck before Trent ripped me off him.

"Get your bitch under control." He swiped at the scratches and scowled. But I saw the hint of fear in his eyes. I was right.

"Trent, his hands. His knuckles are bruised." I pointed as Ethan backed away, discomfort twisting his ugly face.

Trent practically vibrated with anger. "Let me see your hands."

"Fuck off." Ethan turned his back.

Trent took a step to follow.

"No. Let him go. It's not worth you getting hurt. I'll text Monroe right this minute."

"What's going on?" Hawthorne stayed close.

"Ethan's a fucking asshole. That's what." I gripped his arm and squeezed. "Thanks."

"Welcome. If he pulls that again, I'll gang up with Trent, and we'll see if we can't drop the big guy."

"I'm down." Trent put his hands on my cheeks. "You sure you're okay?"

"Yes."

Coach Carver yelled for Hawthorne to practice his fake. I darted to the sideline and texted Monroe my suspicions. He responded almost immediately that he was on his way to question Ethan in person. A half hour later, Monroe arrived and escorted the wildebeest into the locker room.

Trent shot me a look from the field. I didn't text Landon about it. Getting his hopes up wouldn't help him recover. I couldn't be sure it was Ethan, but the bruises on his hands were pretty damning.

A short while later, Coach Carver dismissed Hawthorne and me to class. I waved at Trent and trotted to the women's locker room, my mind swirling with whatever Ethan might be telling Monroe.

I stripped and showered, the warm water reviving me

from the chill of outside. My back was starting to get sore from where I'd landed on it. Otherwise, I was in good shape. I wrapped a towel around my midsection, then walked back to the locker area.

Then the lights went out.

There were no windows, and I was the only one in the locker room.

"Shit." I couldn't see my hand in front of my face, literally. I tried it.

Reaching out, I felt along the row of lockers and eased toward the door that led to the stadium's inner hallway. My memory served me well, and I skirted the sinks, vanities, and lockers until I was close to the door.

"Princess." It was a whisper that sent a shudder through me.

I began to back up, but he must have known where I was. His palm crushed down on my mouth, and he pressed me into the bank of lockers. He was huge. I tried to scream and push him, but he slammed me against the metal, jarring me into silence.

"Telling the cops about me?" He pressed against my mouth until I thought my lips might split open.

I slapped him, the blow glancing off his forehead as I struggled to escape. He gripped my wrist and squeezed until pain ripped through my arm. I whimpered and gasped against his palm.

"Shh." His voice cut through the blackness. "Don't fight so much. And don't worry about the cop you sicced on me. I didn't tell him shit. Said he could talk to my lawyer. I'm not going anywhere."

I tried to shove him off, but it was like pushing against a brick wall.

"Play along, princess. You owe me this for sending that detective to ask me questions. And if you don't cooperate, I can hurt your little pal again whenever I want. He didn't even put up a fight. He was out cold after the first hit."

Hot tears burned in my eyes as he pressed against me, and I couldn't breathe.

Then I was blinded. Someone had flipped on the lights. Ethan turned. I filled my lungs and screamed as Trent yanked him backwards and slammed him into the tile floor.

Hawthorne dashed to me. "Did he hurt you?"

I couldn't respond.

Trent had settled on Ethan's chest and was throwing punch after punch. Ethan tried to defend himself, but Trent's fury seemed to only grow stronger each time he connected with a sickening thud. Hawthorne moved in front of me and pulled me to his chest so I couldn't see it anymore.

"Did he hurt you?" He hugged me as I shook.

The door creaked open and yells bounced off the walls of the room. Coaches and players swarmed around me, but I buried my face in Hawthorne's chest and wished it was all just a bad dream.

"Get off me!" Trent's voice shook with raw anger. One more sickening thud, and then it was over.

"Cordy." Trent's voice at my side. He stroked a hand down my hair, and Hawthorne eased me into Trent's arms.

I couldn't think, couldn't process what had just happened, or what would have happened if Trent and Hawthorne hadn't shown up.

"Can someone tell me what in the hell is going on in here?" Coach Sterling's roar quieted all other voices.

"Trent and I heard some weird noises when we were walking past after practice. We opened the door, but the locker room was dark. We almost left, but then we heard Ethan threatening Cordy. Then we flipped on the light. He had her pinned against these lockers, his hand over her mouth."

The room shifted, all the anger fading and recognition of what almost happened hitting everyone at the same time.

"Do you all need me in here?" Detective Monroe's familiar voice rang out.

I peeked around Trent, though his arms tightened as if he were afraid I'd run. "Ethan admitted to me he hurt Landon, then h-he tried to…" I couldn't finish my sentence.

Detective Monroe knelt next to Ethan who had both hands pressed to his bloody nose and mouth. Unlatching a pair of handcuffs from his belt loop, he clicked them open. "Ethan Granger, you're under arrest. You have the right to remain silent." His words faded away as Trent squeezed me close.

"Are you hurt?"

"No. He didn't get a chance to do much." I rubbed the back of my head where it had been pressed against the lockers.

Trent scooped me up and carried me toward the back of the locker room. He sat on one of the benches and held me as Coach Sterling approached.

"Cordy?" He swiped his ball cap off his head and sat on the bench opposite us. "I had no idea. No idea Ethan was capable of such a thing. If I had, he wouldn't have been on the team. I swear. Are you hurt?"

I stared at him, his weathered cheeks and sunburned brow. His eyes usually had a glint of calculation, but at that moment they were damp with concern.

"I'm not injured." I turned my eyes to Trent. "Thanks to you. And to Hawthorne." Though I was safe in Trent's arms, I was still shaken, the shock of Ethan's assault registering only on the lowest levels.

"He's off the team, and if I have anything to say about it—and I do—he'll be expelled before he bails out of jail. I promise you. I'll speak with the administration about getting you a guard. I need you to feel safe. You are part of this team, a very important part. I understand if you don't want to be part of it anymore after this." He scrubbed a hand down his face, looking far more tired than he ever did when he yelled at us on the sidelines. "But I want you here. You belong here, on the field."

I shook my head. "Ethan can't run me off this team. Not a chance. And I don't need a guard, but I would ask for something else."

"Anything. If it's in my power, it's yours."

"I'll feel safer if Trent can dress out with me. Here and when we're on the road."

"It's..." He scratched his jaw. "It'll raise eyebrows up the chain. I'm not sure if I can agree to that."

Trent pulled me closer. "All you have to agree to is that I will watch out for Cordy. I'll stand guard whenever she's dressing out."

Coach raised a gray eyebrow. "Will that be inside or outside the women's locker room?"

He shrugged. "As far as you're concerned, outside."

Coach chuckled. "Plausible deniability. Is that what we're doing here?"

"Pretty much." Trent's voice was backed with steel. He wasn't going to take no for an answer.

"Cordy, you sure you're okay with this?"

I wanted to say I could take care of myself, but Ethan's attack had proven me wrong. Having Trent around would go a long way toward making me feel safe. "Yes."

"It's unorthodox." Coach sighed and settled his ball cap back onto his head. "And you can bet your teammates are going to talk. But if that's what it takes to keep you, I'll approve it as long as you two are the only ones. I'm pretty sure if any other women are in the locker room, they'll make their objections known."

"Trent?" I looked up into his green eyes, one of the eyelids starting to swell. "Oh shit, did Ethan hit you?"

"I don't feel a thing. Don't worry about it. And yes, I'm all for it. I don't think Coach could keep me away from you after this, anyway. I don't want to let you out of my sight."

Overprotective? Yes. Comforting all the same? Hell yes.

CHAPTER THIRTY-ONE
TRENT

"I KIND OF FEEL like I should join the team. I can kick almost as well as you." Landon looped his arm around Ellie's shoulders and leaned over the wall to look down at Cordy and me on the field. His face was still yellow and a sickly green in patches, but he was healing more every day. He'd managed to sit through the entire game against the Bears, and I caught him cheering like a nut after every one of Cordy's field goals.

"I think you've lost your mind. That's what I think." She tucked her helmet under her arm.

"Congratulations." Ellie smiled at me. "Think we'll make the playoffs?"

"Looks like it. As long as we can defeat the Devils next week." I reached up and shook hands with Landon. It had become our greeting over the past week, a simple, oddly formal handshake. But it seemed to work, and if it made him hate me less, I was all for it.

"Let's just say, for the sake of obvious argument, that we win next week," Landon eyed the cheerleaders on the field behind us. "How do you see our playoff chances?"

A couple of students passed by, yelled, and reached

down for high fives from me. Landon rolled his eyes, and Cordy grinned.

I smacked her ass, and she squeaked. "Good game, kicker. And, to answer your question, our chances are looking good. I think we'll get in. If we advance depends on how one through three stack up in the rankings. Number one plays number four, and numbers two and three play each other."

"I want the Eagles." Cordy bounced on the balls of her feet.

She'd muffed the kick at the very start of the season against the Eagles, which resulted in that disastrous touchdown. But after we defeated everyone else on our schedule, she was jonesing for another piece of them. Problem was, now that our best defensive lineman was in lockup for assault, we would have to run a strong offense to have any chance of coming out with the win. I had a disciplined line to work with, but if the Eagles could score on our defense with ease, we were doomed.

"Hey, Trent." A fan, completely decked in Bobcat attire with his face striped in white and blue paint, stopped next to Landon. "You going into the draft, man?"

"That's a while away, so I'm not putting too much thought into it. We need to get through our season here first." In truth, I had put plenty of thought into it. I'd already submitted myself to the Draft Advisory Board. They would grade me and, if all went well, I'd get invited to the Combine prior to the draft, with the end goal of getting on a team—a team that would most likely be far away from Billingsley and Cordy.

A harsh camera light cast my shadow on the brick wall ahead of me.

"Paparazzi on your six." Landon pointed.

I turned and got a face full of lens and a microphone. "How has the loss of Ethan Granger affected team morale?" The reporter shouted her question as I grabbed Cordy's elbow and hustled her toward the tunnel.

"Save it for the presser." I started a jog as she peppered me with more questions.

"Any truth to the rumors you and Ms. Baxter are an item? Was Ethan kicked off the team because of Ms. Baxter?" She followed behind us until we made it to the safety of the tunnel and security stopped her.

We trudged down the slope to the inner corridor. At the bottom, Cordy headed to the right.

"Left." I grabbed her shoulder pads and turned her.

"Yeah." She faked a confident tone. "I was just testing you, making sure you know the layout of the Bears' stadium and stuff."

"Sure you were." I laughed and fist bumped a couple of passing players.

They smiled at Cordy, genuine warmth in their eyes. Something about Ethan's attack on her had galvanized the entire team. She was one of us, and our team had rallied around her on and off the field. No longer just the Mav, she was welcomed into the men's locker room during the Coach's halftime speech and treated like any other teammate. Despite all the acceptance, she still showered and dressed out in the women's locker room. With me.

I pushed the locker room door open for her, my pads pressed against hers as she walked ahead of me.

"Aren't you supposed to be stationed outside?" Cordy glanced over her shoulder.

"I feel that, in the interests of your safety, I should stay a little closer."

"My safety, huh?"

"Right. I'm here to protect you. Keep an eye on you. Especially right now, since you need a shower."

"You do." She smiled and loosened the tie at the end of her braid.

I wholeheartedly agreed. "I was thinking the same thing. Let's save water and shower together."

She walked to the benches and pulled her braid loose. "I don't think that would be proper. After all, we're teammates. We should keep things professional." Gripping the hem of her jersey, she lifted it over her head and tossed it to the bench.

"Have I ever told you how sexy you look in pads?" I let my gaze slide down her body, and my cock hardened almost instantly.

"You may have mentioned it."

I pulled off my shirt, then lifted my pads from my shoulders. After unlacing my pants and cleats, I stripped down to nothing. She watched every move, and when her eyes focused on my cock, I could almost feel her on it.

She licked her lips. *Jesus.*

"Get naked." I leaned back against the gray lockers and crossed my arms over my chest. I didn't want to crowd her, not after what had happened with Ethan.

She glanced to the door.

"It's just you and me. You're safe."

"With you? Always." She locked eyes with me and unlaced her shoulder pads, then lifted them off. When she peeled her sports bra over her head and her delicious tits popped free, I had to force myself to stay where I was. I needed my mouth on her, but I wanted her naked first.

"I love the way you react to me. It's like every time you see me, it's the very first time." She finger-combed her braid the rest of the way out and let her silky brown hair fall over her shoulder. I gritted my teeth and stood motionless, my eyes taking in every one of her curves as she slid her pants and pads down her legs. She stepped out of them, then sat and removed her cleats and socks.

"Panties, too." I wanted to see her little patch of dark curls, and hoped they were already wet for me. Just me.

"Give me a minute." She shot me a playful look through her lashes.

She stood and slowly stripped her panties off.

I gripped my shaft, as if that would somehow relieve the pressure already building inside me. "Do you have any idea how beautiful you are?"

She glanced up to the fluorescents. "In this lighting?"

"You'd be beautiful in the dark."

She laughed, but I meant every word.

I had to taste her. Covering the distance in a second, I took her in my arms. She melted against me as I held her up. Her soft skin rubbed against mine, her hard nipples begging to be sucked.

My tongue caressed hers, and she moaned when my fingers tangled in her hair. The scents of grass, dirt, and sweat mingled as we kissed. My fingers roamed her back, all the way down to her toned ass. Then I gripped her hard and ground my cock against her hot pussy. She was wet for me, just like I wanted.

She moaned into my mouth at the sweet friction. I slanted my mouth over hers, plundering her lips and setting us both alight.

She pulled back, taking a breath, her eyes half-lidded. "Press conference."

"They can wait." I walked her to the showers and hit the faucet. The water shot out cold.

She jerked against me, and I bit her shoulder as the shower began to warm. Her sweat tingled on my tongue, and I licked up to her neck.

Then I turned her so the water poured down her hair.

"Trent." She ran her nails down my back as I pushed her against the cool tiles.

"I'll make it quick." I leaned back to gauge her reaction. "It's okay if you don't get off, right?"

She crinkled her nose, and I laughed.

"Calm down. Kidding. Only kidding." I set her on her feet. "Here. Let me prove it to you." I dropped to a knee, the warm water spraying onto my back. Lifting one of her legs over my shoulder, I darted my tongue between her folds to find her delicate nub.

She curled her fingers in my hair as I stared up at her and let my tongue run wild on her pussy. Her trembling thighs sped me along. I wanted her to come all over my mouth. Sliding two fingers inside her, I finger-fucked her until her hips met me stroke for stroke, my mouth sealed around her clit. She squeezed my hair hard enough to hurt, then came on a strangled cry, her pussy pulling my fingers in tighter as I kept licking her.

When her orgasm was nothing but aftershocks, I stood and lifted her right leg. Pressing into her always felt like coming home. I slid into her tightness and shared her taste with a kiss. She wrapped both legs around me as I seated myself as deeply inside her as I could go.

The water pelted us, its wet slap onto the tiles weakly disguising the sounds of skin on skin as I fucked her against the wall. She moaned as I lifted her higher and wrapped my lips around her hard, wet nipple. I loved the feel of her nails on my skin, the taste of her in my mouth. She arched her back and spread wider. Each one of my thrusts hit her deep, and my balls ached to release inside her. I switched nipples and gripped her ass, using my arms to move her up and down on my shaft just how I wanted.

She gasped and pressed herself to me, rubbing her breasts against my chest as I pistoned inside her. I ran my fingers up her neck, her cheek, then pressed my thumb inside her mouth. She closed her eyes and sucked, treating it as if it were my cock.

"Fuck, that's going to make me come." I slipped my thumb out and pressed it to her clit, splaying my fingers along her hip.

Leaning back, I watched her pretty pussy take every inch of me in each deep stroke. Her upper back rested against the tiles, her eyes on me as I fucked her and swirled my thumb around her clit.

She ran her nails down my chest, the slight sting making each plunge even more enjoyable. Her breaths became labored, and she closed her eyes.

"Watch me. You're so beautiful when you come."

"Oh my God." She bit her lip and dug her heels into the backs of my thighs. "I-I'm there."

"Good." I let myself go, fucking her hard and fast as her hips seized and a low moan rushed from her lips.

My load shot up my shaft, every nerve ending in my body focused on Cordy as her pussy milked me. I gave her every drop, groaning and thrusting, losing myself completely in her. I leaned in, pinning her with my body as we both took deep breaths and tried to come back down.

"I love you." I kissed her before she could start debating with herself on whether she should say it back. I wanted her to say it; my heart was desperate for the words. But I wouldn't push her. I knew what I felt, and I hoped one day soon she would admit she felt the same.

CHAPTER THIRTY-TWO
CORDY

I STEPPED UP THE familiar front steps to my father's house, Trent at my elbow. We'd arrived just before noon, and it was Thanksgiving. A Billingsley Bobcats flag, faded but flown with pride, hung beneath the porch awning.

I'd talked to Dad on the phone only a few times while he was in rehab, and this was my first time seeing him since he got out. My nerves were in knots, and I tried to prepare myself for disappointment.

"It'll be fine." Trent's rich voice gave me a modicum of comfort.

I wasn't so sure. "What if he's drinking again?" The question had been rattling around in my brain for the entire trip here. I'd ignored the rolling hills, not even noticing when the ground became covered in snow. My worry grew with each mile closer to home. What if he'd relapsed?

"Have faith in him, okay?" Trent knocked on the faded front door, the once-white paint now a dingy gray.

"I'm trying."

"Chin up, kicker." He smacked my ass.

I rubbed the sting through my leggings and glared up

at him. He winked, and I didn't know if I wanted to murder him or jump his bones.

The door swung inward, and a man who looked a lot like my father but with brighter eyes, a clean-shaven face, and a bigger smile welcomed us in.

"Daddy?" I knew my eyes had become comically wide, but I couldn't believe the transformation.

"Come on in out of the cold." He shooed us in, and the smell of roasted turkey and something sweet filled the air. Mrs. Trapper bustled around the kitchen, a worn calico apron tied around her waist.

Dad shook hands with Trent. "Cordy told me what you did for me. I thank you, and I'll pay you back just as soon as the coal company comes through with my severance."

"Please don't." He ran a hand through my hair and rested his palm at the small of my back. "If it makes Cordy happy, then it's money well spent as far as I'm concerned."

"That's mighty kind of you, son." Dad clapped him on the arm. "I can at least offer you some good vittles. Mrs. Trapper is cooking up a storm, and we're in for some tasty eats."

My vision blurred as I stared at my dad. He looked like he did in old pictures I'd seen of him. Like the ones of him in the shotgun wedding ceremony with my mother. My grandfather—literally—had been holding a shotgun in the photo.

"Is something on my face?" He rubbed his smooth cheek, and I was certain he knew what a big change this was.

"You look so good." I hugged him and sniffled as tears tried to overtake me. The soft flannel of his shirt brought back so many warm memories that I squeezed him even harder.

He patted my back. "It's okay. Don't cry. I was afraid of this. Don't be upset."

I pulled back and stared into his clear, light brown

eyes. "You're back. You're really here."

"It hasn't been easy." He shook his head. "Sometimes I want a drink so bad it hurts, but then I kept thinking about this." He patted my cheek. "About making you proud of me. That's the only thing that kept me away from a bottle. You." He turned to Trent. "And now you. The both of you."

Trent smiled, genuine pleasure showing in his eyes. "Thanks for having me. I was afraid I'd miss turkey this year since I didn't really have any Thanksgiving invites. Mom decided to spend the holiday in the Bahamas."

Trent looked like a giant in the small two-bedroom, one-bath home. The ceilings were only seven feet high, so Trent was in grave danger of knocking his head on the light fixtures if he wasn't careful.

Dad scratched his temple. "Cordy mentioned your mom's a tough nut to crack."

"She is." Trent's smile faded. "Things are difficult at the moment."

"Going to get better." I may have said it a little too brightly.

Trent raised an eyebrow but nodded. "Right. They will. In any case, I can't wait to try Mrs. Trapper's cooking. Thanks again for the invite, Mr. Baxter."

"Oh, don't call me that. Nobody calls me that except the cops when I'm in the drunk tank."

Oh my God. I put my hands to my face, but the embarrassment didn't abate.

"Kick your shoes off and stay a while." Dad motioned at us, and we handed him our coats. The house didn't have a coat closet, so he just draped them over the back of his worn recliner.

"And just call me Clarence or Dad if you want. No formalities needed around these parts."

Trent nodded in thanks. "That's very kind of you."

My dad cleared his throat and glanced to the kitchen. "Well, that's enough nonsense. You two have a seat at the table. I think the food's almost ready."

We walked the few steps through the door into the kitchen and dining area. Mrs. Trapper had laid out a beautiful turkey, stuffing, and plates of vegetables.

She hugged me, pressing me to her with her wrists since her hands still had flour on them. "Welcome home. Sweet tea's already on the table. I'm just waiting on the pumpkin pie to come out of the oven." Trent got the same treatment, with an added kiss on the cheek.

We edged around the table, skirting the window that looked out onto the small side yard, and took our seats. Dad didn't sit at the head of the table. He never had, as far back as I could remember. He'd always sat across from me and asked about my day, what was going on in school, what my dreams were.

Today was no different.

"So, are we going to bring home the championship?" He sipped his tea and looked at Trent with hopeful eyes.

"Well, it's hard to say." Trent leaned back, the antique spindle chair creaking under his weight. "Unless the Gators have a particularly strong showing in their division championship, we'll likely be ranked at number four and have a playoff berth."

"Them Eagles are going to be number one. I can feel it." Dad scowled.

"Good. I want to play them." I grabbed the roll of paper towels and handed them out as Mrs. Trapper sat down next to my father. "Sooner rather than later."

"That's my girl." Dad tucked his paper towel into his shirt.

Mrs. Trapper laughed.

"Oh, you love it."

She shook her head, then jumped, her cheeks turning red. I suspected Dad had goosed her under the table, but I didn't want to go anywhere near that thought.

Dad said a brief, and only slightly profane, prayer, and we all dug in.

"So, Trent, tell me about your family." Mrs. Trapper heaped a second helping of potatoes onto his plate.

I marveled at his ability to put away food and turn it into muscle. Jealousy was far too mild a word.

"We're originally from New York State, but there's a family tradition of going to school at Billingsley. My dad loved it so much, he built a home only about an hour away from campus. That's where I spent my summers when I was growing up."

"I thought your accent was a little too clipped to be from the south." She poured a healthy serving of gravy on top of his potatoes.

"Right. Anyway, my father played for the Bobcats, so I was raised a Bobcat through and through."

"I can't tell you how proud I was when my Cordy told me she was going to college, and Billingsley at that." Dad beamed, and my heart melted even more. "I'm sure your dad feels the same."

I almost choked on my roll. "Dad, let's not talk about—"

"No, it's okay." Trent set his fork down. "My dad passed in July."

"Oh, I'm sorry." Dad bowed his head.

"It's fine. I had so many great years with him. He had a rare form of leukemia. And you're right. He was extremely proud when I chose Billingsley, and even prouder when I became the starting quarterback last year."

"He should be." Dad recovered. "Any talk about the NFL?"

"Some." Trent began to eat again. "Nothing for certain yet."

"I hear those scouts go to practices almost constantly. Is that right?"

"I've seen quite a few." I glanced at Trent. We hadn't really discussed what would happen after the spring. He'd graduate, of course, but what then? I supposed I couldn't make any demands on him, especially considering I was too chicken to tell him I loved him. Even so, the thought of him leaving spoiled my appetite.

"Well, I've seen you and Cordy play every game. They even let me hog the TV at the facility, so I got to watch every weekend. I don't know much about the draft, but the announcers seem to. They think you'll go in the first two rounds." Dad raised his glass and tipped it toward Trent. "Good Lord willing and the creek don't rise."

My unease at the thought of being separated from Trent grew. Mrs. Trapper seemed to notice, because she changed the subject to the upcoming winter festival.

After we each had a slice of her pumpkin pie, we settled into the living room and caught up some more. Dad was full of coal mine gossip, and Mrs. Trapper seemed content to just listen to his stories. They were a handsome couple, and I was happy that Dad had finally found someone to spend time with. That she was someone I trusted to take care of him and keep him on the straight and narrow? Even better.

The day eventually waned, and Trent and I said our goodbyes. Mrs. Trapper loaded us down with leftovers, and we hugged our way out the door.

"Keep it up, Dad." I kissed his wrinkled cheek. "I've never been more proud."

"Thanks, honey. I'll be watching for that playoff spot."

"I hope we get it."

"You will, and you'll show them Eagles a thing or two about heart." He kissed my hair and I stepped back, the frigid, smoke-scented air swirling around us as the sun set behind the hills.

"We'll be seeing you at Christmas, right?" Mrs. Trapper drew her white shawl closer around her shoulders as she stood in the doorway.

"Of course." Trent placed his hand on my waist. "My dad always loved Christmas, so I want to celebrate it big for him this year."

His certainty, the ease with which he spoke to my dad, the way he complimented Mrs. Trapper's cooking— everything about him made the words "I love you" dance along the tip of my tongue. But it remained trapped there instead of awkwardly blurted.

Dad smiled and hustled Mrs. Trapper back into the cozy house. "Looking forward to seeing you in a few weeks. Now get on in the car before you two catch your deaths of cold." He waved as we walked down the front steps. Trent opened my door for me, as always. We drove down the pothole-filled road that led out of our small hollow and back onto the main highway.

"Was that okay? Did you like the food? What about my dad? I'm sorry he asked about your dad. That must have been hard. I'm sorry the house is so small. But it's sort of—"

"Cordy, take a breath." He pulled my hand to his lips and kissed it. "It was perfect. I was with you. I wouldn't have cared where we spent the day, as long as we were together. And the house was perfectly fine. Your dad and Mrs. Trapper were great company."

"Thank you. I l—" I took a deep breath but I couldn't stop myself. My emotions were like a volcano inside me, the top blown off and everything rising to the surface. "Trent, I love you."

I screamed as the car swerved off the road and onto the gravel shoulder almost a hundred yards back from the ramp to the highway.

"What? Was there a deer?" I turned and looked out the back window.

"Cordy." Trent put his hands on my cheeks and pulled my face to his. His eyebrows were drawn together as if he were concentrating. "Can you repeat that?"

"Oh." I wrapped my fingers around his forearms as a smile took over my lips. "I said I love you."

He closed his eyes and smiled as if the sound was sweet. "Say it one more time. I just want to make sure."

I laughed, joy rushing through my veins. "I love you."

He kissed me with an exuberance that made my heart beat double time. I was so afraid to give him those words that when I finally did, his response was all-consuming. In that one kiss, he gave me all of him, but still managed to take my breath away.

He pulled away. "Get in the back seat."

I blinked. "Wait, what?"

"I want to seal the deal."

I laughed. "We aren't married. You don't have to consummate."

He kissed me again, more urgently this time. "With you, I do. I've waited for so long, wanting you this whole time. I need to feel you. Backseat. Now."

That tone—it was like his desire for me made him regress to the mean, as if he were a more primal version of himself. It turned me on to an alarming degree.

He jumped out of the car, and I tentatively opened my door. He ran around and pulled it all the way open, helped me out, and then eased me into the backseat. Walking back around to his side, he slid in next to me and tangled a hand in my hair.

"I'll never want anything the way I've wanted you." His kiss seared down to my soul, and his hands were rough in my hair and along my body.

He leaned me back, pressing his chest against my breasts, and sending tingles of pleasure shooting through me. Pulling my hair, he angled my head so he could deepen our kiss, and his tongue alone was erotic enough for me to press my thighs together to keep the ache at bay.

I slid my hand down to his pants and caressed his thick shaft through his pants. He groaned into my mouth. The more I stroked him, the more I wanted him inside me.

He seemed to read my mind and hitched my sweater up, yanking it over my head and tossing it to the floorboard. Pulling my bra cups down, he fastened his mouth around one of my nipples.

He licked until I was panting, and the windows fogged up. He leaned back and picked at the waistband of my leggings. "Are these pants or what? Doesn't matter. I want them off." He grabbed one of my boots and pulled it free while I did the other. In a few moments, I was bare from the waist down.

His hands went to his pants, but I pushed them away.

"Let me." I unbuckled his belt, undid the button, and unzipped the fly. He ran his fingers up my thigh and slid them through my slick folds. I bit my lip as he began to rub my clit in small circles. I shoved his pants and shorts down his hips, and his cock sprang free. I bent over and licked the underside of his shaft.

"I need you." He pulled me up and lifted me so I straddled him. Face to face. "I want you to get off on my cock." Reaching between us, he rubbed his cock head against me and positioned himself at my entrance.

I sat down on him slowly, impaling myself until I shook from the sheer pleasure. He cupped my breasts and pressed them together, sucking my nipples as I began to ride him. Headlights passed, but I didn't care. He was all I could think about, and how good he made me feel.

"That's it." He groaned as I leaned forward, pressing my breasts into his face. His hands went to my ass and squeezed as he rocked his hips up to meet me.

I bore down harder on him.

"Grind that pussy on me." He gripped my hips tighter and pressed me down.

"Trent." I pulled his head back and took his mouth as I rode up and down on his cock, my clit getting perfect friction against him with each of his thrusts.

He rubbed his tongue against mine at the same tempo, our bodies completely entwined with each other as he pushed me toward my orgasm.

My legs began to shake, but he only gripped me harder, forcing me to enjoy every little point of contact. He kissed to my neck, then ran his teeth along my shoulder. I pressed down on him, working the thick length in every pleasurable way imaginable. My breath caught in my throat as tension built in the pit of my stomach. I was a slave to my hips. They ground on his cock until I came, repeating his name on a low moan. I couldn't stop the rolling waves of pleasure, and he bit my shoulder as he thrust up hard. His cock kicked and filled me as I took his grunts and groans with a steady kiss.

When we were spent, I let my forehead rest against the seat back and took in gulps of air.

He ran his hands up and down my back, then pulled me close to him in a gentle embrace. "I'm yours. Always."

I pulled away and ran my palm down his face before grazing my lips against his. "I guess you sealed the deal."

He thrust inside me again, his cock still hard enough to send a wave of heat through me. "Maybe we should double seal it. Just to be sure." He turned and lay me on my back, still inside me.

"I think it's probably better safe than sorry." I giggled as he pressed down on top of me and stole my laughter with another kiss.

CHAPTER THIRTY-THREE
CORDY

"THAT'S WAY TOO MANY jalapenos." I frowned as Landon scooted a handful of diced peppers into the pot of cheese dip.

"Don't be a pussy." He stirred them in until the gelatinous orange cheese hid the danger within.

"When does the good stuff start?" Ellie had folded herself into a side chair in the living room and was texting furiously.

"They like to go through all the highlights from the year before they announce the four playoff teams. Be patient." Trent tossed a piece of popcorn in the air and caught it in his mouth.

Of the four of us, only Landon and I were proficient enough to be in charge of food for the playoff selection get-together I'd planned. He'd healed up nicely, no signs of Ethan's handiwork lingering on his handsome face.

Things were different, though. Our relationship had shifted. The change was almost imperceptible, but I could feel it. He didn't share as much with me as he had before. I couldn't tell if that was a result of his relationship with Ellie or mine with Trent. But he was here, and we talked every day just like we used to, so I was thankful.

A clatter sounded from the living room. I looked over as Trent tried to fish the remote off the floor, but only sent it skittering under Ellie's chair.

The announcers were laughing. I turned to the screen. There I was, in all my blue and white glory. My muffed kick from our early season game against the Eagles was playing in an untold number of households across the U.S. I'd memorized the play—the way the ball hit my own player and flew straight up, how the lineman ran past me and then dragged me all the way to the end zone.

"It's been called the Kick Six of the Century. And after that replay, I don't think I can add anything else." One of the announcers guffawed, and I rolled my eyes so hard it almost hurt.

Trent sent me a sheepish glance. "I tried to change it. Sorry."

"It's cool. I mean, it *did* happen." I attempted to ignore the peals of laughter from the two announcers and made a mental note to send Kirk Herbstreit a rude tweet. He was cute, but he could stand to be taken down a peg or ten.

I grabbed a bowl of salsa and a bag of chips and set them on the coffee table.

"Thanks." Trent patted the leather next to him. "Take a break for a minute."

"I have to finish the taco bar."

He pulled me down into his lap and nuzzled my neck. "There's a particular taco bar I'd like to finish."

"Gross." Ellie switched to texting with one hand while scooping salsa with the other.

"You need to work on your inside voice." I giggled as he ran his fingers over my stomach through my team t-shirt.

"Maybe I should just take you to the bedroom for a private chat."

I laughed louder when he tickled my ribs. "Stop!"

"No." He nipped at my ear.

"Hey, I'm trying to work over here," Landon grumbled from the kitchen.

I disentangled myself and stood. Trent's thick erection was on full display through his athletic shorts. I snagged a throw pillow and tossed it to him. He didn't take his eyes off me, the look in them making me forget what I was doing for a second.

"Taco bar." I forced myself to walk away from him, but the image of me riding him like a rented mule once Ellie and Landon left for the night was a small consolation.

"How many presents under that tree are for me?" Landon glanced to the overdone Christmas tree in front of the big windows that looked out onto the park.

Trent had told me how his father loved Christmas. The stories of his dad dressing up as Santa Claus and visiting children in the hospital, giving outrageous gifts, and spreading holiday cheer during the entire month of December touched me, especially because Trent was so fond of those memories. So, to keep his dad's spirit alive, I'd gone a little overboard. The tree, the mantle, and any available surface had some sort of Christmas decoration on it.

"I don't know. Are you on Santa's nice list or his naughty list?" I slid the taco shells into the oven.

He leaned against the counter, his worn Pantera t-shirt looking decidedly non-festive. "I would have to fall firmly in the naughty camp."

I set the timer and walked past him to the fridge. "Well, in that case, I don't know how many presents you can legitimately expect."

I tried to snag every ingredient for the tacos that my arms could hold, but it didn't quite work.

"Let me help." He took the salsa and lettuce from me.

"I didn't get any soft tortillas. I hope that's okay." Snagging the cheese, sour cream, and onions, I backed away and turned to the bar.

"You know my thoughts on crunchy versus soft tacos." Landon joined me.

"I do. 'Soft tacos are hard tacos' ugly cousins.'"

"Perfectly quoted and completely correct."

Trent stood and walked over. His dick situation seemed to be under control again. Thank God. That would have been awkward.

"They're building it up some more." He surveyed the bar. "But the announcement is imminent."

"Cool." I tried to tamp down my nerves, but I burned for the chance to face the Eagles again. The Kick Six replay only added fuel to the fire.

Trent's phone rang. He snagged it off the coffee table and froze.

"What is it?" I started dicing the tomato.

"Mom."

I stopped mid-chop. She hadn't contacted him since she'd stormed out of his apartment.

"I'll take it in here." He hurried to his bedroom and closed the door.

I forced myself to keep chopping, though I was desperately curious as to what his mom wanted.

It didn't take long for me to find out.

Trent's voice started low and then rose, contention in every note. "Mom. Mom. Listen. No. I'm not coming without Cordy."

His voice grew quiet again, but tension permeated the air.

Landon coughed. "So, who wants nachos?"

"I do!" Ellie finally stopped texting and came over to the bar. "Is this real meat? Where's my tofu?"

Landon shook his head. "I refuse your attempts to profane my tacos. Meat or GTFO."

I strained to hear any more of Trent's conversation with his mother, but the bedroom was quiet.

"I'll just have veggie tacos."

Landon gaped. "You're going to eat a taco without any meat. Seriously? I thought I knew you."

Ellie walked around the bar and hugged Landon from behind. "I'll get my meat another way."

"Okay then." I turned my back on them and rinsed my hands off as Trent came out of the bedroom.

His eyes were stormy as he walked to me.

"What happened?"

"We have an invitation to the Carrington Estate for Christmas Eve dinner."

"Both of us?" I dried my hands on a dish towel.

"Yes. If you don't want to go, I understand. We can celebrate here."

"You'd pass it up for me?"

He cocked his head to the side. "Are you serious? Where I go, you go. If you aren't welcome somewhere, then neither am I."

His answer was perfect, just like him.

I pulled him into a hug. "I think we should go."

"If you want to, we will. But if she's rude to you—"

"Then you'll let me handle it." I pulled back and peered at him. "I'm a grown woman. I can hold my own, even against her. Maybe we can work out some sort of truce."

"I like your fight, but she's a tough opponent."

I dug my nails into his sides. "Are you saying I'm not tough?"

He laughed and picked me up, bringing me to eye level. "If you and my mother get into it, I may just hide under the dining room table until the destruction is over."

I kissed the tip of his nose. "Don't worry. I won't hurt her too bad."

"Thank you."

"Hey, they're announcing!" Ellie ran to the living room and turned the volume up.

My nemesis, Herbstreit, was announcing the top four teams. We all scurried into the living room.

"We've finally reached the moment we've all been waiting for. So, without further ado, the fourth ranked team in the nation, according to the playoff committee, is the Billingsley Bobcats."

We went wild—screaming, jumping, high-fiving, hugging. Trent picked me up and spun me around. I laughed when he almost knocked the TV over, but he didn't seem to mind. He kissed me until I was breathless and boneless.

Yells erupted from the park outside, and the entire town was no doubt hooting and hollering about their team making the National Championship playoffs.

"I can't believe it." I grinned so hard I worried my face might crack.

"Number three, according to the committee, is the Rangers." Herbstreit revealed their names on a digital bracket board.

We all sat down, tacos forgotten, as the commentators discussed the picks and gave their opinions on who numbers one and two should be.

"Come on. Eagles need to be number one. I want them right out of the gate." I willed Herbstreit to do the right thing.

He stood in front of the bracket and announced that the Tigers had been selected as the number two team. And, as there was only one other no-loss team left, he filled in the top of the bracket. Number one—the Eagles.

"Yes!" I rocketed to my feet and fist-pumped like I was in a music video from the nineties. "Yes! Yes! Yes!"

Trent yanked me into his lap and kissed me again. "I love it when you get scrappy."

"Get used to it." I bit his jaw, and he squeezed my ass.

Landon stood and clapped. "Taco time!"

Our phones were going crazy with notifications. I called Dad and could barely make out his words, he was so excited. Mrs. Trapper congratulated us, too.

Then I put my phone on silent, enjoyed the company of my friends, and had a wonderful taco Tuesday.

CHAPTER THIRTY-FOUR
TRENT

"IT'S GOING TO BE fine." Cordy powdered her nose for the third time since we'd left Billingsley to drive to my mother's house. "She already loves you. I'll just have to convince her that I'm not so bad. Doable."

I took the interstate exit and drove up the curvy road that led to the Carrington summer home, one of many, but my favorite by far. "She's never been a warm person, Cordy. Not like you."

"I get that. I do." She clapped her compact closed. Her forest green dress gave her skin an even more luminous glow, and the way she'd done her hair made her look like a silver screen bombshell. Beautiful.

"She's just a hard woman."

"It's because she thinks I'm after your trust fund." She turned to me, her face a total deadpan. "And I am, of course. I set up this whole two-year estrangement and all just so I could eventually get my hands on your Scrooge McDuck-sized vat of cash."

I laughed, the tension easing a little as she put her hand on top of mine. "Are you going to dive into it and swim around?"

259

"Every day. Twice on Sundays." She smiled, at ease despite the fact that we were walking into a lion's den.

"As long as you're doing it nude, I'm all for it. That's a particularly nice mental picture."

She snorted. "As if there is any other way."

I sped past the smaller houses at the base of the mountain, their Christmas lights warm in the cold night. Far above, the lights of my parents' house shone through the trees every so often. Mom's phone call had taken me by surprise, especially given the way we'd parted. But she mentioned how Dad wouldn't have wanted us to be apart on Christmas. I agreed with everything she said until she made it clear Cordy wasn't invited. Not a chance.

Mom had eventually given in, but I knew she would do everything she could to convince me I was making a mistake. Maybe Cordy could change my mom's mind. It seemed impossible, but Cordy had surprised me plenty. Maybe she'd come out on top in the battle with my mom. Either way, Cordy was my future. If Mom couldn't accept that, we had nothing more to discuss.

"This is your house?" Cordy's eyes widened as I climbed the snaking driveway.

"Not mine, but yeah."

Most houses in this part of the country were built of logs or painted in such a way as to blend in with the amazing Appalachian scenery. That didn't work for my mother. Our house was a sprawling light gray mansion with large marble columns—imported from Italy—at each corner. A porch wrapped around the front with a separate balcony above that looked out on the sleepy valley below.

"I've never seen…" Cordy gawked at the immaculate lawn that tapered into well-kept flower gardens and then the darkened forest.

"I guess Mom had sort of a *Gone with the Wind* image when Dad told her he wanted to build a house in Tennessee." I shrugged.

"This is unbelievable."

I pulled up the drive along the side of the house and parked. "It's just a house. It's filled with things. They're just things. Hey." I put my fingers under her chin and drew her gaze away from the house and back to me. "You're more important than any of this."

"I-I'm just…" A corner of her lip turned up in a smirk. "I'm just glad that I picked you as my trust fund target. I chose wisely."

"Jerk." I kissed her.

She ran her hands down the lapels of my blazer and turned her head to give me more access. I took it, running my tongue along hers.

I placed my hand on her knee and skimmed up the smooth skin of her thigh.

She grabbed my wrist. "This is a terrible time for that!"

I pushed farther, my fingertips grazing her panties, and leaned into her, reclaiming her mouth. It was always a good time for me to touch her, taste her. Easing farther, I twitched her panties to the side and ran my fingers along her soft skin and down to her entrance.

Her breath hitched when I slid my finger inside. I laughed into her mouth as my cock grew into a full salute in my jeans.

"Trent, we can't." She pulled back, panting, but she didn't try to push my hand away. Her cheeks were highlighted with pink, and her eyes glittered in the fading twilight.

"You sure?" I slipped another finger inside her, and she bit her lip.

Pumping in and out slowly, I watched as she came undone, her lips parting and her moans growing as I stroked her. I moved faster, then pulled my fingers from her and rubbed her slick clit. Watching her like this, completely under my control, was like a shot of testosterone straight to my cock. Her chest heaved, and she worked her hips along with my increasing tempo.

When she threw her head back, I sucked her neck. She came in a crescendo of moans and writhed on my fingers as I sucked at the sweet spots on her neck and shoulder. When she relaxed into the seat, I pushed my fingers inside her once more, then drew them to my lips and licked them clean.

"That is…easily…one of the…hottest things I've ever seen." She said the last part on a hard whoosh of air.

"Perv." I climbed out of the car before she could retort. I gave her a minute to adjust her dress and powder her nose for the fourth time. Breathing in the cold air, I tried to calm my nerves. Hearing Cordy come while moaning my name went a long way, but the storm that was brewing inside the house would dampen anyone's spirits. It also dampened my erection, which was a good thing.

Cordy stepped out, her black heels clicking on the pavement as we walked to the front door. "Don't worry." She hugged my bicep. "I'll protect you."

"I feel so much better now." I turned the door handle and allowed Cordy to walk ahead of me.

"This is just as beautiful as the outside." She stared up at the chandelier, the huge Christmas tree in the sitting room, and the numerous silver, gold, and green decorations that graced the foyer. Smells of ham and savory spices scented the air. The cook must have been hard at work. Everything in the house screamed "Christmas".

Mom had kept the tradition. It was bittersweet, knowing that my father wouldn't get to see it this year. His portrait hung in the sitting room above the fireplace. It was painted when he was in his prime. My five-year-old self sat on his knee, and we both smiled down at me.

"Is that you?" Cordy followed my gaze to the image.

"My father and me, yes."

"I see where you get your good looks." She walked to it and craned her head back. "He was a stud."

"He was." Mom's voice echoed in the foyer, and she

strode into the sitting room. Her red sweater and green skirt were festive; her pinched expression was not.

Cordy whirled. "I'm sorry. I meant no offense."

Whereas a normal person would respond with "none taken," Mom simply stared down her narrow nose.

I stepped between them. "How was the Bahamas?"

She took a sip from her wine glass. "Bearable. Though the servants there hadn't aired out the house to my satisfaction when I arrived. It's always been hard to find good help. Have you ever worked in a service profession, Ms. Baxter?"

I wanted to cut this off, to shut Mom down as surely as I had done at my apartment. Instead, I stayed silent and trusted Cordy. She'd told me on what seemed like an endless loop that she would take the lead with my mother. So I let her.

"Yes. Actually, I used to wait tables when I lived in Gray Valley." She kept a pleasant smile on her face as she approached my mother. "I got pretty good at it, if my tips were any indication. Have you ever waited tables?"

My mother scoffed. "Me?"

"Sure. My dad has always said the quickest way to test someone's mettle is to give them a job they don't want to do."

"Your father." Mom smirked. "What does he do?"

"Nothing." Cordy kept her composed smile. "He used to work in the coal mines, but he got laid off."

"And he hasn't worked since, I take it?" She took a larger drink of her wine as Cordy moved even closer, no fear in any of her movements.

It was like watching a lion tamer, though I wasn't sure which one of them held the whip.

"No. He's never done anything except work in the mines. He did try to work as a stocker in a local hardware, but that didn't turn out very well."

"So he can't hold down steady employment?" Mom glanced at me, as if to say, "*See? She comes from horrible stock.*"

"It's hard for him, especially since he's a recovering alcoholic."

Mom stilled and narrowed her eyes. *Oh, shit.*

"Something smells delicious." I cut in despite Cordy's numerous warnings.

Mom glanced to me. "Chana is cooking like always. Let's go in. It should be ready any moment." She turned on her heel and headed across the foyer, past the grand staircase, and to the hall that led to the formal dining room.

Cordy gave me a stern shake of her head, but took my offered arm. "I had it under control." Her whisper was barely a hiss.

"I know." *I didn't know.* "You were doing fine. I'm hungry is all."

She crinkled her nose and peered up at me. "You're so full of shit."

"Yes." I nodded and followed my mom into the dining room. Three place settings were laid out at the far end of the table. The head seat—where my father always sat—remained open, and I fought away the memories of him sitting there, because with them came a sadness that I tried to ignore.

"Chana!" Mom's sharp bark made Cordy jump.

Chana hurried through the side door from the kitchen. "Everything is ready."

"Go ahead, then. Thank you." Mom sat and motioned for us to do the same. She took the wine bottle from the table and refilled her glass. I wondered how much she'd already had.

I pulled Cordy's chair out and helped her get settled, then sat to her right, both of us facing Mom.

"Have you thought any more about what I said? About Carlotta?" Mom lay her napkin in her lap as Chana began setting platters of ham, deviled eggs, green beans, and corn along the center of the table.

"Carlotta isn't going to happen. I haven't seen her

since I started dating Cordy."

"Her brother is up for re-election soon. It's the perfect time for you to hit the campaign trail with him. Get your face out there. With Carlotta by your side, you would make a pretty picture for the press."

"She's pretty, but that's about it." My conversations with her consisted of her telling me what she bought on her last shopping trip.

"Pretty is all you need. The rest will come in time."

I clenched my jaw, but a side glance from Cordy had me relaxing. "And to be honest, I'm certain she doesn't miss me. She never liked me that much."

"I find that hard to believe." Cordy patted my thigh, then frowned, likely realizing she was playing into my mother's hands.

"As do I." Mom took full advantage.

Cordy doubled down. "Trent is by far the kindest, smartest, and best-looking man I've ever met. On top of that, he's not snobby. He doesn't care where I come from. We spent Thanksgiving at my dad's house, and"—she swept her gaze around the room—"it's nowhere near as grand as your lovely home. Trent didn't mind. He was gracious, well-mannered, and impressed my father to the point where he calls and asks to talk to Trent instead of me."

I laughed. "He calls to talk football. That's the only reason he wants to talk to me."

She gave me a withering glare. "I play football. I know football as well as you do, if not better. So that is definitely *not* the reason he wants to talk to you."

"Better than me?" I forked a piece of lettuce and brought it to my mouth, the vinaigrette tangy on my tongue. "You must be kidding."

"What?" Cordy set her water glass down and turned to me. "I know more about football than you do. NCAA rules, anyway."

"Pfft."

"You don't believe me?"

"Not a chance. You might know soccer rules better, but not football."

She set her fork down. "Try me."

"Seriously?"

"Yes, seriously. Do your worst."

"Okay then." I rolled some obscure rules around in my head and settled on one. "What happens if I'm running the ball and fumble at the one-yard line—not that that would ever happen of course—but let's just say, for this hypothetical situation, the ball gets knocked loose at the one and rolls into the end zone and out the back. What happens?"

"What down is it?" She stared hard at me.

I tried to maintain my poker face, but her question told me she didn't know the right answer. "First down."

She tapped her finger on her chin, and I could sense my mother listening intently. When Cordy's smile emerged, I knew she'd been teasing me with her question. "Downs don't matter in that situation. If you fumble out of the end zone like that, it's a touchback. You pretty much screwed the pooch, and we'll have to kick it away to the other team."

Shit. "That's right."

My mom made a *hmph* noise and grabbed a roll from the bread basket.

"Now it's my turn to ask you one." Her grin widened, and she sparkled under the crystal lights.

"Please." I knew the NCAA rulebook almost as well as the constellation of freckles on her inner thigh. "I got this. Hit me."

"We'll see." She drummed her fingers on the table. "Let's say Coach decides to punt, and Hawthorne runs out onto the field with the punting team."

I focused on her, my mother's prickly attention fading. Competition was my caffeine. "Yeah."

"So the center hikes the ball back, but it's short. The

ball hits the ground and bounces up. Instead of scrambling for it, Hawthorne sees an angle and runs up and kicks it. He gets some good leg behind it, and it sails through the uprights. What happens?"

My mind whirred. If the ball was punted and landed out of the back of the end zone, then it was a touch back. I went over the play in my head, imagining Hawthorne kicking just as Cordy described. She piled some ham and mashed potatoes on her plate, then licked the gravy off her spoon as she stared at me with a confident, sly look. It was hot, definitely a good look for her.

"Well, Trent? Cordy answered your question quite a bit faster." Mom watched me. Was that a hint of amusement in her eye? And I couldn't help but notice she'd used Cordy's first name instead of the cold "Ms. Baxter."

"Okay." It had to be a touchback. Cordy was just trying to psych me out. Surely.

"Yeah, Trent. What's the answer?" She took a big bite of ham.

"Fine. It's a touchback."

Cordy made an obnoxious buzzer sound, and Mom jumped and put her hand to her mouth.

"Oh." Cordy glanced at her. "Sorry about that. But no, Mr. I-Know-Everything-About-Football. You are incorrect."

I threw out the only other option. "It's a field goal?"

She nodded. "Right. Because the ball hit the ground first, it's treated like a field goal attempt. It's called a drop kick. They used to do it all the time back in the old days. I think Doug Flutie is the only guy who's ever done it in modern football times." She put her water glass to her lips and leered at me over the edge.

"Are you sure?" I bit a roll with a tad more forcefulness than necessary.

"Google it if you don't believe me."

"You usually say that when you're pulling my leg." I

pinched her thigh.

She smacked my hand. "This one time, I'm serious."

"Okay then. I believe you. No Google necessary."

"I don't like electronics at the table." Mom took a larger gulp of her wine.

"Seems like a good rule." Cordy nodded. "Phones are so distracting."

"I—" Mom stopped, then gave Cordy a glare, as if she were angry about what she was going to say. "I quite agree with you."

I hid my amazement. But inside, I felt like I'd just watched the most thrilling Super Bowl of all time, and Cordy was doing a celebration dance in my Mom's end zone.

Instead of gloating, I made small talk about college. I tiptoed around the NFL subject before Mom got going on a tirade against one of the teams she owned a large chunk of. After we'd finished and the hour grew late, Cordy and I stood to leave.

"Cordy, can I have a word?" My mom's severe tone raised the hackles on the back of my neck, but Cordy accompanied her into the sitting room as I hovered around the staircase.

Playing on the steps had been one of my favorite pastimes when I was a child. Standing there as an adult, I could almost see my dad, memories of him and me racing up the stairs ingrained in my memory. When I was younger, he always beat me. By the time I was a teenager, I dusted him every time. And then he'd grown so sick that the only way he made it up the stairs at all was if I or someone else carried him.

He'd been like a frail bird in my arms toward the end. But the sparkle never left his eyes. He'd stayed true despite the pain, the fear, and the heartache he was going through. I gazed around at the Christmas lights and fir swags. They didn't carry the same joy as in years past, but I couldn't ignore how my mother had taken care to use the decorations Dad liked best. Our shared pain couldn't stop the love we had for him. Nothing could.

"I miss you, Dad." My voice was a whisper. I hoped he heard me, wherever he was.

Cordy and Mom emerged from the sitting room, and I walked to them.

"Ready to go?" I wanted to get Cordy as far away from my mother as possible. We'd done our duty and visited for Christmas.

"Sure." Cordy draped her arm through mine. She had a friendly smile on her face—unusual for anyone who just spent one-on-one time with my mother.

"Mom?" I couldn't read her face.

"Come here." Mom opened her arms and gave me a hug, the powdery smell of her perfume familiar and oddly comforting. I returned her embrace, surprised by how much I'd missed her in the short time since our falling out. She pulled away first and squeezed my elbows. "Have a safe trip back."

"We will."

She walked us to the door, and Cordy threw her arms around Mom. Mom's eyes widened in surprise, but then she patted Cordy on the back as if she were an over-friendly pet that my mom didn't quite know what to do with. I'd take it.

Cordy didn't seem to mind. She stepped back to my side and beamed. "Thank you for having us, and Merry Christmas."

Mom's chin trembled slightly. "Merry Christmas to you, too." She straightened her back. "And thank you both for coming."

Holy shit. I was too dazed to respond as Cordy led me out onto the porch and to the driveway. Mom closed the door, but watched us through the side windows.

"Did you put something in her drink?" I asked as I opened Cordy's door for her.

She looked at me through her lashes, her amber eyes

dark in the low light. "Oh ye of little faith."

I closed her door and hustled around to the driver's side. "Don't get biblical on me, country girl. What did she say to you in the sitting room?" I drove down the driveway, the lights below twinkling through the wood smoke that blanketed the valley on cold nights.

"Did you know that your grandfather had a problem with alcohol?"

"What?"

"She said when she was growing up, he'd drink himself into a stupor at least a couple of nights a week. She didn't say he was violent, but I assumed it from the way she spoke about him."

"No." I ran a hand down my face. "She never mentioned that. I had no idea."

"He never overcame his problem. She wanted to tell me that she was glad my father wasn't going to go down the same path as hers. I told her it was all because of you. That you paid for his rehab and didn't even tell me until after the fact."

"What did she say?"

"Nothing. She just gave me that look. You know the one where it's like she's looking straight down into your soul, but you can't tell if she's happy or angry with whatever she's found there?"

I knew that look plenty well. "Yeah."

"And that was it, really. I wanted her to see me, the real me. Warts and all. It's the only way she can make a decision on whether she wants me in her life or not. I can tell she's sad, still grieving over your dad. Hey." She reached out and took my hand. "Are you okay? I know it must have been hard without your father with you this year."

"It was." I quieted when I felt my throat close up.

"I understand." She leaned over and kissed my cheek, then turned on the radio to a local station. They played only holiday tunes this time of year.

By the time we were on the interstate, she had me singing along—and completely off-key—to every Christmas song that came on.

When we reached the apartment, we sat in front of our twinkling Christmas tree, her in my lap as I played with her hair. She was perfectly snuggly in flannel pajamas, which I planned to remove before we got in bed.

She turned to look at me, and took my face in her small hands. "This has been the best Christmas I've ever had."

I smiled and nuzzled her nose. "Same here."

CHAPTER THIRTY-FIVE
CORDY

THE MASS OF BODIES behind me felt like a single organism, one bent on crushing the life out of the Eagles' season. I stood at the head of the line, Trent at my side, as we listened to the music pumping through the stadium. A steady roar of the crowd rolled through the newly built venue, and anticipation thickened the air.

The Bobcats were pegged as the underdog, with the line in Vegas giving the Eagles a seven-and-a-half-point advantage. But the bookmakers didn't know us. They didn't know our team. We would end this game with a win, and the Eagles would return home empty-handed. After that, we would play on the biggest stage of all—the National Championship game.

"You ready?" I bounced at Trent's elbow, excitement coursing through me.

Trent looked down at me, a smirk creeping up under his eye black. "Not as ready as you are."

"Shut up. I'm excited. It's okay to be excited."

"Don't be a hero out there." He patted my ass as our fight song played. "Let's go!"

Coach Sterling had already taken off, heading for the

sideline. We followed, running through the smoke to the sound of eighty thousand people cheering or booing. I ran straight for the practice net behind the benches and began to set up my kicks. Hawthorne was there doing a few extra stretches. Trent huddled with Coach Sterling and his linemen, double-checking strategy for the game and getting ready to go to work.

We won the coin toss, and opted to defer to the second half. The Eagles swarmed the opposite side of the field, their red jerseys painting the sideline.

"You're on." I clapped Hawthorne on the back as he ran out with the kickoff team. The band seemed louder in the professional stadium, and the sound echoed. The crowd noise receded to a low hum as Hawthorne got set. The hum grew into a yell, and then into a deafening roar of "go Cats go" as he kicked the ball to the Eagles.

Their returner caught it at the five and gained ten more yards before being brought down at the fifteen. We settled in for a grueling game. The loss of Ethan had weakened the defensive line, and the Eagles took full advantage. On their first possession, they drove down the field with a series of running plays. When they got to our twenty, they fumbled and we recovered. Bobcat nation breathed a collective sigh of relief.

Trent took the field, and so it went, team against team. The game remained scoreless after first quarter. Trent threw a bomb in the second quarter, and we moved close enough to try for a field goal. Hawthorne trotted out. I held my breath as he lined up the shot from the thirty-one, a forty-eight yard field goal.

The snap went well, and he managed to get it up and high, but it veered barely left, missing by only a foot, if that.

Trent patted Hawthorne's helmet as he ran past. Coach Carver didn't even say a word of correction to him; his execution was perfect, but the ball didn't go his way. Nothing to be done.

"Don't sweat it." I punched him in the arm.

His wry smile didn't reach his eyes. "That pretty much sucked ass."

"Next time. You'll hit it next time."

He nodded and plopped on the nearest bench. "Right."

"You just needed to warm up a little. You got this."

He stared up at the closed dome over our heads. The temperature was a perfect seventy degrees or so, no matter how frigid it was outside.

"You can stop now." He ran a hand through his bright red locks. "But I appreciate it."

We soldiered on through the second quarter. Trent got the team into scoring position again. On the next play, he handed the ball off to our running back. A defender shot a gap and tackled the runner immediately. The ball came loose. The Eagles fans shook the stadium when the ball was scooped up by another defender. Trent made the tackle and kept him from running it back for seven points, but the damage was done. What little momentum we had was gone, dissolved under the harsh stadium lights.

I dashed out to the edge of the sideline as Trent ran in. He went to Coach, and they argued for a few moments before Trent stalked off. Then he stopped, put his hands on his hips, and stared at the ground for a few long seconds. Then he seemed to shake it off and motioned at our running back to keep his head up. I smiled. He was pissed, but he was a leader above all. They put their heads together as our defense worked on holding off the Eagles onslaught. The clock ticked down until only thirty seconds remained in the first half.

If we could get to halftime without a score, we could start fresh when we received the ball first thing in the second half. The Eagles had made it to a first down in Bobcat territory, but the clock wasn't on their side. With only a few seconds left, they sent out their kicker.

I whispered all sorts of jinxes, and Coach Sterling

tried to ice him with a time-out. Despite all that, he kicked the field goal as time ran out.

We went to halftime down by three points. I stayed with the guys and hurried into their locker room. We milled around, some of the coaches going over assignments with certain players. I downed a cup of water and walked over to Trent.

"Feeling okay?"

He wiped his face with a towel. "Making it. I think we have a strategy figured out. Throwing it in the flat seems to work best, and they have a hard time—"

"Take a knee!" Coach barked.

We all hit the floor, Trent on one side of me and Hawthorne on the other.

"No one thought we would be in this situation. Those bookies in Vegas? They're sweating us right now. The Eagles? They're sweating us right now. Three points? I could wipe my ass with three points and flush it down the goddamn toilet!"

A deep yell went up around me. Since my main function was to make three points, I took a slight bit of umbrage, but I decided it wasn't the best time to broach the subject.

Coach stared hard at each player, stopping on every set of eyes as he looked around the room. "Now, we've had tough fights all year. We haven't come through unscathed, but we will come out on top." He whipped his hat off his head and shook it at one section of players. "The Eagles? Their schedule had more creampuffs than the bakery down the street."

A few chuckles went up, and Hawthorne snorted.

"We have strength of schedule, strength of character, and above all, strength of team!"

A round of yells went up as Trent stood and walked into the center of the circle. There was no hint of nerves in his stance. Gone was the boy from speech class. In his place stood a man, a leader; our quarterback. "We're better than these guys. Ever since our loss, I've watched each and every one of you grow over the course of the season. I've watched you scrape and claw your way to have a chance at this game. I've watched you have each other's back." His eyes lighted on mine, and the love I had for him filled every corner of my heart. "I've watched you sacrifice. All for this chance at redemption. Well guess what?" His voice rose into a thunderous yell. "That chance is here. That chance is now. We just have to take it!"

The entire team leapt to its feet, and raucous yells created a deafening din as Trent's enthusiasm spread from player to player. I yelled right along with them, feeling the moment. Trent held up a hand, and we quieted, all eyes on him.

"We play for each other. I know who I'm playing for." His gaze returned to mine before he swept it over every player in the room. "This team, all of you. You play Bobcat football, and I guarantee you they won't be able to stop us. The season has come to this, our final choice between being nothing and being champions. I choose to be champions. How about you?"

I thought the roar before was deafening. But this one felt like it might pop my eardrums. We shook the walls with our desire to win, our need to right the wrong from earlier in the season. A new energy pumped through the room, and I couldn't wipe the grin off my face.

Coach clapped Trent on the back. "Let's get out there and destroy them!" He headed out of the locker room, the team at his heels.

We sounded like a freight train barreling through the tunnel and out onto the field. I'd never seen the team this amped up, and the same electricity flowed through me. I wanted to do just what Trent had said—play for him, play for my team, and crush the Eagles. The crowd seemed to sense it, and the noise grew as we hyped them by raising our arms and egging them on during kickoff.

We took the ball at the twenty and ran it to the fifty

before our runner was tackled. Trent set up and dismantled the defense play by play until he was five yards from the end zone. On third and five, he threw a perfect spiral to the front of the end zone, and the stadium boomed its approval.

I ran out, lined up, and kicked the extra point. We were up seven to three, and it remained that way as we entered the final quarter of play.

"Hold them. We have to hold them." Hawthorne and I stood beside each other and watched our defense struggle on the first set of downs.

Our defense gave up two first downs, then finally stopped the Eagles' running game on the third set of downs. They kicked the ball away, and we gained good field position at the forty thanks to a shanked punt.

Trent ran out, the familiar number nine in control of the field of play. He went three and out, never even close to the first down thanks to a sack and a false start. The good field position didn't help us, and Trent jogged back to the sideline. Our defense was tired, but had to get back out onto the field.

They were still fighting, but worn down. Play after play, the Eagles drove down the field. Then I watched as Ethan's replacement missed a tackle and the runner cut up the middle, dodged to the right, stiff-armed a defender, and high-stepped it into our end zone.

"Shit." I rubbed my temple.

Their kicker made the point after, and just like that, we were down by three points.

"Double shit." I checked the clock. Their offense had whittled it away prior to the touchdown until only five minutes remained in the final quarter. That could be an eternity on a football field or a snap of a finger, depending on who had possession.

The Eagles kicked it off to us and pinned us down at our own eighteen-yard line. Trent methodically took the team down the field, keeping an eye on the clock as he did so. The Eagles had been double covering our best receiver the entire game, so Trent changed to more of a run-based strategy, employing short passes in the flat to get out of bounds and keep the clock from ticking away too much.

Four first downs later, and he was at the Eagles' twenty-yard line.

"I can't believe this," Hawthorne said. "He may pull it—"

I clapped my hand over his mouth. "Are you trying to jinx it?"

He shook my hand off and stared at our offense. "He needs to get the play off."

"He's got time." My hands were sweaty as Trent ran down the line and changed the play.

"Play clock is down to seven. Game clock only has twenty-nine."

"Shh."

Trent yelled for the ball, and the play went into motion. Trent tried to hand the ball off, but the runner bobbled it. Trent yanked it back before a defender creamed the runner. He ran toward the end zone, got a couple of good blocks, and stretched for the touchdown right as a defender threw a shoulder into him. It was a hard hit, and I heard the crack of contact.

I gasped and ran down the sideline. He hit the ground, and the ball rolled from his grip. One of the defenders tried to pick it up and run with it, but the refs whistled the play dead. Trent had been down at the two-yard line when the ball came out, and video replay confirmed it. He didn't get up, just flopped onto his back, his chest rising and falling at a rapid pace.

The trainers ran out to him. I only stayed on the sideline because Hawthorne held my elbow.

"He's okay. He'll be okay." I didn't know if I was reassuring myself or Hawthorne. Probably myself.

When Trent sat up, the stadium went wild, and when he rose and trotted to the sideline, there seemed to be a collective sigh of relief.

Coach yelled to the offensive line coach. "Call time!"

I dodged through the players and ran to his side.

"What is it?" Coach Sterling bent his head to hear the trainer's answer, his face darkening at each word.

"We have no damn depth at quarterback." Coach glanced at Green, the second-stringer, and shook his head. "He's not ready."

"Trent?" I scooted around to face him.

"It's my shoulder. They think it's dislocated or something worse. Right arm." He winced as a trainer pressed on his shoulder blade.

"He's out." The trainer didn't even flinch when Coach let loose a stream of invective that would have killed a nun.

"What about Green?" Trent shot the kid a look. I'd seen him in action. He wasn't ready. Great potential, but his mechanics needed work.

An idea started rolling around in my mind—it was foolish, over-the-top, and definitely not well thought out.

"Green's all we got." Coach Sterling spit on the turf. "We're about to shit the bed in the playoffs."

"I can play." Trent pushed the trainer away who was feeling on his arm.

"Yeah?" Coach poked him in the shoulder, and Trent winced. "That's what I thought. I'm not having a first round draft pick ruin his arm on this game. It's Green." He turned and yelled to the offensive coach. "Call time again."

"One left, Coach."

"I know that, goddammit! Call the next one, too!"

"Put me in, Coach. I'm ready to play." I blinked. "Should I have sung that?"

"What are you on about, Baxter?"

"Trent can't play, Green will lose the game, but I can win it."

"We need more than three points, Baxter. Three

points will land us in overtime with a quarterback who can't play!" He turned to walk toward Green, who still sat on the bench with a dazed expression.

"Wait! Not three. Six!"

"Six?" Coach whirled.

"Six." I stared up at him. "Put me in. They'll think we're trying to tie it for overtime. It'll be a fake. I'll run it to the end zone. Just give me the chance."

"That's crazy." The crafty glint in his eye undermined his words. Then he shrugged and waved the idea away as if it were a troublesome fly. "Besides, Trent can't even hold the ball."

"No, she's right." Excitement lit Trent's voice. "Listen, Coach. We always practice the fake where I throw the ball over my left shoulder. I can do that fine. Nothing wrong with my left arm." He clapped me on the back. "And I put way more faith in Cordy than Green."

The offensive coach called for our last time-out.

"That's gutsy as hell." Coach scratched his forehead and looked from me to Green and back again. "A gutsy move. You got the balls for this, Baxter?"

"I was born with them, Coach. They just haven't dropped yet."

He laughed, the insanity of my plan likely fueling the chuckles more than my joke. He sobered and considered me one more time.

I pulled my helmet on. "Trust me. I can do this. The play I'll make out of this will replace that 'Kick Six of the Century' on every highlight reel."

"Time's up, Coach!" We were out of time-outs.

Coach put his hands on his hips. "Well, hell. Get out there. Let's see what we can do."

Adrenaline coursed through my veins as I cut through the line of players and ran onto the field with my kicking team.

"You got this," Trent said. "Just follow the plan. Make it look natural. Take your steps like usual. They won't know what hit them until you shove it down their throat in the end zone." He knelt as our teammates lined up on the two-yard line, right hash. I'd have to get to the corner and cut around to the end zone while taking care not to step out of bounds.

"I got this." I squashed the memory of the Kick Six and focused on the play clock ticking away.

My team depended on me, and I refused to let them down like I had at the start of the season. My head and my heart were in the game. With Trent holding for me, I couldn't lose. I took a deep breath and ran onto the field. The crowd quieted, or maybe I just shut them out. I ran the play in my mind over and over again.

The defensive line was set, and my teammates lined up in front of me. It was go time.

Marking off my steps, I did my usual set up. I stopped and lined up, then motioned for the hike. As soon as Trent signaled, I set the play in motion by running to the left. He tossed the ball, and it slid into my hands. Tucking it under my arm, I pumped my legs as fast as I could. Trent jumped up, sprinted, and threw a hard block that gave me a little room on the outside. I darted to the edge and sensed grasping fingers as the defenders tried to hem me in. I was so close when I felt a hand on the back of my jersey.

Time stood still, the crowd went silent, and all I saw was the white line that separates the winners from the losers. I stretched my arms out, holding the ball ahead of me, and dove for the end zone.

EPILOGUE
CORDY

THE SMELL OF FRESHLY mowed grass and dirt filled my nose as I stared out at our home field. The stands were overflowing with fans for our season opener against the Lions. Billy the Bobcat did pushups in our end zone, and the hum of excitement energized everyone on the field.

"Coin toss, captain." Hawthorne elbowed me. I, along with two other team captains, ran out and did the honors.

Running back, I spotted something that made my heart skip a beat. I veered off toward the right where all the visitors stood with their special bright blue lanyards. Trent didn't need one, of course. Everyone recognized him. He was the starting quarterback for the Bucks, one of the top professional teams in the country.

His team was based in New York, but he would fly his mom, my dad, and me to his games. After Christmas, his mom had taken a new approach with me. When she told me that my relationship with Trent reminded her of how she and his father had been in their early days, I knew we'd turned a corner. Things had thawed between us, and our relationship had become so warm that even Trent was amazed. Our little cobbled-together family was new, but didn't lack in the love department.

"Hey, kicker." He gazed down at me and smiled.

"Hey, QB." I stood next to him as we got ready for kickoff.

"I miss this."

"You do this every Sunday."

"Not with you."

"I like to do other things with you." I shot him a smirk.

"Do you have any idea how hot you look with eye black on? Have I ever mentioned that?"

"Just a few hundred times."

He smacked my ass and yelled "good game" as if that somehow covered it.

I laughed and leaned into his arm. He was dressed in a nice button-down and jeans. It was odd that I was dressed out and ready to play while he had to stay on the sideline. I, of course, took the opportunity to rib him about it.

"You'll be riding the pine for the whole game. Are you okay with that?"

"I could try for another year of eligibility if you want me back."

"Oh, I don't know if that would be a wise choice on my part." I whistled. "Our new quarterback was a five-star recruit."

He puffed out his chest a little. "So was I."

"Well, he's really tall."

He stood straighter. "So am I."

"He doesn't hog the shower in the women's locker room."

He glared down at me. "Cordy."

"Kidding. Well, not really. He doesn't hog it because he's not in there."

"Better not be."

I bumped my hip into Trent's. "I'm going to be pretty

sweaty after this game."

"Yeah?" He licked his lips.

"I'll certainly need a shower."

"I agree."

"Maybe you could come help me soap up. You know, for old time's sake?"

He grinned. "Oh, I'm certain I can manage that." Looking me over, he stopped at my hands. "I thought you were going to wear it?"

"I am wearing it."

I reached inside my jersey and pulled on the chain around my neck. My ring popped out, and I held it up to him. The Billingsley B was imprinted on the top, and "National Champions" flowed down each side.

"Where's yours?"

He waggled his fingers, the matching ring flashing in the lights.

"When is kickoff?" I frowned and stared down the field, wondering why the kicking team was still on the sidelines.

"I think you need a new ring."

I smirked. "I'll get one at the end of this season."

Since when did the stadium get so quiet?

"I was thinking one with less gold and more diamonds."

I turned to him slowly and only then realized our image was on the huge screens above each end zone. When I looked back, he was on one knee, holding up a ring with the largest diamond I'd ever seen.

My knees turned to jelly, and I was struggling to stay conscious.

"Cordelia Elaine Baxter, will you marry me?" His eyes swam with emotion.

I put a shaking hand to my face. "Oh my God."

He smiled. "Can I take that as a yes? My heart's kind of on the line here. More importantly, we're delaying kickoff, and the team—"

I bowled him over, and we landed in a heap on the turf. I kissed him as he wrapped his arms around me. The stadium erupted around us as we made out on national TV.

"Yes...yes...yes." I said between lip locks.

He laughed and sat up, then took my hand and slid the ring on. The crowd ramped up again as he pulled me to my feet.

"Look." He turned me around and pointed out his mom, my dad, Landon, and Ellie in the stands right behind us. My dad grinned like a madman and tried to hug Trent's mom. The attempt was comical and ended in a half-hug truce.

"I love you." It was all I could think or say as I met his eyes again.

He picked me up and twirled me, my head going foggy as he kissed me. "I love you too."

Tears blurred in my eyes as he set me down and gave me one more long kiss.

Our kickoff team ran out on the field, and Hawthorne shot me a thumbs up as he dashed past.

Trent grinned, his handsome face alight with joy. "Now give it back. I'll hold it while you go out there and kick some ass."

ACKNOWLEDGEMENTS

I watch football. A lot of football. I roll with the Tide every season. Before starting this book, I researched the hell out of the mechanics of kicking field goals. I watched footage of amazing college and NFL kickers. I did my homework and relived the terrible Kick Six of Alabama's 2013 season. I felt up our football and slept with it (ok, maybe I didn't sleep with it … but all the rest is true).

Despite my in-depth research of men in tight pants with balls, Mr. Aaron read my draft and marked all the football sections with a red pen. So, I tweaked, and re-arranged, and changed yardages, and redid whatever he said didn't seem quite realistic. Mr. Aaron knows, because he played football. Don't tell anyone, but his nickname during his football days was Quiet Storm, and he was the best damn linebacker, like, ever. {{I just asked him who the greatest linebacker of all time is, and he said "Dick ButtKiss." I laughed. Then I realized he was serious. Then I looked it up, and it's actually "Dick Butkus." *Awkward.*}} Point is, Mr. Aaron knows the game. He even tells the TV announcers the correct rules before they get told in their earpieces. Vern and Gary have nothing on Mr. Aaron (if you get that ref, you are a fan and I salute you).

So, my number one thank-you goes to Mr. Aaron for setting me straight on "real" college football. He made the football parts of this book as realistic as possible while I made the sexy parts as hot as possible, as I tend to do.

Also, thanks to the tip of the spear—Rachel and Viv. Y'all are always the first ones in, and your feedback is invaluable. Neda, thanks as always, for keeping my promo going while I'm in my writing cave or adding more filth to my Tumblr. Trish Mint gave me some excellent beta input. Keep it #Mint, my dear. Next, a big high-five goes out to everyone in the Acquisitions. You ladies (and a few gents) are fabulous readers, and I can always count on your support.

My next book, Tempting Eden, is a modern reimagining of *Jane Eyre*. It's slated for release in late September. I've included the first chapter for you to get an idea of just how modern it is, and I hope you enjoy it.

Thanks, as always, for reading.

xoxo,
Celia

CHAPTER ONE
EDEN

"I DON'T GIVE TWO shits if the entire development goes down the drain. That's exactly what will happen if you go with anyone else. Give me the business and see all the units sold. Go elsewhere and get used to having a 'for sale' sign permanently in your window." I tapped the screen and ended the call.

He would call back. Developers always did. I hurried across the sidewalk toward my building, the tallest in the city.

I looked up. Impossibly bright blue eyes caught my attention. That's all it took. My left heel caught in a grate, stuck as sure as if it was superglued to the spot. I tried to take another step with my right foot to anchor myself. Mistake.

My coffee sloshed to the top of the travel cup, shooting like a geyser through the small opening before I let the cup go entirely. It crashed down, ending in a small explosion of caffeine and foam at my feet.

I pulled my left foot from the offending shoe to take a steadying step, but when my bare foot came down, it turned to the side, twisting as sure as a corkscrew. It was over then. Gravity would have its due. My momentum carried me toward the concrete at an alarming pace.

The blue-eyed man caught my elbow and easily pulled me upright. "Whoa."

"Get off." I yanked my arm away. "You made me drop my coffee."

"What?" He cocked his head to the side, the sun illuminating his angular jaw and handsome features. "Let me help."

"You've done enough. I don't need your help." My ankle was screaming, my shoe was still stuck in the grate, and the sleeve of my white blouse was streaking brown from the coffee. I'd dropped my blueprint binder. It lay open, the pages turning and turning, as if the breeze were the fastest reader of all time. *Shit.*

I realized I'd let out a string of some of the vilest profanity allowed this side of the Mason-Dixon line, but no one cared. People kept passing by, not even offering a glance to the grate's newest victim. It was just that commonplace. I made a mental note to call the Pilot Group, the building's owner, and have the damn thing fixed once and for all. Thornfield paid a small ransom each month to ensure our business presence on the top floor, and maintenance was part of the package.

"You *definitely* need my help." He took my elbow again as I glared up at him.

"I'm fine." I went to step back for my shoe, but my ankle gave a decidedly painful twinge. More curses, these perhaps even more colorful than the last.

His thick black brows lowered, encroaching on the blue that had led me to this state of affairs. "You twisted your ankle."

"No shit, and no thanks to you." I glanced down to my notebook. How the hell would I manage to pick it up and make it to my office?

He bent down to retrieve my shoe. His back was broad beneath his suit coat. Built was the word. I hadn't seen him before, or at least I thought I hadn't. I was pretty sure I'd remember him. Those eyes at the very least. They were impossible, beyond beautiful, more startling than oddly colored contacts.

He gingerly removed my shoe from its metal prison. The leather heel was scraped and ruined. I'd have to take it in for repair. I added it to the long line of things in my life that needed fixing.

He scooped up my binder and returned to my side. I just stood, helpless and with the injured foot up and resting on the tips of my toes. In my skirt suit, I looked like the corporate karate kid about to do the crane kick and win the tourney. The thought was so ridiculous and out of place that I laughed at myself, more like a harsh bark.

He gave me a stoic look that revealed nothing. I tamped down my temporary amusement.

I just needed to get to my office and recover what little shred of dignity I still had left.

The day was already teed up to be full of difficulties. This start really wasn't that out of character.

"Let me help you to your office." It wasn't a request. His hand returned to my elbow, a steady pressure.

He was sure of himself, walking the fine line between confidence and cockiness with the skill of a tightrope performer. I wondered if he was working without a net.

But it didn't matter what he said or how he said it. I wasn't in a position to say no. I would make a spectacle of myself trying to get to my floor in this state. "Sure. You owe me, since all this is your fault. Get me to the elevator bank, then I should be all right to make it from there."

"If you say so." He smirked and squeezed my elbow lightly. I hopped along, struggling toward the door, so much so that he did away with pretense and simply wrapped his arm around my waist, allowing me to use him as a crutch. I caught a whiff of his scent—masculine with some sort of tantalizing aftershave. Definitely not an aqua velva man, thank God.

He was tall so that even jostling along on the one remaining heel kept my eyes at the level of his shoulder. His arm tightened even more, lifting me to keep the pressure from my injured ankle. He didn't slow his gait, just manhandled me along like a package under his arm. He was hard against me, and I couldn't help but mold to his metal, my curves melting into him.

I looked up, taking in his profile as he half-carried me into the high rise. He seemed younger than me, though I was only twenty-eight. His dark hair was cropped close. There wasn't even the hint of a shadow along his jawline; clean-shaven and professional. His neck was long, almost too elegant for a man. His lips were full and a rich plum color, a perfect match to his light brown skin. Handsome by any standard. And those otherworldly blue eyes were stunners.

He hit the elevator call button. I noticed he didn't have a band on his ring finger. That's what I did—noticed details. Details were the sort of thing that could make or break a person. I wasn't the sort to ever allow myself to be broken. Not anymore.

We stood in front of one set of shiny gold elevator doors, making the silly bet that it would be the one to open for us instead of the five others. I looked at us, standing together, covered with a hazy gilded finish. Me short and fair, him tall and dark. We made an interesting pair, standing too close, looking too familiar for strangers.

The doors slid open before I could ponder any further. We'd won the elevator door bet. That was something, at least. He swept me into the enclosed space, and I got a waft of him again, rich and masculine.

"Floor?" he asked.

"Forty-two." My real estate brokerage, Thornfield, took up the entire floor, abuzz with salespeople working on some of the largest real estate deals and buildings in the Southeast. Well, it wasn't *my* company. I was just a senior vice president of sales, overseeing a number of the pricier projects.

I'd been away for a week, checking over an almost-finished development in midtown Atlanta. Nothing fancy, just some lofts for DINKs (dual income, no kids) near some of the livelier spots. They were coming along nicely, and with another small infusion of Gray's money for higher end interior finishes, they'd be ready to take to market. I was poised to make a nice profit on them now that the real estate sector was back in full swing. The money would go a long way to make my life easier, if only in the short run.

The stranger hit the button for my floor, but didn't hit any others. He must have been skipping his floor to take me to mine first. Was there no end to his Southern gentleman behavior? I smirked.

"I can take it from here." I pushed my elbow into his ribs.

He only tightened his grip. "I'm going your way."

His strength made some of the wires in my brain cross. I wanted to escape, but I also tingled in all the wrong places.

A few others hurried into the elevator before the doors closed, saying their good mornings to each other or giving friendly nods. I nodded back and watched them as they watched me in the reflective panels.

The whoosh of gravity pressing down made my ankle ache as the blood rushed into it. I put more weight on my good foot, scooting closer into the stranger at my side. His hand slid down a little lower on my waist, onto my hip so he could hold me even more tightly. His hand was large against me, spanning the fabric of my skirt and top with ease. His constant pressure was making me warm.

I glanced to the mirrored door again and saw he was watching me. His gaze was trained on my legs and leisurely made its way up my body until he caught my eye. He didn't look away, even though I'd basically caught him eye-fucking me. He was certainly bold, whoever he was.

The ride slowed as it approached the twenty-fourth floor.

I hated relying on him, hated the fact that he easily held me in place, but something in me thrilled at his self-assured touch, all the same.

"I can make it from here." I put more force into my voice than necessary.

"All right." He smirked again and let his arm drop.

I winced when I put my foot to the ground. His warmth was gone, and goose bumps rose along my skin. I wanted him back. I didn't have a plan for making it the rest of the way to my office. He still held my binder and ruined shoe under his other arm. My coffee was long since lost, the delicious contents feeding the treacherous grate outside instead of my caffeine addiction.

"You sure you can make it by yourself?" That. Fucking. Smirk.

The elevator stopped, and three men stepped off, leaving one more passenger and floor before mine.

"Yes."

The elevator pinged again. The last passenger got out, leaving me alone with the stranger as we finished the ride to the top.

He continued studying me in the mirror. I felt my cheeks pink as he watched me, his silence embarrassing me. Well, embarrassing wasn't the right word. His silence was heavy, not the comfortable, affable sort that was to be expected on elevators.

"You missed your floor." I gave him my ugliest glare. I needed something to break the quiet between us that seemed to double every second, larger and larger.

"I haven't."

The elevator stopped at the top, Thornfield's domain.

"But this is *my* floor." It sounded stupid when I said it, like I was a child with a toy and I refused to share.

He remained silent and offered his arm. I ignored it. Fuck him.

I took a step and struggled to keep my cry of pain in my throat. He looped his arm around my waist and helped me into the lobby. He didn't ask permission, just used his strength to reinforce my weakness. I hated it and basked in it all at once.

Sasha rose from the receptionist desk, hands going to her face in an over-dramatic gesture. Her nails were done in vivid red, with the pinkie sporting some intricate design, complete with glittering crystals. "What happened?"

"The grate got me."

She wrinkled her nose. "I hate that damn thing. It's ruined more shoes of mine than I care to mention." Sasha picked up her phone's handset and punched a button. "Mr. Fairfax, you're needed up front."

"Let me go." Why was my voice breathy?

"All right." He slid his hand from my waist, skirting the top of my ass with his fingers before letting his arm fall to his side.

His touch was too intimate, too knowing. I didn't want to, but I glanced into his crystalline eyes. He didn't turn away, just kept me in his gaze as Sasha prattled on about the grate.

I hopped a step away from him. "My office manager will come get me. You can go."

"I didn't catch your name." He gave me an easy smile, too easy. He was toying with me.

"I'm Ms. Rochester." I straightened my back despite the pain in my ankle.

"Jack England." His voice was deep and smooth, not a scratch in the rumble.

I noticed Sasha staring him up and down like she was taking his measurements. I couldn't blame her. Though obviously an asshole, he was beautiful in all the ways a man should be.

"Well." The pain burned in my ankle as I reached for the binder and my ruined shoe. "Hand me my things and you can go about your day."

I sounded dismissive. I knew it. Mason called my demeanor haughty, among the many other things he called me these days. But now wasn't the time to think about those moments, those words.

Jack England didn't seem to take offense at my tone, but he didn't move either.

Allen Fairfax, king of all things in the Thornfield office, came around the corner. He smiled, warmth beaming out of him in a way I envied. Fairfax was a genuinely nice person, the kind that are hard to find. He was rounded in the belly and graying on his head, but he had a jaunty walk, as if he were still a teenager with the world laid out before him. As a distant cousin, I'd known him long before I began working at Thornfield, but we'd grown closer over the past few years.

"Ms. Rochester, what have you done to yourself?" He narrowed his eyes at my naked foot and then looked at Jack. "Hurt your boss on the first day? That must be some sort of record."

I looked up sharply as my heart sank. "Boss?"

Fairfax smiled, the crow's feet at the corners of his eyes showing his age. "Yes, Ms. Rochester, Jack here is your new assistant."

"Wha-what happened to Jenny or whatever her name was? You know, the one with the hair." Jenny, darling redheaded Jenny, had decided that her best look was dreads. It wasn't.

"Once she realized you were clear of the building last week, she took her leave." Fairfax kept smiling, laughing at my chronic problem of vanishing staff.

"Why?"

He raised his eyebrows with a "you know why" look.

Truth be told, I wasn't too well-liked as a boss. Jenny had tried my patience on several occasions over the course of her weeks-long employment. Her time was up, anyway. They never stayed for more than a month. I ran them off in short order.

They all had the same complaints in their exit interview—Ms. Rochester was too demanding, too high strung, too much of a brooder, too brash, and the list could go on *ad finitum*. Of course, all those things were true. So what?

I was sure that somewhere out there was an assistant who could appreciate me. *Surely.* I gave Jack a look, wondering if he'd be the one. Doubtful. He was a cocky asshole. He'd be out the door in no time.

The clock started ticking in my mind, counting down the days until he says he's found greener pastures elsewhere. Maybe I could run him off even quicker. What was Fairfax thinking, hiring a man?

"There weren't any more qualified candidates?" I glanced at Jack.

"I think you'll find me perfectly capable." He wasn't flustered in the least, his steady confidence like a calm body of water.

No one had ever been so unflappable in my presence. I didn't like it.

"Just try him out." Fairfax's smile and the amused twinkle in his eye grated on me.

But my ankle hurt too much to continue arguing. Besides, I had plenty of tactics to get rid of assistants posthaste. Jack wouldn't last. "Somebody help me to my office."

Jack took my elbow again before Fairfax could get close enough to offer aid.

Fucking hell. His touch was firm and sent a tingle down my spine. I sighed at my body's reaction. "Just do that thing you did before. It helped."

Jack obeyed and wrapped his arm around my waist, lifting me as I toddled along on my one good foot. He led me to my corner office and lowered me into my desk chair. Fairfax followed us, obviously highly amused with my current plight.

I motioned to Jack. "Put the binder on my desk. Send

my shoe out to Lenny's two blocks over for repair. Tell Len I want it back this morning. No later. If he gives you guff, tell him I'd be more than happy to speak with him about it. That'll shut him up."

Jack nodded.

"Fairfax, call Pilot as soon as you walk out of this office and tear them a new asshole over that grate."

He tipped his head. "I'll get it taken care of."

"Tell them they're lucky I don't sue."

Fairfax chuckled. "They'll feel lucky enough already that I called instead of you. You scare them to death over there."

"They're lucky I don't take this ruined shoe and shove it up their backsides."

"I'll tell them that for you, too."

"Good."

"Well, I'll let you two get to know each other. Holler if you have any issues." Fairfax left, still laughing at my pronouncements of lawsuits and shoe violence.

Jack didn't acknowledge my threats. He was a man of few words and even fewer tells. What was he thinking? That I was a bitch, like all the rest of them thought? I could generally get a decent idea from most people, but he was a puzzle. His face, calm and angular, gave nothing away. His eyes followed my movements, though. He seemed to take in details. That was a good thing. Details were everything in my business.

"Why did Fairfax hire you? What sort of training do you have? Degrees?" I leaned back in my chair and crossed my hurt ankle over my knee to inspect it more closely.

He looked away, out the window that gave a broad view of the few skyscrapers in downtown Birmingham.

"I graduated from Alabama this summer with a bachelor's and master's degree in finance. I also—"

"How were your grades?"

"Summa cum laude." He didn't say it with pride. There was no chest puffing or faux self-effacing commentary. Just a simple fact. He'd gotten out with the highest honors.

Maybe Fairfax hadn't totally screwed up this hire. Jack might be useful for the month he lasted. He was young, and green as a spring bud, but his grades said he was smart. Smart could get you a long way. Clever or cunning? Even further. A few years back I was just like him, before I'd worked and schemed my way to the top ranks of a multi-million dollar company. It helped that nobody had been minding the store.

The Thornfield CEO, Mr. Hurst, hadn't darkened the office's door for almost two years now. He'd retired in some sunny island nation and let the vice presidents and other agents do all the work, sell all the real estate, and keep him fully stocked in piña coladas. I envied the bastard something fierce. But his absence helped me work my magic on his clients, getting their business and making money off every high dollar enterprise I could. Making money was the name of the game, and I had debts that couldn't be ignored.

"Why come to work for me?" I rubbed the skin along my ankle. It was starting to swell and would be black and blue by the end of the day. I would have Pilot's ass for this.

"Thornfield is one of the biggest real estate brokers in the Southeast. I figured it would be in my best interest to learn the business." There was something in his voice. It wasn't quite eagerness, more of a scientific curiosity.

"You don't have any problems being an assistant to a woman only a few years older than you?" The question came out cold, like most of my words. I wanted to test him, needed to know if he could take it.

He seemed laid back to the point of almost having no reaction. Cool, thoughtful. But I sensed something, something under the surface, hidden. Or maybe I only wanted there to be something more to get a rise out of him. I tended to be like that. Poking, prodding, and pushing to the hard limits. Hence the month-long tenure of most assistants.

"None." He met my eyes, no fear or apprehension there. He was steady, at ease. I hadn't shaken him one bit.

I frowned. "How old are you, anyway?" My curiosity won out over the employee handbook restrictions on asking about age, gender, or any other no-nos.

"Twenty-five. How old are you?"

I wanted to smile at his boldness. He'd already shown more backbone than my prior two assistants combined.

"Twenty-eight. Why such a late bloomer? Shouldn't you have graduated a few years ago?"

His gaze strayed back out the window. Though his face was expressionless, I felt like I'd gotten to him, if only a little, with the question.

"I wasn't able to go straight to college after high school."

"Why not?"

"Family issues." His voice softened, making him seem even younger.

Lord, I knew all about those. I'd had enough experience with "family issues" to last a lifetime. He didn't offer any more insight.

"And where are you from originally?"

He turned his head, looking out toward the crisscrossing railroad tracks and industrial buildings, toward the poorest areas of town. "Lowood."

Surprising. Few had the ability to make it out of such humble beginnings. Maybe he was a person of pure will, one who was always meant to rise. I never had to worry about whether I had what it took to make it. I came from a prestigious family. If Jack had looked through the window behind me, he could see my family manse perched high atop Red Mountain, looking down at the city with an arrogant, if beautiful, façade.

"Do you still have family in Lowood?"

"No."

"Your parents?"

"They don't live there."

Where do they live?"

He shrugged.

I should have stopped prying, but his quick answers made me want to know more. "No aunts or uncles?"

"Several, I've been told, but I don't know where they are."

"Brothers or sisters?"

"Maybe. I don't know."

Maybe? He was definitely a hard case of some sort. I was intrigued.

"So, no family connections. How did you get recommended for this position?"

He turned back to me, stoicism still threading through his expression. "Mr. Fairfax knows my godmother, Ms. Temple. She recommended me for the position."

"So you do have family, then?"

"She lives in Homewood, not Lowood. And she's not blood."

I let the silence return, giving him a reprieve. I'd done enough prying...for now, anyway.

I let my ankle go and leaned back in my chair. I could swear when I crossed my legs at the knee, his nostrils flared the tiniest bit. It was the most reaction I'd seen yet. Interesting.

"Well, Jack, this is a beginning. I don't want any dead weight on my team." I pinned him with a stare. "Piss me off, I'll cut you. Fuck something up, I'll cut you. You already have one strike against you for that shit at the front door."

"That wasn't my fault." He shook his head.

"You were holding the door for me at a ridiculously awkward distance. That's what made me trip. I was trying to get to you, and then I actually looked at you..." My cheeks heated. *Jesus, Rochester, get your shit together.*

His smirk returned. Cocky bastard.

I waved my hand at him. "We're done here. Get with Fairfax if you haven't already. He'll give you pointers on how I like my day run."

"He gave me a crash course last week, so I intend to hit the ground running." He gave another perfunctory nod before turning to leave. He was a good dresser, his medium gray suit hitting him in all the right places. It helped that he had a stunning body: broad back, narrow waist, and long legs.

The only thing that gave away his humble beginnings was his accent. It was faint, barely noticeable. Still, I could detect a certain local dialect—one frowned upon in the Rochester family social circles. He must have taken pains to erase it, to make himself sound as if he came from one of the more affluent suburbs, like Homewood where his godmother lived. Little things like that would be of no moment to the average ear, but a born-and-raised snob like myself could hear it right off, even if I didn't ascribe any import to it. That was more of an old guard issue; one that I hoped would die off.

Still, he was definitely different. Not in the color of his skin or his accent, but in his bearing, his confidence. He was not what I expected to find in my newest assistant. I stared at the frosted glass doors long after he was out of view. This was going to be an interesting month.

Sign up for my mailing list to be the first to know when Tempting Eden is released (no spam, promise): http://www.aaronerotica.com/newsletter.html

DARK ROMANCE BY CELIA AARON

Sinclair
The Acquisition Series, Prologue

Sinclair Vinemont, an impeccable parish prosecutor, conducts his duties the same way he conducts his life-- every move calculated, every outcome assured. When he sees something he wants, he takes it. When he finds a hint of weakness, he capitalizes. But what happens when he sees Stella Rousseau for the very first time?

Counsellor
The Acquisition Series, Book 1

In the heart of Louisiana, the most powerful people in the South live behind elegant gates, mossy trees, and pleasant masks. Once every ten years, the pretense falls away and a tournament is held to determine who will rule them. The Acquisition is a crucible for the Southern nobility, a love letter written to a time when barbarism was enshrined as law.

Now, Sinclair Vinemont is in the running to claim the prize. There is only one way to win, and he has the key to do it—Stella Rousseau, his Acquisition. To save her father, Stella has agreed to become Sinclair's slave for one year. Though she is at the mercy of the cold, treacherous Vinemont, Stella will not go willingly into darkness.

As Sinclair and Stella battle against each other and the clock, only one thing is certain: The Acquisition always ends in blood.

Magnate
The Acquisition Series, Book 2

Lucius Vinemont has spirited me away to a world of sugar cane and sun. There is nothing he cannot give me on his lavish Cuban plantation. Each gift seduces me, each touch seals my fate. There is no more talk of depraved competitions or his older brother – the one who'd stolen me, claimed me, and made me feel things I never should have. Even as Lucius works to make me forget Sinclair, my thoughts stray back to him, to the dark blue eyes that haunt my sweetest dreams and bitterest nightmares. Just like every dream, this one must end. Christmas will soon be here, and with it, the second trial of the Acquisition.

Sovereign
The Acquisition Series, Book 3

The Acquisition has ruled my life, ruled my every waking moment since Sinclair Vinemont first showed up at my house offering an infernal bargain to save my father's life. Now I know the stakes. The charade is at an end, and Sinclair has far more to lose than I ever did. But this knowledge hasn't strengthened me. Instead, each revelation breaks me down until nothing is left but my fight and my rage. As I struggle to survive, only one question remains. How far will I go to save those I love and burn the Acquisition to the ground?

EROTICA TITLES BY CELIA AARON

Forced by the Kingpin
Forced Series, Book 1

I've been on the trail of the local mob kingpin for months. I know his haunts, habits, and vices. The only thing I didn't know was how obsessed he was with me. Now, caught in his trap, I'm about to find out how far he and his local cop-on-the-take will go to keep me silent.

Forced by the Professor
Forced Series, Book 2

I've been in Professor Stevens' class for a semester. He's brilliant, severe, and hot as hell. I haven't been particularly attentive, prepared, or timely, but he hasn't said anything to me about it. I figure he must not mind and intends to let me slide. At least I thought that was the case until he told me to stay after class today. Maybe he'll let me off with a warning?

Forced by the Hitmen
Forced Series, Book 3

I stayed out of my father's business. His dirty money never mattered to me, so long as my trust fund was full of it. But now I've been kidnapped by his enemies and stuffed in a bag. The rough men who took me have promised to hurt me if I make a sound or try to run. I know, deep down, they are going to hurt me no matter what I do. Now I'm cuffed to their bed. Will I ever see the light of day again?

Forced by the Stepbrother
Forced Series, Book 4

Dancing for strange men was the biggest turn on I'd ever known. Until I met him. He was able to control me, make me hot, make me need him, with nothing more than a look. But he was a fantasy. Just another client who worked me up and paid my bills. Until he found me, the real me. Now, he's backed me into a corner. His threats and promises, darkly whispered in tones of sex and violence, have bound me surer than the cruelest ropes. At first I was unsure, but now I know – him being my stepbrother is the least of my worries.

Forced by the Quarterback
Forced Series, Book 5

For three years, I'd lusted after Jericho, my brother's best friend and quarterback of our college football team. He's never paid me any attention, considering me nothing more than a little sister he never had. Now, I'm starting freshman year and I'm sharing a suite with my brother. Jericho is over all the time, but he'll never see me as anything other than the shy girl he met three years ago. But that's not who I am. Not really. To get over Jericho – and to finally get off – I've arranged a meeting with HardcoreDom. If I can't have Jericho, I'll give myself to a man who will master me, force me, and dominate me the way I desperately need.

***

A Stepbrother for Christmas
The Hard and Dirty Holidays

Annalise dreads seeing her stepbrother at her family's Christmas get-together. Niles had always been so nasty, tormenting her in high school after their parents had gotten married. British and snobby, Niles did everything he could to hurt Annalise when they were younger. Now, Annalise hasn't seen Niles in three years; he's been away at school in England and Annalise has started her pre-med program in Dallas. When they reconnect, dark memories threaten, sparks fly, and they give true meaning to the "hard and dirty holidays."

Bad Boy Valentine
The Hard and Dirty Holidays

Jess has always been shy. Keeping her head down and staying out of sight have served her well, especially when a sexy photographer moves in across the hall from her. Michael has a budding career, a dark past, and enough ink and piercings to make Jess' mouth water. She is well equipped to watched him through her peephole and stalk him on social media. But what happens when the bad boy next door comes knocking?

Bad Boy Valentine Wedding
The Hard and Dirty Holidays

Jess and Michael have been engaged for three years, waiting patiently for Jess to finish law school before taking the next step in their relationship. As the wedding date approaches, their dedication to each other only grows, but outside forces seek to tear them apart. The bad boy will have to fight to keep his bride and Jess will have to trust him with her whole heart to make their happy ending a reality.

F*ck of the Irish
The Hard and Dirty Holidays

Eamon is my crush, the one guy I can't stop thinking about. His Irish accent, toned body, and sparkling eyes captivated me the second I saw him. But since he slept with my roommate, who claims she still loves him, he's been off limits. Despite my prohibition on dating him, he has other other ideas. Resisting him is the key to keeping my roommate happy, but giving in may bring me more pleasure than I ever imagined.

***

Cash Remington and the Missing Heiress
Sexy Dreadfuls, Book 1

I'm the best operator in the entire agency. The plum assignments—always mine. So when an American heiress goes missing, I'm the guy they call to get her back. Rescuing Collette Stanford is my mission. What I do to her after that is purely up to me, as long as she makes it back to the States in one piece. I'll kill the bad guys, get the girl, and get a little taste of what the heiress has to offer. None of this is negotiable. I'm Cash Remington, and I never miss.

Cash Remington and the Rum Run
Sexy Dreadfuls, Book 2

I plunder the sea, steal what I can, and never look back. It's a pirate captain's life for me. When my crew and I discover a destroyed ship floating on the endless waves, we scavenge it for every scrap of cloth and every morsel of food. Inside, I find a treasure—gold, gems, and a girl. I'll ravage the girl, spend the gold, and use the gem to buy the ship of my dreams—the Gloomy Lotus. At least that's the plan—until the Kraken, a whirlpool, and a six-headed beast attack my ship. Despite the danger, I still intend to have my way with the girl. Nothing can stop me. I'm Cash Remington, and I take what I want.

***

Zeus
Taken by Olympus, Book 1

One minute I'm looking after an injured gelding, the next I'm tied to a luxurious bed. I never believed in fairy tales, never gave a second thought to myths. Now that I've been kidnapped by a man with golden eyes and a body that makes my mouth water, I'm not sure what I believe anymore. . . But I know what I want.

ROMANTIC SPORTS COMEDY
BY CELIA AARON & SLOANE HOWELL

Cleat Chaser

Kyrie Kent hates baseball. She hates players even more. When her best friend drags her to a Ravens game, she spends the innings reading a book... Until she gets a glimpse of the closer—a pitcher who draws her like a magnet. Fighting her attraction to Easton Holliday is easy. All she has to do is keep her distance, avoid the ballpark, and keep her head down. At least, all that would have worked, but Easton doesn't intend to let Kyrie walk so easily. When another player vies for Kyrie's attention, Easton will swing for the fences. But will Kyrie strike him out or let him steal home?

Cleat Catcher

What happens when an unrepentant Cleat Chaser meets the player of her dreams?
Nikki Graves has a history of going through the baseball roster with an eye for talent—the kind of talent that keeps things spicy between the sheets. But, once she meets Braden Bradford, catcher for the Ravens, her talent scout days are done. He's the one.
Braden has never met a woman like Nikki, and he can't get enough of her smart mouth and big heart. But life isn't always as direct and certain as the connection between

Braden and Nikki. When family objections and career trajectories begin to crowd the plate, will Braden be able to keep his catch of a lifetime?

About the Author

Celia Aaron is the self-publishing pseudonym of a published romance and erotica author. She loves to write stories with hot heroes and heroines that are twisty and often dark. Thanks for reading.
@aaronerotica
aaronerotica.com

Printed in Great Britain
by Amazon